"The sun is always rising. We cannot hold back the day."

—Aline St. Julien

Blockchain entry, refracted view

> 5780.151.0621
>
> _KaitlynnSkye_orange_bellis perennis_3_1/1
>
> _LaToyaNull_black_gladiolas palustris_1_1/13
>
> Reparative charm to LaToya from Kaitlynn Skye in
>
> > consideration of 17 credits immediate exchange and
> >
> > one future favor TI.
>
> Nest Alpha_Pending
>
> 5780.213.0660

WILDSEED WITCH

Fortunes & Frenemies

MARTI DUMAS

AMULET BOOKS · NEW YORK

Cataloging-in-Publication Data has been applied for and may be obtained
from the Library of Congress.

ISBN 978-1-4197-7273-3

Text © 2024 Marti Dumas
Book design by Deena Micah Fleming

Printed and bound in the United States

10 9 8 7 6 5 4 3 2 1

Amulet Books are available at special discounts when purchased in quantity for premiums
and promotions as well as fundraising or educational use. Special editions can also
be created to specification. For details, contact specialsales@abramsbooks.com
or the address below.

Amulet Books® is a registered trademark of Harry N. Abrams, Inc.

ABRAMS The Art of Books
195 Broadway, New York, NY 10007
abramsbooks.com

GLASS, NOT GLASSES

*P*eople are simple. You just have to give them what they want.

My dad's family is magic, so he wanted his family to be magic, too. Everyone thought he would marry a girl from a legacy family in the city, but he fell in love with a witch from down the bayou. What could some well-connected witch give him that she couldn't? My mom may not be a belle demoiselle, but she is a witch, and that's all he wanted. That's what he told the rest of the Charbonnets when he brought my mom home. How was he supposed to know how much my mom needed her family to prop up her magic? Away from her country cousins, no one could see how the old spells and incantations—the ones I'm not supposed to listen to—had made her magic look bigger all along. How was my dad supposed to know that once my mom turned her back on her family, the magic she had would fade back to a trickle? After all, my dad can't see my mom's magic. But I can.

Daddy sees me, though. Ever since I can remember, he called me a belle demoiselle. That's why he named me LaToya. "Victorius one." Because I always win. This time won't be an exception.

I got out of the twin bed in my great-aunt Regina's sewing room and tucked the quilt back into place. Auntie Regina said she'd pieced it together to tell a story of our family's history, but I didn't have time to worry about the past. It was the first day of school. I needed to look to the future.

My uniform was hanging on the back of the door, pressed and starched and looking brand new. Auntie Regina made sure one was ready for me every day. She didn't know that I wasn't going to the Academy. Or that I was supposed to be in Paris on an exchange program with all the other girls. Or that my family's business was going under despite all the magic my mom was supposedly throwing its way. All Auntie Regina knew was that my mom was "too good" for her kind of magic now but that I actually wanted to learn it. That was enough for her to let me stay at her house as long as I kept going to school every day. And every day, she taught me something new. Like the day I bought my mom a restoration charm from the finest fézur in 3Thirteen and sent it to her like it was a gift from Paris. It came with lagniappe: a bottle of special, rejuvenative water. Auntie Regina laughed and said that water tasted like it came right out of the Mississippi River.

"But the bottle," she said with a smile, one eye crinkling more than the other. "That glass is something special. Just like you."

I didn't know what she meant at first, but I kept the bottle anyway, right next to my bwat d'herbes. The bwat d'herbes was supposed to be for my mother, but my grandmother slipped it to me before she died. The box was polished leather and filled with potion things. It was common stuff like coffee, turmeric, and hibiscus tea, but every once in a while, I managed to add something new, like a unicorn hair from the grounds at Belles Demoiselles.

Unicorn tea is supposed to be better than rose-colored glasses but only lasts a few minutes. Auntie Regina helped me brew the potion, but when it was done, she left me alone. I was glad. I didn't want her to see me fail. Selling the unicorn hair wouldn't have saved my family's business, but once I used it, there was no going back. I poured the brew over the bottle carefully so that every drop collected in the teacup underneath without making a mess. The liquid was useless. The magic was in the steam. Water vapor passed over the surface of the glass and, through it, I could see the truth. An intention laid out with mathematical precision, somehow churning inside the glass. A spell you could touch.

The tea cooled and the magic in the glass turned back to a shimmer. The unicorn hair wasn't wasted, though. That glass was special, like me. It was worth seeing. And there was definitely a way to use it.

I tucked the uniform blouse into my pleated skirt and slipped the blazer over it. My two french braids looked neat and perfect for a day at the Academy. I would put a wig on after I left the house. Even if my mother drove past me on the street, she wouldn't know who I was. She'd never suspect her daughter was a girl with locs.

I felt bad wasting the money Daddy had spent to send me to Paris, but it gave me three more weeks. Three more weeks to set things up so that no one would have to worry. Not my mom. Not my dad. And definitely not any one of the Charbonnets. None of them would be able to look down on us. How could they when we'd be right on top?

CHAPTER ONE

BEADS AND TREES

Knowing you can do magic isn't the same as knowing you are magic. I didn't really get that until I was at school, standing under a bead tree, holding on to my best friend, Luz, for dear life. No one was chasing us. I was chasing myself, hoping against anything that once she saw the real me, Luz would still want to stand next to me. A witch. And maybe not a good one.

I'd known I was a witch for weeks. That doesn't seem like a long time, but trust me, when it's the summer before eighth grade, those weeks feel like an eternity. Especially when you're afraid to show everyone who you are because you kind of don't know yourself. My whole life was smashed to pieces that summer, and suddenly it was time to build something new.

Magic sloshed against my skin. I looked up into the canopy of oak trees, focusing all my love, my hope, my fear on the aqua beads hanging over the front walk. Luz squeezed my hand. After hiding my magic from her all summer, I was finally going to do a spell and let her see that part of me. It was a freedom spell. A gift from my step-mother, and this was the perfect place to do it. Anywhere else, my magic might have gotten out of hand. I was a wildseed, after all. But our school was on a sanlavi. The sanlavi kept my power inside me like a Band-Aid wrapped a little too tight. It almost hurt, but I was glad it was there because no matter how much my power tried to leap out, the sanlavi held it in. It made sure that no matter how wild it was, it would only be charm, not magic.

Mo lib.

To lib.

So lib.

No lib.

With every word of the freedom spell, I felt lightness build inside me like helium in a balloon. It weighed less than nothing, but from the pressure of it, I thought I might burst.

Luz smiled. I tried to smile back. I wanted her to see the charm in me. I wanted her to know that even if I had made mistakes, the power in me was good.

I looked down at the roots of the tree, and something gave way. The magic pushing against my skin exploded like I was always afraid it would. But instead of covering the world with the flowers that came whenever I made mistakes, it unleashed the wind. A tiny hurricane right where Luz and I stood.

In New Orleans, we run from hurricanes. When we see them coming, we pack up and leave, if we can. I expected Luz to run, but Luz stood there with me, wind whipping our hair, shaking beads out of the trees, freeing whatever had stopped people from doing magic in this place.

It was only supposed to be charm, I thought. *It was supposed to stay inside me.* But magic still sloshed against my skin, and I knew it was everywhere, just like the beads all over the ground. Sanlavi or not, nothing was holding my magic back. The only thing keeping my power from changing the world was me.

I took a deep breath and remembered who I was. A witch. A daughter. A friend. And the magic I'd accidentally unleashed curled back to where it belonged, flowing between my dolphin, my fleur-de-lis, and me.

The wind stopped. It had sent my phone flying, but all I cared about was Luz.

"Are you OK?" I asked, my whole body clenched tight.

Luz wasn't a witch. Maybe she couldn't take it. Maybe the protection charm I gave her wasn't enough to keep her safe. Even if the magic was mine, it could still hurt.

But Luz was laughing. "I'm fine," she said. "But that was wild. Are you sure it was only charm?"

I shook my head, confused at first. "It wasn't charm," I said, a new feeling washing over me. "That was definitely magic."

My magic. My magic made a storm and, suddenly, I felt free.

That whole summer, when the Belles Demoiselles witches were saying "charm, not magic," I thought they were lowkey teaching us to be weak. Demure. The bad kind of careful. But they were teaching us to be powerful and I just didn't get it. I didn't learn what charm really was until my stepmom, Sandy—aka, HitchedandFree on Insta— told me. Sandy's a witch, too. She said charm is the magic you use to change yourself. That sounds small, but standing under that tree with Luz with beads scattered everywhere, it felt big. Maybe not safe, but powerful. Like endless possibilities.

I'd spent all summer afraid of magic the same way I was afraid to learn to ride a bike. If I'm being honest, I'm still afraid of bikes. Everybody should be—they go so fast. There's nothing to stop you from hurtling into something headlong, just a helmet and scraps of fabric on your elbows and knees to soften the blow. Even if you're careful, you still might get hurt. But that doesn't stop you from riding.

Magic is like that. And when magic is in your DNA, every mistake you make points right back at you. Even the ones that look like pretty flowers. But no matter how many mistakes I made or how many people kept telling me I was wrong, right there under that tree I knew that not even a sanlavi could stop me from being what I was meant to be: magic.

Luz cocked her head to the side. "I thought you said you couldn't do magic at school because of the sanlavi."

As if on cue, my self-appointed nemesis, LaToya, appeared to test me. She shouldn't have been there on so many levels. The old me would have been bothered just seeing her face. But I was standing in my favorite place in the world—Riverbend Middle—hugging my best friend in the world, Luz, in our matching jeans and shoes hand-painted by my linked sister, Dee, in the aftermath of a storm I made. LaToya did not bother me one bit. Not even when she tried to make me look stupid in front of a group of kids who shouldn't have even known what magic was.

"She told you this is a sanlavi?" LaToya scoffed. "Typical."

From the look on her face, she may as well have called us "ignant."

"Magic Lesson 10, you guys," LaToya said, whipping out her valley girl/teacher voice to talk to the kids behind her. "Sanlavi comes from the Kouri-Vini words meaning 'without life.' Since magic is life, no one can do magic on a sanlavi. The land just can't support it. But see the trees? The grass? Does this place look like it's without life to you? And if we were standing on a sanlavi, would I be able to do this?" LaToya asked, forming a fuchsia gladiolus in her hand. I wondered if she was still trying to call that thing a "sword lily."

"See?" she said, sliding her signature flower's long stem into the lapel of her blazer. "Not a sanlavi. Even a basic witch could see that.

9

This is what happens when fake witches spread fake information just to impress people."

I heard somewhere that you're not doing life right if nobody's hating on you. Well, I must have been doing my life right because LaToya was still hating. Dee ran in with our other linked sister, Angelique. Neither of them were fighters, but they flanked me like they were ready to throw down if they had to. Angelique and I weren't on the best of terms, so it felt good that she would have my back even if she was mad. But right then, I didn't need my coven to defend me, because there was nothing to defend. The old me would have been scared or angry or at least annoyed that LaToya was out here doing magic in public in front of people who shouldn't have known magic existed, but thanks to Sandy's spell, all I felt was free.

LaToya rolled her eyes and motioned for her little crew to walk away. I poured some magic on the ground behind them. Morning glories formed like I knew they would. My only regret was that my kitten wasn't there to soak it all up.

"Tomorrow, I'm bringing Othello," I said, when LaToya and her crew were out of earshot.

"You're gonna bring a cat to middle school?" Luz asked.

I smiled. Luz had a lot to learn about witches and cats.

"He's been here before," I said. "But the magic was all clogged up then. He'd like it better like this." I liked it better like this.

My magic had ripped off the Band-Aid squeezing everything in. I could breathe.

"Hasani, what happened?" Angelique asked. She and Dee both looked concerned.

"Hasani? Hasani!" Sandy was calling out for me from wherever my phone had landed. "Are you OK, girlie?"

"We're OK!" I shouted in the direction of Sandy's voice.

The four of us popped out of our group stance and started looking for my phone. It was way on the other side of the tree, face down on a root. I picked it up, expecting the glass to be shattered, but it was fine. I smiled, grateful that my dad made me decorate my ugly, shatter-resistant case instead of buying a flimsy cute one. Not that I'd tell him that. He didn't call me, anyway.

"Sandy!" I said, wiping a chunk of dirt off the front camera. "I did the spell! I think it worked!"

Sandy's face beamed back at me through the screen.

"And, Sandy! You know that weird sanlavi barrier thing at my school?" Sandy nodded to get me to keep going. "It's gone! Your freedom spell is amazing. We can totally do magic here now." A week ago, that would have been a bad thing. Now it sounded amazing. Like I was free to be me—all of me.

"You are amazing, chica! I didn't doubt you for a minute! How do you feel?"

"Good," I said. "Really good."

All my friends had gathered around to see Sandy on the phone screen.

Sandy smiled even bigger. "From the sound of it, you freed every bead in those trees. I'm surprised nobody got hit."

"Me, too," I said.

"I guess it was *luck*," Sandy said, pressing on the word "luck" so much that it could only mean she was about to say something about my mom—"and your mom isn't even there." Told you. My mom's a kismet, which makes her as uncontrollably lucky as that joke made Sandy unbelievably corny. I rolled my eyes but not too bad. Even a cool Sandy was still Sandy.

"Do you mind if I tell your mom how your first freedom spell went?" Sandy asked. "Or do you want it to be you?"

"You can tell her," I said. It was Sandy's spell, after all.

"Yay! I'm gonna call her now before I run to the doctor. Talk to you later, chica. Byeee!"

Angelique had stepped away from the phone, but I could feel her smiling in my direction. She was glad Sandy and I were cool. I was, too.

"Need some help?"

I jumped, a little surprised to hear _AnnieOaky_'s voice. Her name was Anne Johnson, but she'd always be _AnnieOaky_ to me. _AnnieOaky_ had been my very first fan on YouTube and, unfortunately, the very first person to cross over to #TeamLaToya. That made me nervous, but as Angelique said, you can't tell people who to be friends with. I tried not to think of it as LaToya pulling the wool over Annie's eyes. I tried to think of it as Annie seeing something in LaToya that I couldn't. I mean, even Angelique and Luz had hung out with LaToya for a bit.

It was nice to see Annie without LaToya, though. Most of that crew had left. As far as I could see, the only ones left were Annie and this girl named Jenny.

Jenny, who was wearing my faux-freckle look, gave a little wave. "Wassup, Hasani?"

The last time I saw Jenny, it was weird. I guess it would always be weird when people who had known me since kindergarten acted more like fans than friends. At least she called me "Hasani" this time instead of my YouTube channel name, MakeuponetheCheapCheap.

"I thought y'all went to get coffee," I said.

"Oh, they're grabbing coffee first, then coming back to help clean up the beads," Jenny said, tucking a wedge of blonde hair behind one ear. "Since Anne and I don't drink it, we figured we'd get a head start."

"Some of them are *glass*," Annie said, like she'd never heard of anything more dangerous in her life. "Safety first!"

I looked around. Unless people were gonna be barefoot, glass beads wouldn't be any worse than the plastic ones. But beads were all over the grass, the benches, and the walkways. Basically, they were everywhere. If we didn't clean them up, someone would fall for sure.

"You didn't have to come all the way back," Angelique said. "I was just about to go get a custodian."

Normally I would have teased Angelique about Riverbend Middle not being like her fancy private school, but I decided not to push it. Angelique was being cool, but not enough time had passed since our first big argument for me to be messing with her yet.

"Seriously. Y'all don't have to stay," I said. "We got it."

"It's our school, too," Jenny said. "Plus, you know how Miss Amber gets."

Jenny and I had known each other for a long time, but since we weren't friends-friends, I was not about to tell her that the beads getting knocked out of the trees was one hundred percent my fault. I may have been a wildseed, but apparently, unlike LaToya, I was too much of a belle demoiselle to talk to random kids about magic.

Jenny was right about Miss Amber, though. All she was gonna do was hand us a broom.

"Thanks," I said.

"Mudbug Pride!" Jenny responded, which wasn't nearly as weird as that time she did my outro instead of saying goodbye, so I laughed and started picking up beads.

Jenny was a bead-picking-up machine. Surprisingly, so was Angelique. I knew the rest of us had experience picking up fallen beads at Mardi Gras, but if I hadn't seen it with my own two eyes, I would never have believed Angelique Hebert would stoop to pick up anything off the ground.

I scooped beads up and slid them onto one arm, the whole time keeping an eye out for my favorite beads, the aqua strand I looked for every time I stepped on campus. It wasn't in its spot in the trees anymore, so I scanned the ground hoping to catch a glimpse of it among the fallen.

Was that weird? Absolutely. Mardi Gras beads are cool until about two P.M. on Mardi Gras day. After that, they're just more stuff you have to recycle or sort for your neighbor to throw next year in the truck parades. But me and those aqua beads went way back. If anybody was gonna get it, it should have been me. Even if it was broken, I could make it into a perfect collar for Othello.

"Done!" Jenny said brightly. Her left arm was basically a bead hanger. She was holding it out stiff to keep the dirty beads off her new school clothes. A thousand colors, but the aqua one was right in the middle, glistening like it always did.

"I'll take them," I said.

Jenny shook her head. "Don't worry about it. LaToya might get upset. She said to bring them back to her so she can upcycle them. See you at lunch, though?"

Was LaToya queen beeing that hard already? Then I caught myself. Being LaToya's lackey wouldn't kill them, not unless you counted dying of embarrassment from falling so low. It wouldn't have been my choice, but it wasn't my choice. If Annie and Jenny wanted friends who sent them to pick up trash, that was on them. Besides, it felt silly arguing about some dirty old beads. If LaToya wanted to do arts and crafts, good for her.

Whoa. I blinked. *That was different.*

I'd said words like that in my head a thousand times, but I'd never felt them before. No hate. No judgment. Just you do you. I could not believe how light it felt. Sandy's freedom spell must have really been that special sauce.

"Sure," I said, smiling at the lightness. "See you at lunch!"

Annie and Jenny ran off in the direction of the coffee shop. But as soon as they ran off, both their arms jangling with beads, something shifted. It wasn't the freedom. It was something else. Something that made the hairs on my neck stand up. I didn't know if they were standing up on their own, or if the wind had picked up again. It was hard to tell. Because the thing about hurricanes is sometimes everything calms down, and you think where you're standing is "after," when really it's the eye of the storm.

CHAPTER TWO

CIRCUSES AND MONKEYS

"What's wrong with you? You all right?" Luz asked, looking me up and down while I stared at Annie and Jenny. They were way down the block and already too far away to see, but it wasn't them I was looking at. It was my aqua beads hanging on Jenny's arm.

"I'm good," I said, trying to play off the fact that I was legit staring longingly at Mardi Gras beads that probably cost less than a penny. "What time is your dad dropping off Miguel?" Miguel was always a good way to change the subject.

Luz sucked her teeth. "Miguel had a hissy fit about not coming early with me. I told him he can't always hang with us. Sixth graders don't even have the same lunch. But you know he's gonna die if we don't meet him at the gate. You don't mind, right?"

"Of course I don't mind. Miguel is my favorite."

Luz looked like she was about to suck her teeth again.

"After you!" I said. "I meant my Miguel is my favorite after you!"

She fixed her face. "Good. We just got back on speaking terms. I don't want to have to act like I hate you, especially not when we look so cute. It'd ruin the effect."

We did look cute. My mom had actually complimented my makeup. It was subtle. I didn't want it to scream "Makeup YouTuber," but my little touch of cat eye was definitely worth noticing.

"I hate to interrupt this bestie fest, but I don't think y'all know what's happening," Dee said. The look on her face did not match the joy that should have gone with her fresh purple fade.

"You're being entirely too calm," Angelique added. "We need to talk."

Dee looked around. "Is Miss Nancy close?" she asked.

Miss Nancy was the person in charge of driving Angelique around and, trust me, she was always close.

"Maybe. But we can't use my car. My mom's back in town. She—"

Dee put up a hand and shook her head like Angelique didn't need to finish.

"I brought it, though," Angelique said, tapping her purse. "Do you think it'll in work in here now, or should we find somewhere outside?"

"You saw that flower?" Dee asked, lips pursed, head cocked to the side.

Angelique nodded. "You're right. Inside. We need a good spot . . ."

"On it," Dee said.

I had no idea what was happening, but I knew enough not to fight it. Three minutes later, all four of us were crouching under some azalea bushes on the far side of the building and Angelique was using the thinnest trail of magic I've ever seen to sew us into an intention she'd already woven . . . and was apparently keeping in her bag?

Angelique answered the question my eyebrows were asking.

"It's the one from the car. I didn't want to waste it."

I didn't blame her. Weaving intentions looked complicated. Watching her, I might have been able to do something similar with an extender, but without it? No way. The thinnest my magic ever got was like a fat, broad-tip Crayola marker—the kind you give to little kids when they're first learning to write. Angelique's was extra-fine point all the way. No one could say Angelique didn't have skills.

Angelique turned to Luz when she finished attaching the intention to the ground and closed the flap.

"Are we invisible now?" Luz asked. "Like that gift bag my charm came in?"

I smiled. Even with all the drama it took to get it, I was really glad Luz had a fleur-de-lis charm. It wasn't like our Belles Demoiselles charms, but it still made her look like she belonged. And magic or not, she did.

"Exactly," Angelique said. "Although, the bag you're talking about came from 3Thirteen, so the construction is probably much better than this one. Those witches have a lot more practice. But we needed something to make sure that Miss Nancy didn't report back every single thing we said this summer to my mom. Not that we were doing anything wrong. My mom's just a little . . . overprotective."

Understatement.

Luz nodded.

"Also, technically, we're not really invisible. The intention reflects light and sound in a way that makes it really, really unlikely that anyone will notice us. It helps that I was able to anchor it into the ground. It's not perfect, but between that and these bushes, it'll do."

"You good?" Dee asked Luz.

"This is nothing compared to the stuff in 3Thirteen. Yeah. I'm good," Luz said.

3Thirteen got way wilder than what she'd seen. Luz had basically only been in the food court. Although, to be fair, she did see two women leaning on white tigers like floor pillows while they swapped public "recipes" from magazines. Not quite the same as being literally wrapped in magic and trusting it to keep your secrets, but I let it go. There was no point in saying something that might burst Luz's magic comfort bubble.

"So, why are we in here?" I asked. "What's the problem?"

"LaToya!" Dee was looking at me like I was supposed to get it. I most definitely did not get it. "It's not time to be chill."

Angelique nodded. "LaToya just outed you."

"Outed me?" I said, trying to remember what happened. "No one saw me. I didn't sprinkle flowers around until they left. LaToya did it right in front of their faces. She outed herself, not me. She can out herself if she wants to."

"Wait," Luz said. "There's no rule against telling people about magic? I thought there was a rule."

"It's more of an understanding," Dee said.

"Common courtesy," Angelique added. "Like wearing a mask in public when you know you're sick. You don't have to, but it is the right thing to do."

"So, there's no, like, witch police?" Luz asked.

We all answered at once. "There's no witch police."

Luz was not prepared. She put her hands up. "OK. Dang. I got it."

Dee softened it up some. "There kind of was a long time ago, but that didn't go well. Witches are more live and let live."

"So why all the secrecy, then?" Luz asked.

"If you want to tell people you can do magic or whatever, cool. Live. You do you. But how you gon' tell people *I* can do magic and consider that *you* livin'?" Dee shook her head. "Don't make no kind of sense."

"Think of it as witches all having an inherent right to privacy," Angelique said.

"Well, if there's no police, what's to stop witches from outing other witches left and right?" Luz asked.

"Other witches," Dee and Angelique said together.

All of us were thinking of Belles Demoiselles. Those witches kept that sisterhood on lock. Nobody talked about their magic. Nobody.

"But LaToya didn't tell anybody I can do magic," I said, wishing Angelique had woven that intention a little bit bigger. "She only said *she* can do magic."

Dee shook her head. "Nah, fam. Don't let her mind games fool you. LaToya knew good and well she couldn't do magic at Riverbend before just now. She had to. There's no way she didn't try it the first time she stepped foot on campus. But the second she could do magic, instead of being cool about it, she said something to try to make you look stupid. Maybe whatever was blocking up the magic here wasn't a sanlavi, but she knew it was something."

"LaToya is always willing to make somebody look bad to make herself look better." I shrugged. "That's just LaToya."

"Well it's one thing if she does stuff like that around witches," Dee said. "It's another thing when she does that in the street, and she knows it."

I'd never seen Dee this heated, and she'd spent the whole summer with her mom as the world's most toxic teacher.

"Trust me. She just called you out. She did it in a negative way hoping you'd take the bait, and you kind of did. I saw you drip out those morning glories."

"Nobody else saw me!" I said again. It was seriously cramped in there. I was ready to get out.

"OK," Dee said. "Let's say nobody saw you pouring magic on the ground right behind her. Cool. But she got you to respond. And if she's negging you that hard in public, sooner or later, she's gonna do something so big you can't ignore it. Then everybody will see."

"Bigger than me accidentally making a mini-hurricane? That was probably hard to miss."

Angelique shook her head. "It's cloudy and wind happens. As far as anyone is concerned, that was just the beginning of a storm. LaToya is trying to make it bigger. She basically just called us all out."

Dee nodded. "Sooner or later, we're gonna have to answer. Better sooner than later. It'll only get worse the longer we wait."

"We?" I asked, looking back and forth between Angelique and Dee.

Dee gave a look like she wanted to suck her teeth. "We're a coven. We're not gonna leave you out there alone to save ourselves. We couldn't even if we wanted to and, for the record, we don't want to."

Dee and Angelique weren't saying petty witch war, but they didn't have to. At one point I would have been excited to have them ready to fight LaToya with me, but right then, it didn't seem worth ruining the peace over LaToya's insecure party tricks.

"Wait a minute," I said. "Literally just yesterday y'all were telling me how wrong I was about not giving LaToya a second chance. Angelique, you and Luz were *just* hanging out with her."

"True, but that was before she outed you," Angelique said. "I didn't want to believe she could. I mean, who would want to believe that of anyone? It's awful. I wish she hadn't done it, but what she just did was basically saying, 'pistols at dawn.'" Angelique shrugged like there was nothing else we could do. Except there was something we could do: not go to the duel.

"She called me a fake witch, not a witch."

"Same difference," Dee said.

"How?"

"If she keeps pointing at you, how long do you think it'll be before people really look?"

"OK." Luz put her hand on my arm. Her nail polish exactly matched our shirts. "I wasn't gonna bring this up because, I mean, leave the past in the past and all that, but you're right. LaToya and I were hanging out a lot."

I know.

"I've never heard her come right out and say Hasani is a witch, but she does call Hasani out a lot. Not by name, but it would be really hard not to know who she's talking about. She's dropping hints. Big hints. Like in that book. The one with the creepy drawings where the witches wear wigs to blend in."

"*The Witches*?" I said.

"Yeah. That one."

"You hate that book."

"No," Luz corrected. "I just like the chocolate factory one better. Anyway, LaToya's been schooling people on the telltale signs of fake witches while showing she's a real one."

"So she's outing me by not outing me? Reverse outing me?"

"Yeah," Luz said, like it made perfect sense. It didn't.

"Big deal," I said. "Even if that did work, who cares if a bunch of kids think I'm a witch? First of all, who are they gonna tell? Second of all, nobody would believe them, anyway."

Dee shook her head. "People be listening," she said.

"What happened to 'they go low we go high' and 'turn the other cheek' and all that?" I added, feeling bold. Maybe because I already had a mental checklist ready.

"One: She can't tank my YouTube channel. The bitbot Dee built me is way too tight for that."

Dee had to nod to that.

"Two: And, yeah, maybe she could try to influence people but, honestly, she's already doing that. Three: But she can't influence witches, anyway. And four: Now that Luz is wearing a protection charm, she can't influence Luz, either. Do I want LaToya to be queen bee of Riverbend? No. But as long as she can't mess with the four of us, I'm good. Plus, five: LaToya may have thirteen people in her coven, but twelve of them live out of town. If it comes down to it, it's three against one. I think we have to let this one ride," I finished.

"All right." Dee shrugged. "Your call."

Angelique looked a little nervous, but she nodded, too.

"Should we leave this invisible intention tent up just in case?" Luz asked. "No offense, but if something goes down, we might not have time for you to put it together again."

"No offense taken," Angelique replied. "There are probably people outside now, anyway. If we took it all the way down, they'd definitely notice the four of us suddenly sitting in the bushes. I'll open the back flap and we can slip out like that."

There were people in the front yard, but we slipped out of the intention with no problem. The biggest issue was that, out of nowhere, I'd start grinning. I knew what it was, though. LaToya was trying to stir up trouble, and for once, I couldn't care less. On top of that, Dee and Angelique wanted to ride in and do something about her and *I* was the one trying to talk them down. I was the voice of reason. Who knew? Felt good, though.

The sixth-grade teachers acted like human shields, blocking the sixth graders from the rest of us and herding them into the building as soon as they got dropped off, so even though we did make it to the gate before Miguel got dropped off, we didn't get to see him much before school started. I tried to make up for it by giving him a thumbs-up when I saw him in a big clump of sixth graders getting a lesson on locker combinations in the hall. He looked a little green, like maybe he might throw up, but honestly, I'd felt that way when I was learning how to do locker combinations, too. I mean, it looks too simple to mess up, and yet I probably messed it up fifty times before I got it right. Miguel would get it, too. Eventually.

Luz and I had P.E. together right before lunch. It was the first day, so Coach Wil didn't make us dress out, but she did remind us that, since we didn't have Health until fourth quarter, we would be dressing out every day after. That was fine with me. Having P.E. right before lunch meant that, if we showered fast enough, Luz and I would be able to claim a good table AND get a good spot in the lunch line.

My mom always wanted me to pack a lunch, but there were cafeteria lunch days that just could not be missed. The day Thanksgiving week when they served the turkey soup with a grilled cheese sandwich?

Slamming. Gumbo day, of course. But lunch on Mondays was red beans and rice, and nothing topped that. Kids who brought bag lunches got in line for it anyway. So when Coach let us out a couple minutes early to pick gym lockers and put our P.E. uniforms away, Luz and I walked right through the locker room, straight out to the hall, and to the cafeteria to get a good spot. We weren't the only ones to think of that, though. When we got to the cafeteria, _AnnieOaky_ was already there.

"Hey!" I said, dropping my backpack on a chair at the table she was grabbing. "Did you have P.E. fourth period? I didn't see you with seventh graders." Unlike Coach Wil, Coach Davis had made the seventh graders dress out and start off the year with push-ups.

"No," Annie said nervously. "I have Ms. Simmons fourth period."

"For English Language Arts? Y'all are lucky. Ms. Simmons never let us out early last year."

"She didn't let us out early. I asked to use the bathroom and just didn't go back. I wanted to get a good table."

Annie looked guilty. I don't think she was cut out for that cuttin' class life.

"Don't worry about it," I said. I mean, I would have worried about it, but she already did it, so . . . "If Ms. Simmons notices you can just say you got your period or something, but she probably won't notice."

"Cool"—Annie looked pained—"but . . . I was saving this table for LaToya and Jenny and everybody. I—"

She was looking between me and my backpack like there was some problem.

"Oh!" I said, grabbing my bag. It hadn't occurred to me that Annie might not want to sit with us. Awkward.

"My bad," I said. "We'll get another table."

Annie half looked like she wanted to cry. She was literally wringing her hands. I've only read that in books.

"I would sit with y'all," she said, "but LaToya asked me to save a table, and this is the biggest one and it barely has enough chairs. Y'all understand, right?"

"Of course!" I said. "No worries!"

Luz tried to catch my eyes with an *Are you sure?* look, but Sandy's freedom spell must have worked wonders. Sandy had made it up by trial and error. She tried to explain it to me, but the only thing I really knew was that it worked. This was a perfect example. I liked Annie. Really. But it was like, suddenly, I was free from the feeling that I had to save her. It's not like I hadn't warned her about LaToya. If she wanted to walk down that road, skipping classes for LaToya, that was on her.

"You're not mad, are you?" Annie asked.

I shook my head. "Of course not," I said. "We'll just grab another table."

Annie looked relieved. "OK. Good. I just didn't want to hurt your feelings by sitting with LaToya over you this time. It's just, I couldn't *not* sit with her today, you know? Not after what she did for all of us."

Luz made a face. "What did LaToya do?"

Annie hunched her shoulders while she talked, like somehow that would make her whisper even quieter. "There was a spell on Riverbend Middle. Kind of a curse. It kept kids from doing magic. That's why no one who came here could do it, even if they were from magic families. And this morning, LaToya broke the curse!"

"*LaToya* broke the curse?" Luz's voice sounded like she was about to tell Annie about herself, but I put a hand on Luz's arm. Sandy's spell + my magic ≠ LaToya but, honestly, it wasn't worth it to say anything. If LaToya wanted to claim she cured the sanlavi, let her.

"That's cool," I said.

"Isn't it?" Annie chirped. "Most of us won't get into the school where LaToya learned magic. I guess they're super elitist. But LaToya says she'll teach all of us herself. She already has been, right, Luz? But I'll sit with y'all tomorrow."

"No worries," I said again.

Annie smiled. I tugged Luz's arm so she'd follow me across the room.

Luz looked like she was ready to burst. We didn't make it five steps before she grumbled, "She should be thanking *you*."

"Don't worry about it," I said. "But you know what you should be worried about?"

Luz looked at me.

"Today is red beans and rice. And red beans and rice means cornbread," I said. A cheap shot, but Luz laughed and let the Annie thing drop. When cornbread is that sweet and buttery, nobody wants to miss it.

We grabbed a small table on the other side of the room, left our stuff for spot dibs, and managed to get through the line before Dee and Angelique got there.

"Cornbread?" Luz asked, holding up two perfectly yellow squares for Dee and Angelique to choose from. "You're gonna want it before we tell you what you-know-who told our seventh-grade friend."

Correction. Luz had not let the Annie thing drop.

Angelique politely declined the cornbread, but Dee grabbed one and took a huge bite.

"That's good," she said. "Not as good as mine, but really good."

"I got the hookup." Luz grinned.

I grinned right back. You'd think Luz was the one with the charm because ever since sixth grade, the cafeteria ladies had given Luz special treatment. Today, it was *three extra pieces of cornbread* worth of special treatment.

"Talent." I grinned.

Luz fake-angrily tossed a piece of cornbread at me. I caught it and started eating, even though it was crumbling in my hand. She laughed. By then, she got the joke. After a bajillion years of sneaking around, witches hardly ever called themselves "witches." People like my mom who had magic but couldn't control it were called "gifted." People who could control their magic were called "talented." Technically, people like Luz were called "untalented," but I don't think she'd have been so cool about anybody calling her UNtalented. I mean, who would be? Hopefully she never heard that part. But the way she kept wanting to go to 3Thirteen, maybe we'd find out she was magic, after all.

"Not a gift or a talent," she said, "but I do have a secret."

"What?" I asked, hoping it wasn't anything like the size of the one I'd sprung on her.

"A birthday card," Luz said.

Eyebrows went up all around the table.

"In sixth grade I overhead Mr. Raymond telling Miss Bonita happy birthday. When teachers have birthdays, everybody makes a big deal out of it, but the only person I heard say happy birthday to Miss Bonita was Mr. Raymond, so I made her a card. I didn't think it would be that big a deal."

"I guess it was to her," Dee said.

"That makes so much sense," Angelique said. "Low-wage workers are often overlooked and underestimated." *Like Wildseeds?* "It's like people consider them less valuable as people just because their jobs make less money."

How would you know? I thought, but I definitely kept that one to myself. It was a struggle to keep my face smooth without throwing a little charm on it, but I managed. Angelique and I were linked sisters. She would have seen the magic at work.

Luz motioned for us all to lean in.

"I don't want to keep looking over there, but will one of you check on Annie and see if she looks OK to you? When Hasani and I saw her earlier, she was definitely giving brainwashed vibes, like 'blink once for yes, twice for no.'"

"Do you think she's being influenced?" Angelique asked. How Angelique got her voice to carry without ever being loud was beyond me. It was right up there with how she never seemed to sweat.

"I don't know. That's what I'm asking Dee. If she is, maybe we can get her one of these." Luz tapped her fleur-de-lis charm. It looked like our fleurs-de-lis, but instead of storing magic, Luz's deflected it, making her immune to witch influence as long as she was wearing it.

A charm like Luz's wasn't a bad idea, but after the whole thing with Sandy and Kaitlynn and the unicorn poop, I doubt we had enough credits left.

"They're really expensive," I said.

"Angelique got it." Luz winked.

"Not cool," Dee said.

"My bad. You're right," Luz said. "When I get rich, I don't want y'all to assume I'm paying for everything, either. Sorry, Angelique."

"That's OK," Angelique said. "I couldn't afford it, anyway. 3Thirteen doesn't take fiat money like dollars or euros, and when I joined, I didn't get a lot of credit."

"You didn't?"

Angelique shook her head. Luz caught Angelique's embarrassed look and mercifully switched topics.

"There must be something we can do. Not saying who Annie can be friends with or anything, but just so she knows we're still here for her."

The table Annie saved was full except for one seat that was obviously still being saved for LaToya. All the other kids were talking and laughing, looking at things on each others' phones and stuff, but not Annie. She was sitting stiff as a board, staring at the door.

I found myself saying a mantra in my head. Or maybe it was an incantation. I couldn't remember which was which.

Not my circus, not my monkeys.

Not my circus, not my monkeys.

34

I don't know where I got that one from. It's kind of confusing when you think about it, but in my head, it had a good flow.

Angelique stood up. "I'll go check on her," she said. "We were supposed to touch base about getting snowballs after school tomorrow, anyway."

I did not think that was a good idea. It's not like Annie didn't know where we were. We were sitting in plain view in the cafeteria. And she knew we would've liked to sit with her. But between the freedom charm and "not my circus, not my monkeys," I didn't try to stop Angelique from going over there. Dee sighed, but she didn't say anything, either. Angelique was halfway across the cafeteria when the universe decided she shouldn't. And by the universe, I mean Ms. Coulon.

"Angelique Hebert and Hasani Schexnayder-Jones, please report to Ms. Coulon's room. Angelique Hebert and Hasani Schexnayder-Jones, please report to Ms. Coulon's room."

Angelique didn't pause until the loudspeaker said Ms. Coulon's name. Among other things, Ms. Coulon was the teacher in charge of Mathletes and the person who let Angelique be a captain her very first year on the team. I could almost see her calculating. Friends > Mathletes? Or Mathletes > Friends?

Mathletes won.

I got up, too.

"We'll be right back," I said. "We have Mathletes today. Ms. Coulon probably wants to check in with us about it before the meeting. Watch my tray?"

Luz nodded and I ran to catch up with Angelique.

I hoped Ms. Coulon was calling us about Mathletes, but an all-call at lunch on the first day of school was not her style. Ms. Coulon planned ahead. She had already sent us a list of expectations and a schedule of the topics for the first six meetings. Part of me already knew she was calling us about the wind and the trees. It didn't help that on the way out the door, I saw Annie was holding my aqua beads.

FAVORS, NOT FAVOR

Hasani gives herself way too much credit. She's only been a witch for like half a week, and, so far, she's lucked into everything she has, including that dolphin charm. She's practically a kismet. It's gross. Real witches don't sit around waiting for luck to happen. We put in work.

That's why I jumped at the chance to work with Kaitlynn. Kaitlynn doesn't even have a black card, but she'd worked her way into a shop on the fifth level of 3Thirteen. People hate on her, but that's all it was. Hate. I could see right through them. They were just jealous because Kaitlynn was killing the game and, when it came down to it, none of those witches were willing to work hard enough to do what she does. But I am. That's why Kaitlynn picked me. Maybe Hasani could blow beads out of some trees, but that was a baby trick compared to what those trees could really do.

The kids in my new crew were all laughing and drinking the free frozen lattes my "aunt" had given them like party favors. Both my parents are only children, but it was way easier to call Cassidy my aunt than to explain who she really was. Cassidy was pretty and brown with a long, thick ponytail and slender chin. We didn't really look related, but Cassidy played along and that's all that mattered. She worked for Kaitlynn, too, but I wasn't going to waste my life running one of Kaitlynn's coffee shops like Cassidy. My black card said I was bound for better things. Kaitlynn could have waited like a hundred years to name the future favor I owed her, but she already knew I was great and could do great things. That's why she chose seventy-seven signatures. For a witch like Cassidy, getting that many signatures would have been impossible, but Kaitlynn knew I'd deliver.

Cassidy gestured me over to the counter with her head.

"Back in a tick," I said brightly, pushing my new locs over my shoulder as I got up from the table. Since Cassidy was supposed to be my aunt, I went. But if she thought she could boss me around just because she was playing along, she had another thing coming.

"How much longer?" she asked.

I looked up at the clock. The real date was small on the bottom like a serial number, but the time was clear as day. 8:01.

"School's at eight thirty. We won't be late. Thanks, Aunt Cassidy," I said, loud enough for everyone to hear.

Cassidy lowered her voice. "So, this was the favor, right?"

I made sure no one was paying attention before I scrunched up my face. "Absolutely not," I said. "I haven't even named my favor yet."

"Well, you better name it soon. Or am I supposed to give away free drinks every day until you decide? Sooner or later, Kaitlynn's gonna catch on."

"Maybe," I said. *You can't decide when I decide. That's what "time immemorial" means. You shouldn't have entered a contract with me if you didn't understand it, Cassidy.* "But they're not supposed to be from Kaitlynn. You're the one who owes me a favor."

Cassidy touched the thick ponytail laying across her shoulder. It looked fake, but every bit of it was hers. My chevelure potion had worked wonders. So had my reflection paste. Her nose was the spitting image of her sister's, just like she wanted. It would only last for a day or two, but it was worth way more than free coffee.

"Fine," Cassidy said, tossing her braid behind her back. "But don't blame me if Kaitlynn finds out about your little suitcase in the walk-in fridge."

My wrist buzzed. I glanced down at my watch. There was a message from Anne.

Jenny and I got most of them. Do you want them all? It's a lot.

"Just the glass ones," I said into the watch, then tapped its face to press Send.

Cassidy had the nerve to stand there with her arms crossed, looking at me crossways. Was she trying to ruin our cool-aunt cover? It didn't matter. If there were glass beads to go with the glass bottles, I didn't need her anymore, anyway.

I pulled my phone out of the inside pocket on my blazer and tapped the 3Thirteen app. My open contract with Cassidy shimmered in a purple dot on the right-hand side of the screen. I tapped it and said "Final."

Cassidy looked relieved. She should have been.

"Don't worry about my suitcase," I said. "I'll pick it up at lunch."

Maybe Hasani was good for something. For once, her dumb luck was going my way.

CHAPTER THREE

SPARKLES AND EYES

Ms. Coulon's room was on the third floor. When we hit the second-floor landing, I turned on a little charm, letting some of the magic that always flowed beneath my skin slow down my breathing and cool me off a little. I didn't want Ms. Coulon to see me sweat.

It was just a little charm, but I knew Angelique would see me do it. She was my linked sister, so even without rose-colored glasses, she could always see my magic. I didn't care. Angelique already knew how much of a mess I was, and even if I couldn't stop the flow of it before we got to Ms. Coulon's room, Ms. Coulon wouldn't be able to see it at all. All she would see was calm, cool, collected cocaptain Hasani reporting for duty.

I was getting used to the cocaptain thing. I still felt some type of way about it, but Angelique was great at math. Angelique was great at organizing. Angelique was great at everything. Of course she should be one of the captains. And as her friend, I was happy for her. I was a little less happy for me that I didn't get to do it alone, but that didn't stop me from being happy for her.

As we hit the third-floor landing, I turned to Angelique to tell her that. I was going to say something cool and supportive like, "Angelique, I'm really happy we're cocaptains," or "Angelique, I'm glad I get to do this with you," but when I looked at her, I was too shocked to say anything. Angelique was charming herself. Not her hair, which was always the world's most perfect coils, but her cheeks and neck and hairline. I think she was even using a little charm to brighten her eyes.

"What?" she asked when she saw me staring. "The stairwell is barely air-conditioned and it's ninety-eight degrees outside. I don't want to be sweaty when we get to Ms. Coulon's room, either."

I smiled. LaToya and Annie and everything that had happened that morning felt a million miles away. I really was happy we were doing this together.

"Come on, cocaptain," I said. "Let's go talk to our adviser."

The moment we walked in, I knew we were in trouble. Old Hasani never used to get in trouble. Witch Hasani seemed to get in trouble all the time, especially with the belles demoiselles. I'd learned so much over the summer, but somehow I still kept getting stuff wrong. At Belles Demoiselles, I got in trouble so much that I could smell it coming.

Ms. Coulon was not a yeller. Her voice was always smooth and calm no matter what was happening. But the way she was looking at us over her glasses when we walked in was yelly enough.

"Never in a million years did I think two talented young ladies barely out of charm school would do something like this."

"Talented young lady" is witch speak for "witch." We had known Ms. Coulon was a witch for only a day. Less than a day, actually, since she didn't show up to our inaugural Self-Care Sunday until it was almost over, but it seemed perfectly normal. Like, once I knew I was like, *Duh. I should have guessed that.* The weird part was finding out that Ms. Coulon was friends with Sandy. That I would not have guessed.

"Charmed girls performing magic on Carrollton Avenue in broad daylight without so much as an intention to refract the view?"

It wasn't really a question. It was an accusation.

Any hope I had that this might have been about Mathletes flew out the window.

"I meant for it to be charm, not magic," I said. "It must have leaked out. I'm not that good at holding it in."

"That is the understatement of the century," Ms. Coulon said, her lips a thin line. "Angelique, I must ask. Does your mother approve of what you've been up to?"

I shrank back.

Angelique clicked into adult mode.

"We apologize for disappointing you, Ms. Coulon. I think I can speak for both of us when I say that that's the last thing we'd want to do. We were under the impression that this school campus is on a san-lavi, so we thought charm was the only thing that could happen here. And to answer your question, no ma'am. My mother did not know what we were going to do this morning, and if she knew it would turn into magic, I'm sure she would not approve."

Part of me thought Angelique was gonna say something about how she wasn't technically even on campus when I blew the beads off the trees, but the rest of me knew Angelique was more clutch than that.

I said it for her. "Angelique isn't to blame. The only thing she did was help pick up beads off the ground. I'm the one who did a spell. I'm the one who made the mess. I should be the one apologizing."

My Belles Demoiselles training kicked in and, without thinking, I started trying to remember who I was. I did it to make a better impression on Ms. Coulon, but the weird thing about trying to remember who you are is that, suddenly, you remember who you are.

"Wait a minute," I said, stopping Angelique in the middle of an extended apology for being the person who helped me get the ingredients. "Stop apologizing, Angelique."

Angelique gave me a look. It was quick, but I knew what it meant. One of Angelique's superpowers was softening up adults to get them on her side, which, in this case, was *our* side. If she stopped apologizing, it would ruin it. But I wanted to ruin it.

"We don't need to apologize," I said, shoulders back, chin parallel to the floor, "because we didn't do anything wrong. Actually, we did a bunch of things right."

Ms. Coulon sat back in her chair a little, like she was going to let me dig my own grave. "Go on," she said, steepling her fingers in front of the glasses hanging around her neck. It made the beads on the chain holding them look like stained glass. "There are no name drops or any other shenanigans in my room, nor will there be. And I assure you that my intentions are impeccably woven. Speak freely."

But Ms. Coulon didn't have to give me permission to keep going because I had no intention of stopping.

"First of all, I saved this school from a termite infestation, and I saved the termites, too."

"You did that alone?" Ms. Coulon said from behind her tent of fingers.

"Well, I had help."

"Aimee," Ms. Coulon filled in, but I didn't confirm or deny. My Animal Affinities teacher, Miss Lafleur, had helped me. Her first

45

name was Aimee, but witches were weird about having their names dropped. The longer I was a witch, the more I understood why, though, and I had no intention of being on Miss Lafleur's bad side.

I just kept rolling with the facts and left Miss Lafleur out. "I used an extender and literally drew them out by hand. Then, on top of that, I don't know if you noticed . . . well, you had to have noticed . . . there was a thing stopping people from being able to do magic at Riverbend Middle. That's the reason the termites got trapped on campus in the first place instead of flying away on their own. I fixed that, too."

Ms. Coulon should have been saying "thank you."

You're welcome.

I didn't say it out loud, but I did think it. I was feeling free, but I wasn't feeling froggy. No need to take it that far.

"You misunderstand me," Ms. Coulon said, putting her glasses back on her face. "Or perhaps I'm not making myself clear. I'm well aware of the 'thing' that was stopping people from doing magic on campus. I helped make it. You essentially undid about fifteen years of my work when you freed it this morning, but I'm not upset with you. I just want to know how you did it. So, please. Start from the beginning. I'm all ears."

"Wait a minute," Angelique said. "You're the reason people couldn't do magic here? Not some kind of sanlavi?"

"You have memberships to 3Thirteen. Do you also have library cards?" Ms. Coulon asked.

"I do," Angelique said, standing up even straighter.

Ms. Coulon nodded. "Then I suggest you read up on sanlavi. They are extremely rare—unheard of below sea level—but they do exist. What you were experiencing here was a combination of things, some of which you wouldn't find in the library because, frankly, I haven't shared them with the library yet."

Was that a flex? I leaned back, nodding like, *I see you, Ms. Coulon: doing stuff so cool it belongs in a library.*

"Sandy isn't the only one in our circle of friends who likes to experiment with recipes. Sandy leans on spells. Potions and weaves were my first loves, but they led me to my life's true passion: crystals."

"I didn't know that crystals and weaves were connected," Angelique said, keeping all calm and proper with charm. But the way she kept pinching the fingers on her left hand was a dead giveaway. She was praying Ms. Coulon would say more and itching to write down every word.

Ms. Coulon smiled like she was only too happy to drop a little knowledge. "Oh, yes," she said. "Crystals have all the structure of a weave while being as versatile as potions—if you know what you're doing."

"So . . . you make your own infused crystals?" Angelique didn't exactly sound eager, but even with all the charm she had going, she could not maintain anything like chill.

"Absolutely," Ms. Coulon continued. "The possibilities are endless. Twenty years after I discovered that technique, one of my earliest creations is still in use. The profits I made helped me start a business so I could afford to become a teacher."

"You have to pay to be a teacher?" I asked. I knew teachers didn't make a ton of money, but I didn't know it was like that.

Ms. Coulon laughed. "Not exactly, but without the income from my business I would never have been able to afford to work in education all these years. How the others survive on what the schools pay us is beyond me."

"Oh! So, you have a side hustle selling crystals!" I said. Everybody in New Orleans has a side hustle. Frozen cups. Pralines. Ooey-gooey cakes. Playing music on the weekend. Selling crystals was a new one for me, but it sounded about right.

"It would be more accurate to say that I have a side hustle working with young people, but yes. I have several glassworks, including one in New Orleans and our flagship in Amite. Technically, what we make is crystal, not glass, but the misnomer is intentional. Calling it 'glass' is a fun little thing we do to throw people off the trail of exactly how special they are."

Fun? What about that was fun? What witches thought of as a good time was still beyond me.

"I don't understand," Angelique said. "I'm having trouble making the connection back to people not being able to do magic on campus. Does the crystal you make stop people from doing magic?"

"Mine, no. But other crystals can and do. Talented people have used crystals to create truly terrible things, including an object that has plagued this campus for hundreds of years."

"Worse than a sanlavi?" I couldn't stop myself from shivering. Now that I knew what it was like to be literally cut off from magic, I couldn't imagine anything worse.

"Much worse than a sanlavi. Sanlavi are at least a part of the natural flow of life. If there are places where magic overflows, there must also be places where magic recedes. Natural balance. Riverbend Middle was built on a capture, and there is nothing natural about that."

When Ms. Coulon said "capture," Angelique literally covered her mouth and gasped.

I was just confused. "What's a capture . . . besides not good?" I asked.

"A capture is a prison for witches built by witches. It doesn't capture the body. It captures your magic."

"So it burns you out?" I squeaked. "I thought stuff forcing you to burn out was supposed to be an old wives' tale!"

"Technically, the capture doesn't force you to pour out your magic. It simply roots your magic to a spot. The more you struggle to release your magic, the more you pour out, and the capture captures it all."

Ms. Coulon paused to let the horror sink in.

"Witches are out here building witch jails? So much for being 'live and let live,'" I said.

"We are!" Ms. Coulon cut in. "The gifted and talented are laissez-faire for the most part. We have no central governance. No central rules. There is no one to answer to unless we choose."

No one to answer to? I made a noise. I would have left it at that, but Ms. Coulon gave me a look, so I turned my noise into words.

"Uhhh . . . witches do have rules," I said. "Like, a lot of rules." I know. I was always getting them wrong.

Ms. Coulon shook her head. "You wouldn't feel that way if you were born into it. What you're thinking of as 'rules' are more like customs. Let me give you an example. Say you're walking down the street here in New Orleans and you pass someone. Someone you don't know and have never seen before and might never see again. What do you do?"

"You speak," I said. Duh. I had no idea where she was going with this.

"What do you say when you 'speak'?"

I shrugged. "If it's morning, I say, 'Good morning.' If it's about to get dark, I say, 'Good evening.'"

Angelique chimed in. "Sometimes my dad says, 'How you doing?' and the other person says 'How you doing?' and both of them keep walking without answering."

"And sometimes do you just lift your chin and say, 'All right'?" Ms. Coulon asked.

I nodded.

"And the person you're greeting responds with the exact same?"

Ms. Coulon was making it sound weird but, yeah. That happened, too.

"And can you look at the ground when you're doing all this?"

"No," I said. "That'd be kind of rude. You look at the person you're passing."

Ms. Coulon leaned back in her seat like we had just proved her point. "In New Orleans, that is the custom: the socially agreed upon consensus of how to acknowledge the humanity of strangers when you pass them on the street."

"Why do you keep saying 'in New Orleans,'" I asked. "Don't they do that everywhere?"

Angelique shook her head. "You have to travel more, Hasani. People do not do that everywhere."

"And it's possible that people won't always do that in New Orleans," Ms. Coulon continued. "When people come from other places, they bring their own understandings of what to do when you pass a stranger on the street. If enough of them come at once, they might try to learn our ways, or the consensus might shift, and, if it does, the custom will change."

I frowned. "I like it how it is now. It's nice."

"I like it, too, but that's the way people work, and witches are people. Yes, pockets of witches have customs that have evolved over time, but most of them aren't rules. They're suggestions for fitting in, like 'speaking' when you pass people on the street in New Orleans. It may not feel like it, but you're free to ignore customs. However, that doesn't mean there won't be a consequence." Ms. Coulon looked straight at me, like I knew all about consequences. "Sometimes," she continued, "the consequence is small, like looking rude or sticking out as a new person. But some consequences are bigger. Say, for example, being permanently deleted from the Internet?"

I tried to stop the horror from crossing my face, but I don't know if I made it, because that's exactly what would happen if any of us did anything to reveal the existence of the charm school we'd all gone to: Belles Demoiselles. I already figured Ms. Coulon was a belle demoiselle, but that clinched it. I looked her up and down, trying to see where she wore her Belles Demoiselles fleur-de-lis charm. She turned over her hand so I could see. What looked like a plain silver ring on her left hand had her fleur-de-lis charm on the palm side.

I nodded. Both my charms, the fleur-de-lis and the dolphin, were on a chain around my neck.

"That consequence is relatively new, by the way. Once upon a time, the consequence was that you and your progeny were permanently barred from attending Xavier, Dillard, and Spelman. I'm sure it was something different before those colleges existed. But whatever the consequences are, they only applied to us because we agreed to them. The only rules that apply to a witch are the ones she willingly accepts. Other humans can't say that."

"I would not willingly accept being deleted from the Internet," I said.

"Maybe. Maybe you'd fight back. I doubt you'd win, but that's beside the point because it wouldn't change the fact that you accepted that rule in the first place. Otherwise you wouldn't be a charmed girl. But, wanting to be a charmed girl, you let them have a certain amount of rule over you. Otherwise, witches have no rulers. We've never had a queen or a president or a prime minister, and I doubt we ever will."

"So if witches don't have to follow rules, how do you get anything done?" I asked.

"Witches can only be ruled by consensus. Gather three hundred and thirteen witches. Convince all three hundred thirteen witches to your side, and every witch everywhere is forced to accept the consequence."

"Even a punishment?" Angelique asked.

"Especially a punishment. As you can imagine, there were many witches who've resisted the rulings. Over the centuries, witches got more clever with their weaving, binding each other to agreements with blocks and chains. Of course, witches got out of those at first. They did it themselves with their own charm or were freed by kismets who loved them. Eventually we realized that the bends in the river we used to strengthen ourselves in the moonlight could strengthen the blocks and chains, as well. But people discovered ways to get out of those, too. So over time we developed something far stronger. If you solidify your potions and weavings in crystals and bind those crystals to the roots of the trees, the deeper the tree grows, the more it binds. Eventually, the spell in the crystal becomes a part of the earth itself."

"Whoa," I said, trying to think of what spell I'd want to be a permanent part of the earth. Maybe an animal sanctuary? Ooh! Or a glow-up spot. Like, no matter how rough you felt, if you stood on that spot you'd look like a straight-up deity.

"You can do that even if the spell hurts people?" Angelique asked, her voice shrill. Clearly her mind had not jumped to glow ups. "Just sink it right into the ground and let it grow?"

Ms. Coulon nodded sadly. "And if the tree and crystal are planted in earth that was once carried by the river, the bindings are strengthened by the river's magic. And if the roots of the tree are being fed by the river itself . . ."

"Unlimited power," Angelique said, her voice small. But that only made her words feel bigger.

"Exactly," Ms. Coulon said. "This campus is built on river silt, and before the levees were built, the Mississippi River flooded its banks and watered the roots of all these trees, strengthening the crystal capture that was planted with them. A witch's nature is to be free, so captures are a witch's worst enemy. Our bodies fight our magic being trapped whether we want them to or not. Most times we're not even conscious of it. We instinctively use magic to fight the capture, and when we do, the capture absorbs it. The more magic we use to resist, the stronger the bindings become."

"Like a Chinese finger trap," I said.

"Exactly. The magic of hundreds, maybe thousands of witches have been trapped by this crystal capture. It's the worst kind of punishment: the kind others think you should be able to walk away from."

That was dark.

I stared past Ms. Coulon, my eyes landing on the trees outside her windows. "No wonder my mentor said this spot wasn't on any of the maps," I said.

Ms. Coulon nodded. "Historically, captures do not appear on any maps. When they were in use, they were kept hidden to stop witches from finding and dismantling them. Now they're still left off the maps from the shame of ever having built them in the first place."

"Some people are working to correct the record of history," Angelique said. By "some people," Angelique meant her and her mentor, Miss LeBrun. "We can't ignore the things we've done wrong. We have to own up to them and do something different."

"That's true, and I commend the people doing that work, but this isn't just any capture," Ms. Coulon said. "It's a capture grown and amplified by water from the sharpest bend on the Mississippi, one of the most powerful rivers in the world. It has almost incomprehensible strength."

"Then why aren't we fighting it right now?" I asked.

Angelique gave me a look.

"Seriously," I said. "If we're standing on this incredibly strong capture right now, why isn't it capturing our magic?" A week ago, I would have spilled a little magic just to test it, but I didn't need to. It looped through my body and both my charms, pulsing with every heartbeat like it always did.

"Before I was born, a group of witches who called themselves the Dryades wove an intention through the farthest branches of the trees. They stitched each individual strand so that as the trees grew, the intention would, too. It's quite beautiful." Ms. Coulon turned in her chair to look out the window with me.

"Wait," Angelique said. "You can see the intention?"

Ms. Coulon chuckled. "Only when I look," she said. "Would either of you like to see it?"

Ms. Coulon pulled a brass tube out of a bag hanging on the back of her chair. I always thought that was her teacher bag, but that tube was giving more Astronomy than Math. It looked like a telescope, except there wasn't a skinny end.

Ms. Coulon held the tube out to both of us.

"You go first, Angelique," I said. I wasn't scared, but weaving intentions was Angelique's thing, not mine.

"That's very kind of you, Hasani," Ms. Coulon said, "but there is no need. I have quite a few. We make these at the glassworks." Angelique took the first tube and Ms. Coulon passed me another one from the bag. It was heavy and cold but not nearly as solid as it looked. Like a giant, brass gummy that still managed to stand up straight.

"Weird," I said, watching the metal shiver like Jell-O in my hand.

"The brass is still molten at the center, but don't worry. The outerweave keeps it cool and helps it hold its shape."

I looked over at Angelique. She was already aiming hers at the window, so I put mine up to my face, too, ready to catch it if it flopped down like an elephant trunk in front of me. It didn't. The tube shape held up perfectly.

I closed my left eye and looked with the right one like I would to see through a telescope.

"Both eyes open," Ms. Coulon said.

I opened my left eye and suddenly the trees on the other side of the window were alive with colored lights.

"Whoa!" I breathed.

"Brass glass scopes let you see any intention as clearly as you would if it were drawn by your own mother. They are one of our biggest sellers," Ms. Coulon said, pride in her voice.

I could see why. Through the scope, the shadows of fences and trees and benches were still there, but they were hard to focus on because of all the lights. It was like the whole campus was under a tent of shimmering colors.

"It's like a kaleidoscope," I said.

"Not a bad comparison. A kaleidoscope uses mirrors to reflect objects back and forth. Our brass glass scopes use crystals to reflect objects back and forth. The difference is that kaleidoscopes reflect colorful pieces sitting inside the tube, and brass glass scopes reflect intentions outside the tube."

"Are those the beads being reflected through the trees?" I asked. The wind had knocked a lot of them out. My favorite one was gone, but there were plenty left. And what else besides Mardi Gras could make colors like that?

"A few of the beads will remain visible, but the vast majority of what you are seeing is the Dryades' intention. To the naked eye, intentions look static even to the fleur, but through the brass glass scope it's easy to see how they pulse with movement. Like life."

Angelique was quiet. I could feel her trying to soak up every inch of it. If anyone could become an expert in weaving intentions by staring at a massive canopy of dancing lights, it was Angelique.

"What does this intention do?" Angelique asked.

"It pins magic in place. A yang woven to counterbalance the yin of the capture. I told you before that it's attached to the tips of the branches to grow with the trees. But since roots grow faster than branches, the intention needed rebalancing periodically. At least, that's my theory."

"Your *theory*?" I asked, not taking my eyes off the lights. "You mean, you don't know for sure?"

"Witches don't do much collaboration outside of our immediate circles. More often than not, if you don't watch an intention being woven and talk to the fézur while she weaves it, you might not even find out who made it, let alone how or why. You can only guess the intention's purpose based on what happens. From what I can tell, the Dryades wove this intention to oppose the force of the capture. So instead of sucking your magic out, it presses your magic in."

"Like making you hold your breath," Angelique said.

"Exactly. If you were in a place with poisoned air, holding your breath would be a very good idea. That worked for a while, I'm sure, but by the time I started working here, witches who came to this campus were oozing magic, sometimes without even realizing it. I knew the Dryades' intention needed to be reinforced and amplified so that it could grow faster than the capture, so I developed a crystalized intention that could do it. The more crystals I hung in the trees, the stronger the effect. For the last fifteen years, I've maintained the balance in the trees. Everything was fine until this morning, when I found magic on the ground."

"That's magic on the ground?" Angelique asked.

I pointed my scope toward the ground. Then I winced. There were shimmering puddles of magic all over the front yard. The puddles didn't pulse like the intentions, but they were definitely magic. From the looks of things, LaToya had been out there wasting magic left and right, but, true story: One of those puddles was mine.

"I wonder if this is what the world looks like to Othello," I said. If he was here, there was no way I would have been able to stop him from rolling around in all that.

"The internal structure of a cat's eye was the starting point for the brass glass scope, so possibly. I'd like to think so," Ms. Coulon said. "We used something similar for the beads in the trees."

"You put the beads in the trees?" I squealed. I'd had never, ever wanted to hug Ms. Coulon before, but those bead trees were my favorite. "Those trees are the whole reason I didn't change middle schools.

My mom wanted me to stay here so we wouldn't have to drive across town, but me? I was all about the bead trees."

Ms. Coulon nodded, running her fingers along the necklace holding her glasses. I wondered if those were crystalized intentions, too.

"I can only take credit for a few of them," Ms. Coulon said. "And the kindergartners do most of the work during the shoebox parade. You're a Riverbend lifer, aren't you?"

Lifers is what we called people who went to Riverbend Elementary, then Riverbend Middle, and then Riverbend High School.

I grinned. "Yep. I was trying to convince Angelique to become a half-lifer, but she turned me down."

"I'm sure her mother has other plans," Ms. Coulon said.

"You know my mother?" Angelique asked.

"Of course, Miss Hebert. Everyone in the city knows your mother. She's been trying to be my best customer for years. When Sandy said her stepdaughter's friend, Angelique, was trying to get a spot at Riverbend, I knew who you were right away. I even did what I could to help your mother lean in this direction."

Angelique looked as surprised as I was. "What did you do?" Angelique asked.

"I offered to make a trade for an item she's been after for years if, in exchange, she would seriously consider your request. Looks like it worked."

"Oh," Angelique said. For once, she looked awkward. "Then I guess I should thank you."

"The only way either of you can thank me is by telling me what you did this morning and how you did it. With the Dryades' intention disturbed, the capture should be drawing magic down even as we speak, but somehow, the capture is quiet, too. You've made more progress in one morning than I did in fifteen years. So, please, tell me how you did it."

It was Ms. Coulon's turn to take notes. I started from the top, Angelique filling in what I left out. We told her about me wanting to keep Riverbend magic-free, and the termites, and the spellbook Sandy gave me when she married my dad, and the unicorn poop, and the whole drama around picture jasper and really fresh figs. And how my mentor, whom I still didn't name, by the way, said a freedom spell might work to free the school, but how it really just freed me.

"We should talk to Sandy. She gave me her spellbook. She's the fézur," I said, feeling good about remembering what you call the person who makes a spell.

Ms. Coulon furrowed her brow. "That's Freedom 90, Sandy's ninety-second therapy session for ninety minutes of freedom," she said.

I smiled. "You know it?"

"Of course I know it. I've done Freedom 90 dozens of times. It's amazing. Are you sure you followed it exactly? Did you do it unsupervised?"

"No. Sandy watched the whole time."

Ms. Coulon cocked her head to one side like she didn't believe me.

"She did! She was watching on FaceTime until the wind blew the phone away."

"Well you must have done something different. Our full coven has done that spell on this very campus. We didn't kick up so much as a breeze, let alone a windstorm. Maybe something happened when you linked with your sisters to do the spell?"

"We didn't link to do Sandy's spell," I said. "It was just me."

Angelique nodded.

Ms. Coulon blinked. "Just one of you? Not a full thirteen? Now I see why Aimee was hesitant about taking you on fully. You're so wild."

Angelique stared at Ms. Coulon, wide-eyed. If she had been wearing pearls, she would have clutched them right then. She hated when people called me a "wildseed."

"I don't mean to be insulting, Hasani. It isn't a bad thing. Aimee probably just doesn't know what to do with you. Frankly, I don't, either."

Here we go again. I thought going back to regular school would mean leaving behind the constant feeling that I wasn't quite right. That I didn't belong. But I did belong. Like Ms. Coulon said, I was rooted in this place. Her little comment wasn't going to dig me out.

"I'm a wildseed," I said. "I can't always control it. I try to keep it in, but it's wild. I'm sorry," I said, then I remembered my Belles Demoiselles training. "I mean, please excuse me," I corrected. I wasn't sorry.

Ms. Coulon's face softened.

"I'm guessing quite a few legacy witches have told you something like I just did. On behalf of close-minded middle-aged women everywhere, I apologize. That was wrong of me to think and to say. I'll do better. Hasani, being a wildseed is nothing to apologize for. Maybe legacy witches don't expect much of you. That's unimportant. What is important is deciding what you expect of yourself."

Hit two million subscribers? Have fun with my friends? Help my mom get her tea shop off the ground?

Ms. Coulon gave me the look she uses when she's giving you time to think. Seriously, did she expect me to answer right then? Like, was I supposed to be carrying answers to stuff like that in my pocket to whip out on the fly? Adults were exhausting.

"I don't know," I said.

"Fair enough. But with so many unknowns, I would suggest that the two of you stop any and all magical activity within range of the capture."

"Don't do magic at school? Why? Because I don't know what I want to be when I grow up?" We hadn't been planning on doing magic at school anyway, but still.

"Not knowing is more dangerous than you realize. It may seem stable now, but you don't know what you did to the capture. You don't know if it has been healed or destroyed. You don't know if whatever has been done can be reversed. And you don't know what you want to do with your magic, so you don't know when to give and you don't know when to take. When we don't know things, the wise don't jump in with rushed answers. We move with caution. We pull out a fresh sheet of scratch paper. We work the problem from top to bottom and produce a viable range of solutions. Then and only then do we act. It works for math and it works for magic. Now, will you convey the message to your linked sister, Demi-Rose?"

"Dee," we both corrected.

"Yes, Dee. Until we know more, we should refrain from all forms of magic, including charm. There may not be any negative effects, but we won't know that until we know more."

Angelique and I nodded.

"Should we . . . tell any other witches who might be on campus?" I asked. I mean, not my circus, not my monkeys, but if people might get burned out, it seemed cold not to give them a heads-up.

"Well, I would never presume to know any witch who hasn't made herself known to me, but if there is anyone to whom you feel comfortable passing on a warning, that is entirely up to you."

"Shouldn't we call Sandy? She can help. I know she's not a charmed girl but—"

Ms. Coulon scrunched her nose. "No, no. Let's not bother her," she said. "Sandy has a lot on her plate right now."

Dang. Maybe Sandy did figure out all her spells through trial and error, but it was a little cold to hear her friend acting like she wouldn't be any help.

"I'll see the two of you back here at three fifteen to set up. We want to be ready for the rest of the team by three thirty sharp. Make sure any difficult conversations that need to be had happen before then. Have you studied your teammates' tests to examine their strengths and weaknesses?"

"Angelique has," I said. "She's always on top of things."

"Well then, I'm doubly glad to have her leading the team with you."

Ms. Coulon put her hand out to collect her brass glass scopes. The name could've used some work, but the scopes were sheer perfection. "Can I borrow one?" I asked. "I'll bring it back tomorrow. I want to see if anybody left anything in my room."

"I don't believe in loans," Ms. Coulon said flatly. "The borrower is slave to the lender, and I have never wanted to be a slave master."

Oop.

I blinked.

"Uh . . . OK?" I said, handing it back.

"You can keep them," Ms. Coulon said. "Both of you. Consider them gifts. Perks of being cocaptains."

CHAPTER FOUR

DROPLETS AND BLOSSOMS

"Did you look around Ms. Coulon's room through the scopy-scope?" I asked as soon as we were out of earshot. "Clean as a whistle."

"Except the doorway," Angelique said.

I had not seen anything in the doorway and, believe me, I looked. I was so sure there was nothing there that I made Angelique go back and look again. Sure enough, there were two thin lines of magic criss-crossing the door like a giant X. Even with Angelique literally pointing at them I could barely see them through the scope. They were thinner than spiderwebs and so straight that it looked like Ms. Coulon used a ruler and a pencil sharpened to infinity to draw them.

"She used an extender," I said. "She had to." Besides, until that morning, there was no other way to do magic inside the building. "What do you think they do?"

"She told us. They stop people from leaving name drops and other traps in her classroom."

"You think she made it today?"

Angelique shrugged. "It's not pale blue. That means it's an active weave. There's no telling how long it's been there. The real question is, what should we do about our alternate?"

For a bright, shining moment, I thought Angelique was suggesting we drop LaToya as an alternate on the Mathletes team. Turns out she was talking about telling her Ms. Coulon's warning about the capture. Angelique wouldn't even consider dropping her from the team.

"Hasani, we gave our word" is all she would say.

Back in the cafeteria, Luz and Dee were sitting at the table guarding all our stuff, but unfortunately my lunch was useless since my red beans and rice were ice cold and the line was already closed.

Of course, that's the moment LaToya decided to grace the cafeteria with her presence. She arrived, pulling a flowered suitcase behind her. From that distance, I couldn't tell what kind of flowers were on the suitcase, but I didn't need to see them to know they were gladiolas or, as LaToya liked to call them, sword lilies. Her signature. The way she was smiling and dapping people up on her way in, you would have thought she had gone to school here since kindergarten, not that she'd forced her way in last week.

Not my circus, not my monkeys, but she was definitely playing with influence, maybe even right then.

I looked at Angelique.

"Y'all, we have to tell you something," I said, pulling out my phone to tap out:

School built on witch capture. Don't use magic.

I clicked Send. I don't know why. Angelique and I already knew that info, Luz couldn't do magic, and Dee did not check text messages. I ended up just showing her my phone. She nodded.

"What now?" Luz asked.

"If it's dangerous for us, it's dangerous for her, too. We have to tell her," Dee said.

As if on cue, LaToya unzipped the back of her suitcase and started putting water bottles in front of every person at her table.

"Apologies," LaToya said, fake London accent in full effect. "I just wanted to make certain these were chilled before I brought them to you. Nothing but the best for my besties."

I rolled my eyes. "You know where she got those, right?" I said.

I couldn't help but stare. In 3Thirteen, the matte sheen and gold undertones made those bottles blend in perfectly with the gold and greenery and the strangely luxurious monkey in Kaitlynn's shop. In the cafeteria, bottles of magic stood out, even if LaToya was passing them out like they were Perrier.

LaToya was in her element, flitting from person to person, giving alms to the peasants like any good queen bee. Approaching her then probably had a success rating of less than zero. From the look on her face, Angelique agreed, but we went over there, anyway.

Magic pricked at my fingers. I breathed and consciously forced it to loop through my dolphin and into my fleur-de-lis charm. I don't know if it was nerves or what, but I figured it was better to let Angelique do the talking.

"Excuse me? LaToya?" Angelique said.

Latoya definitely knew we were there. She was just making it hard.

"Oh! Angelique!" LaToya said, switching back to her private school girl voice. "Hi! Everybody, this is Angelique from my Mathletes team."

Her Mathletes team?

Angelique ignored it. I don't know if I could have. Sandy's freedom spell must have worn off, because I was not feeling calm and free. Perfect droplets of condensation blossomed on each water bottle like they had been styled for an ad. Those bottles were dripping with magic inside and out. I tried to focus on something else.

"Can we speak with you outside?" Angelique asked.

"About Mathletes? No! Say it right here. Now that I'm on the team, a bunch of these people are gonna want to join. Right guys?"

"It's not about Mathletes," Angelique said before LaToya could get her table all hyped up.

"What's it about?"

Angelique looked at her firmly.

LaToya didn't budge.

"Camp," Angelique said finally.

"Oh! Camp!" LaToya turned back to her table. "That's code. Remember? The fake ones are always extra secretive. Not that Angelique is fake, but she is a lackey, after all. And look who she works for."

Those fools were all nodding. Even Jenny. It was wild.

I took a deep breath. *Not my circus, not my monkeys.*

"Just leave it, Angelique," I said. "We tried. Now it's on her."

LaToya said something about seeing who's really in charge when we turned to walk away, but Angelique pretended not to hear her, so I did the same.

The lunch bell was going to ring any minute, anyway. I just wanted to grab my backpack, head to Earth Science, and not think about the fact that LaToya was going to be in Mathletes that afternoon, but I couldn't look away from Annie.

Annie was still clutching my beads, waiting for LaToya to look her way. When LaToya finally did look at her, Annie's face was literally flooded with relief as she handed LaToya my favorite one. Annie was definitely being influenced. It was hard to watch. I wanted to run across the room and snatch my beads from both of them. Yank the fancy water from Annie's hand and tell her not to drink it.

Then I saw something that I thought I'd never see. A vine trailing up _AnnieOaky_'s arm like a snake trying to squeeze the life from her. It snaked around her collar before it slowed down, blooming yellow flowers that could have been decoration from where we were sitting. I knew what it was. Cat's claw. I would have known it anywhere as often as pulling it off the house landed on my list of chores.

"Wait. I'm not the only one who saw that, right?" Luz asked as LaToya threw her blazer over Annie's shoulders and hustled her out of the cafeteria.

We all shook our heads. We saw it, too.

AnnieOaky was a witch.

CHAPTER FIVE

SCOPES AND SANDWICHES

As a mantra, *not my circus, not my monkeys* was a solid seven out of ten, but after watching _AnnieOaky_ blossom in the cafeteria, I wasn't even sure a ten out of ten mantra would have kept me calm.

I pulled out my phone to text Sandy, but I couldn't think of what to say, so I texted Annie instead. Annie's mom read her phone sometimes, so I tried to say what I needed without saying too much.

You OK?

Two seconds later, there was a read receipt, and that was it.

I kept finding reasons to open my backpack to check it again when Mr. McLachlan, our Louisiana Studies teacher, couldn't see. When the bell rang, the three dots showed, then disappeared. Showed, then disappeared until finally it said:

I'm good. LaToya's helping.

Thumbs-up. Flower emoji. Book emoji. Heart face.

I showed it to Dee on the way into Earth Science.

Dee raised her eyebrows. Then sighed. Then shrugged.

"What does this even mean?" I asked.

"I guess she got it, then."

I looked at Dee like, seriously? I mean, chill was one thing, but this was over the top.

"I get wanting to protect her, but Hasani, she's not your responsibility. Looks like she never was," Dee said like I was supposed to get it. "You don't have as much influence as you think. She's talented. You might have to let this one go."

Mr. McKinnley started Earth Science, and Dee wouldn't talk after that. Not that she was really being any help.

I tried texting Sandy again. I still didn't know exactly what I wanted to say, so I went with:

Want to hang out?

Sandy always wanted to hang out, but she usually texted about it first.

Your dad and I are going out to dinner. Do you want to come?

Nope. I did not feel like dealing with my dad.

That's all right, I texted.

Tomorrow? Pick you up from school?

For whatever reason, that instantly made me feel better.

Can Luz come?

I'd spring Dee and Angelique and maybe my mom, too, after she said yes to Luz, but Sandy had already peeped my game.

> Can we wait for Sunday for the whole gang? Looking for some quality time with you.
>
> ♥

A few weeks ago, the thought of having "quality time" with Sandy would have made my stomach hurt, but now the idea of having tea with Sandy someplace witchy where I didn't have to talk in code was legitimately making me feel better. Good enough to face the fact that LaToya was in my seventh period.

After Earth Science, Dee left to walk to her coding class at Tulane, but Angelique, Luz, and I all met up outside our Geometry class on the third floor. When LaToya sashayed into room 313, all I did was take a deep breath and exchange shrugs with Luz and Angelique.

When I pulled out my phone again to show Angelique and Luz the weird texts from Annie, a message from Dee was sitting right on the lock screen. *Talented folks don't need saving.*

I know she was serious because she *texted* it to me. Dee never texted.

"She's kind of right," Angelique said, but anything else had to wait for later because walking into Ms. Coulon's class while the bell was ringing was worse than being late.

I don't know what I was expecting. For LaToya to be throwing hexes at me? For her to be saying weird stuff in a British accent just to be annoying? None of that happened. In Math class, she did math. She didn't raise her hand, but she did answer a question when Ms. Coulon called on her. The question was kind of easy. I mean, who doesn't know who Euclid is, but still. There was no gloating attached. LaToya acted like a perfectly normal person. And when class was over and Angelique and I had to stay to prep for Mathletes, she offered to stay and help, too. IN A NORMAL way. Ms. Coulon told her that the job was for cocaptains only and LaToya said she understood and then left without any drama.

"I'm going to go get a fresh cup of coffee from the teacher's lounge," Ms. Coulton said, grabbing her bag off the chair. "I'll have my key with me, so you can close the door if you'd like. Traditionally, the time between the end of the day and the start of activities has been a time for the captain to get into captain mode. Besides, I figured the two of you could use a safe place to talk that's a little larger than your tent. Not that the tent isn't beautifully constructed. It is. Your mother would be proud."

Angelique blushed, but maybe from embarrassment. Who knew what else Ms. Coulon saw with her scopes.

"Thank you," Angelique said. "I'll tell my mother you said so."

"I'll be back by three forty," Ms. Coulon said, closing the door behind her.

Angelique and I didn't talk about anything witchy at first. We just set up the desks and put out the pencils and booklets of scratch paper the way Ms. Coulon wanted them. We still had a few minutes left, so we set a timer and pulled out the scopes Ms. Coulon had given us. I just wanted to see the lights again. The eye shadow palette lights sparked just as much joy as they did the first time and, the longer I watched them, the more I was itching to make a video. I figured Angelique wanted more time to examine that *X* weave across Ms. Coulon's door, but she looked out the window with me. It was peaceful, like lying on your back and watching clouds. Then the timer dinged, we put the scopes away, Ms. Coulon came back smelling like café au lait, and the rest of the team filed in.

I was suspicious at first, but LaToya was chill when she'd left and she was still chill when she came back for practice. She didn't understand anything about the Pythagorean theorem, but she didn't wait for me or Angelique or Ms. Coulon to point it out. She was the one who told us, and she asked a bunch of questions trying to figure it out. She wasn't quite there by the end of the meeting, but she was so determined that I knew she'd get it eventually.

LaToya was a completely different person away from her group. She was so different that I was starting to think maybe it was me the whole time. At least I did until after the meeting.

LaToya offered to help sharpen the pencils and put the chairs

77

back. Ms. Coulon was heading down for another coffee refill but said it was up to us.

Maybe this LaToya would listen if I told her about the capture. If not for her sake, for Annie's. Angelique and I looked at each other, then nodded. LaToya put her backpack on a table and started on the pile of pencils waiting to be sharpened while I pushed a desk across the floor.

"Congratulations, LaToya," Angelique said. From her tone, I could tell she was making a compliment sandwich. Compliment, something to fix, compliment. We learned it at Belles Demoiselles, and despite the fact that all of us knew it, it still seemed to work every time. "You did really well today. I'm glad you made it as an alternate."

"No thanks to you," she said.

Ah! There was the LaToya we knew.

Angelique had already laid down the first slice, though, so she just reinforced it before adding the filling. "I get that you might be a little hesitant to work with us because of things that happened this summer, but I hope you'll listen to what we have to say. It affects you and I guess now it affects Annie, too." Filling. "Annie really looks up to you." Bread.

LaToya nodded for a few seconds before she said anything. "Oh, so now she 'genuinely' looks up to me? I'm not some monster who magicked her into being my friend?"

That statement might have had more impact if LaToya hadn't reached into her bag, pulled out a green bottle, and chugged the whole thing back before she kept going.

"You want some?" she asked. To be fair, I was staring. "Oh! Sorry. It's my last. I already gave the rest to my friends."

Angelique wasn't ready to stop. "I'm glad you're finding a group of friends here. Really. I am. But this school was built on top of a dangerous place for witches, and it turns out that it might be dangerous again. Have you ever heard of a capture?"

LaToya rolled her eyes.

"Seriously? Is that what you were going to tell me? That this place used to be a capture? Duh. If you ever want to actually learn something, let me know. I might let you come to my school. Might." LaToya picked up her bag and dropped the bottle in instead of putting it in the trash, like she didn't even want us to be able to pose with it. "On second thought, no. You couldn't handle it. My school isn't about charm. It's about magic."

Yep. Same old LaToya.

She flounced out. Angelique and I decided to wait a minute before we left. Hopefully she'd be on her way home by the time we got outside. Of course we saw her anyway. She was coming out of the cafeteria still carrying that stupid water bottle. I don't know if it was more annoying that she was trying to make a water bottle trend happen

79

or that, the way things were going, I was pretty sure she would. The one thing I did know was that I had to talk to Annie. If LaToya wasn't going to be straight with her, it was up to me.

Miss Nancy was parked right outside the front gates.

"Come cover for me?" Angelique asked. "I want to pull up my tent, but I don't want Miss Nancy to see me in the bushes. She'll get suspicious."

"The yard is empty. How am I supposed to cover for that?"

"Can you just pretend you lost your phone or something? I need either you or Dee, and you're the only one here."

"You need me or Dee to weave an intention?" Was Ms. Coulon right? Did we maybe link up while I was doing Sandy's spell and I just didn't know it?

"I don't need you to weave it. I can kind of do that without seeing. But if I can't see it reflected in one of y'all's eyes, I can't see how to untie it."

Oh, right! Angelique couldn't see her own magic any more than I could see mine.

"Have you seriously been using the reflections in our eyes this whole time?" I asked.

"It's not like I have rose-colored glasses. Do you have a better idea?"

Angelique was the GOAT for real. I never would have thought of that, but I did have a better idea. The scopes.

Angelique looked like she wanted to smack herself on the forehead, but she nodded and went to discreetly slip into the azaleas. No way Miss Nancy hadn't seen us, but I didn't point that out. Miss Nancy probably knew everything we ever did, anyway. She had that vibe.

"Loved your video," Jenny said.

I jumped. That girl was way too good at sneaking up on people. That was twice in one day.

"Hey, Jenny," I said, trying not to sound as spooked as I felt. I had known her since kindergarten, after all, even if she was hanging with LaToya now.

"Such a good idea. How'd you come up with it?"

"Which one?" I normally remembered which video was coming out when, but since I had a bunch of them scheduled to post and Dee had made me my awesome bitbot, but I hadn't even opened the app to check the comments yet.

"It was 'Cat Looks You Can Rock at School.' I was almost the first commenter. Third," she said.

"Cool. Glad you liked it." This was getting awkward. I wished Angelique would hurry up.

"Definitely. It was super cute. I used to do videos, too."

"You have a channel?" I asked, but as soon as I said it, I knew that wasn't right. "Wait a minute," I said. "You used to do commercials! I remember! 'That's a good car, Mawmaw!'"

I did it in the same baby voice Jenny used to use in those commercials. It was hard not to. It was too cute to say it any other way.

Jenny smiled shyly. "Yeah, that's it. My grandmother says it sparked record sales."

"That's cool," I said. "Why'd you stop doing it?"

"It stopped making record sales, I guess."

Jenny laughed, but it was hard to laugh with her. It actually felt kind of sad.

"Well, anyway, I'm totally gonna rock the modified space buns. And the 'subtle whiskers.' Where'd you get your inspiration?"

"For the cat looks video? I have . . . a cat," I said.

I swear I wasn't trying to make it weirder. It's just, that was it. I have a cat. He inspired me.

"I should have guessed. Does your cat have a name?"

Of course my cat has a name. Even if I just called him 'cat,' his name would be Cat, right? But I didn't say any of that. Jenny was just trying to make an awkward conversation less awkward, so I tried to throw her a bone.

"Are you on Instagram?" I asked. "Because Othello—my cat, Othello—has an Instagram. You could follow him."

"Oh," Jenny said. "I only have WeBop now."

Wow.

Just when I thought I couldn't take it anymore, Angelique rounded the corner. She must have crawled over there through the bushes just so she could play it off and walk out like normal. Of course, not a spot on her. I had never been so happy to see her.

"Oh! There's my friend Angelique," I said. "She's new this year. You've met her?"

"Yeah. We've met," Jenny said. "I guess you have to go?"

"Yeah," I said, pointing at Angelique's car. Miss Nancy was standing outside of it. That meant we really did have to go. "If you ever get Instagram again, let me know. Othello and I will follow you."

"Cool!" Jenny brightened. "And if you ever want to start Othello a WeBop, let me know. I can help you edit or something."

Angelique smiled and we ran off toward Miss Nancy before Miss Nancy started walking toward us.

"What's up with that?" Angelique asked as we hopped inside, ducking one of Miss Nancy's glares.

"Nothing," I said. "She just follows my channel."

CHAPTER SIX

PUDDLES AND PROMISE

"**S**o, did that stuff in the green bottles turn Annie into a witch or what?"

I love Luz. No matter what's happening, she always just gets right to it. Even when everything that's happening is Dee rocking her first college class; Luz convincing the principal to get official uniforms for the debate team; Angelique and I telling the entire story of our day, including the gifts from Ms. Coulon, Mathletes, and post-Mathletes; me still being in my feelings about Jenny getting to those aqua beads before I did, then giving the strand to Annie who clearly gave it to *LaToya*, and then trapping me in a conversation so awkward that I didn't even think to ask about it; everybody taking turns using the brass glass scopes to scour my room and, when we didn't find anything except an invisible bag I was keeping in a box in my closet, great relief that we could say LaToya's name again without activating a name drop; and admiring the roach traps even though I made them and they looked like sloppy kindergarten drawings next

to the tent Angelique wove for us. Not to mention _AnnieOaky_, a girl whose YouTube channel I accidentally tanked when I was getting MakeupontheCheapCheap off the ground, not only being a witch but also blossoming right in front of us. It was a lot, but, as always, Luz was keeping us on point.

"Nah. You either are a witch or you aren't," Dee said without looking up from whatever she was sketching. "Nothing can give you that kind of magic if it wasn't in you to begin with."

Luz looked skeptical, but Angelique nodded in agreement. "There are some things that can raise your power, significantly in some cases," Angelique said. My eyes went straight to Angelique's dolphin charm. Those definitely kicked the power up a notch. "But nothing that can make you a witch if you weren't one already."

"As long as y'all aren't holding back on me," Luz said with a laugh.

"Nah. We're not," Dee said. "You not missing out on much, anyway."

"I don't know about all that," Luz teased, squeezing my YouTube subscribe pillow on her lap. "I could get with having a pink husky who follows me everywhere, but it's cool. Hasani's mom and I can be the not special ones. Wait. What am I saying? Miss Nailah is magic, too!"

"If it makes you feel better, my dad's not magic," Dee offered.

85

"Whose dad *is* magic?" I countered.

Dee looked up and shrugged. We both smiled.

We were just messing around, but Angelique looked offended. "Hey! Don't rag on dads. My dad's pretty cool."

"He is, but that doesn't make him magic. No shade on your dad. Or Dee's. Or anybody's," I added, chuckling at the idea of dad-magic.

Luz was slumped back on my bed with the pillow over her face. "That's not helping, y'all. At this point, I'm basically the only kid we know who *isn't* magic."

Angelique started to say something, probably to point out the fact that most kids we know don't even know magic exists, but I waved for her to stop. Melodrama was kind of Luz's way of processing. She just needed a minute. Sure enough, five seconds later, Luz popped up and said, "Ooh! What if Annie's not really a witch? Maybe she's like your mom. A kismet?"

I shook my head. "Kismets don't make flowers. Wait. Do they?" I looked at Dee.

"Nah. Kismets can't waste their magic. It comes when it comes and does what needs to be done. That kind of magic controls itself, so it's always exactly the right amount."

"Weird," Luz said. But the way she was smiling, I knew she meant the good kind of weird. She was feeling better. "But if it wasn't whatever is in those green bottles that made Annie show her witch side,

it must be because Hurricane Hasani unblocked something"—I gave her a look—"allegedly," she added.

"Hypothetically," I corrected. "But . . . maybe that's it?"

Honestly, I hadn't thought of that. But if I really had done more to fix a capture than Ms. Coulon had in fifteen years, I was way more magical than I thought. I hadn't even done it on purpose.

"OK," Luz said. "So, hypothetically, you freed something and now everybody who has some magic in them might start growing flowers in the middle of the cafeteria?"

"Basically." I winced, expecting somebody in the room to contradict me. Tell me I had a big head or something, but they all looked at me like they figured I could do something like that all along. It was weird. Almost as weird as when Jenny did my outro.

Angelique sighed. "Blossoming at school is the worst."

"Yeah," Dee said. "Even if y'all are not cool, you kind of want your mom when that happens. Glad I was in Vacherie."

No comment from me. Or Angelique.

"Especially with the ones she had growing out of her shirt," Luz said. "I hate those stupid vines."

"Cat's claw. Those vines are worse than yours, Hasani," Dee joked. "At least morning glories don't scratch."

"Ha, ha, ha," I said, throwing a pillow in Dee's direction.

"I like Hasani's flower," Luz said.

I did, too. Morning glories are beautiful, but we both knew that in New Orleans, they were basically weeds. Not as bad as cat's claw, though. I still groaned every time my mom put "Pull cat's claw off the house" on the chore list. Those things really did have claws, and no matter how hard you tried, you could never dig them out. My mom even considered using chemicals to get rid of them. Chemicals! I mean, she didn't go through with it, but even the fact that she thought about it tells you how bad they are.

"Cat's claw is the worst. No offense, Othello," I said. "Your little claws are the best."

Othello was in play mode, but I was in *sit cross-legged on my bed and chill* mode, so I sprinkled some magic down for him to lap up instead.

"You keep overfeeding that cat like that and you gon' have to live in the woods like Miss Lafleur."

I gave Dee a question mark face.

"Because Othello's gon' end up big as a house!" she finished.

I shrugged. Living in the woods with a giant cat actually sounded really good—as long as there was decent Wi-Fi.

"Gonna end up big as a house?" Luz said. "He's already the biggest kitten I've ever seen."

"It was just a few drops," I said. "Don't worry."

Dee's eyes went wide, but she didn't say anything else. Angelique, however, nudged one of the brass glass scopes in my direction. I put the scope to my eye.

"Wow," I breathed. What I thought was a little sprinkle was actually a puddle, and that was what was left as he lapped it up. It had probably been enough for him to swim in at first.

I winced, but it was more like sorry-not-sorry than actually sorry, because no matter how big he got, Othello would always be my adorable little guy. They were right, though. I had no idea I was pouring so much.

"You know I can't see my own magic," I said.

"That's why we find linked sisters," Angelique said. "So we can see each other and keep each other in line. Which is even more reason to be worried about Annie."

"Yeah, Annie's probably a wildseed," I said. "From the way she was acting, I'm guessing she didn't have any cousins or aunties doing magic at home."

"Maybe she'll join LaToya's coven," Luz offered.

Dee shook her head. "Nah. LaToya already has a full thirteen."

"It's forced, though," Angelique said. "It might fall apart any minute."

"Hasn't fallen apart yet," Dee said, "otherwise we would have heard from Thuy."

True. Thuy may have been in LaToya's coven, but she always acted like a friend. And I don't mean acted, as in pretended. I mean acted, like actions. If something that big was up, Thuy would have told us.

"And we all know LaToya isn't above getting a green witch to squeeze her magic. I mean, look at Hasani's hair."

If I didn't know better, I would think Angelique was lowkey insulting me. But she was right. There was no way my hair would be this long and thick if it hadn't literally grown overnight. I still didn't know how to take care of it. People kept asking me to make hair-care videos in the comments, but I couldn't even point them to my mama. She wasn't into doing hair, either. That's why she kept hers shaved.

"I'll give LaToya one point: That chevelure potion did its thing," I said, flicking my braids behind my head. "But you're right. It was shady to give somebody a potion and incantation when you know good and well they don't know what it is. What do they call that?"

"Informed consent," Luz said. "That's the topic of our first debate this season."

Angelique nodded. "Taking that potion didn't hurt you because you're so powerful, Hasani. But LaToya's influence could be really dangerous to a witch who is only promising. Like me."

Dee and I both looked at Angelique.

Only promising? Really?

File that under "Things I thought I'd never hear from Angelique."

Before we joined 3Thirteen, I didn't even know magic had levels. I thought it was just kismets, witches, and regular people. But even if I had known witches had levels, I never in a million years would have guessed that Angelique could be on a lower level than me. Never. Angelique was so . . . Angelique. We tested at the same time to get memberships at 3Thirteen, and I didn't even notice it then, not until Angelique got in her feelings about not having as many credits as me. But this was the first time she ever just came out and said it. I didn't know if I was supposed to hype her up or hug her.

"You're OK?" I asked tentatively.

"I'm not talking about me; I'm talking about Annie," Angelique said. "If there's a potion in LaToya's bottles, it could go really badly for her."

Dee shook her head. "The levels don't matter and neither do potions. LaToya can't influence Annie."

We all looked at her.

"Y'all know what I mean. Maybe LaToya can be a role model or whatever, but influence? Real influence? Nah. Annie's a witch. Not being influenced is the one thing we got going for us. Whatever Annie decides to do, that's on Annie. Same thing for Hasani and all that hair."

Honestly, I hadn't even thought of that. In my head, Annie was always this artistic younger kid I needed to protect. Like Miguel. I guess you grow some flowers and then, bam! You're on your own? Witches are cold.

Luz rolled her eyes a little. "I seriously doubt not being influenced is the only thing witches have going for them. I already mentioned pink huskies, but . . . pink huskies! Anyway, from where I'm sitting, the only thing that makes being a witch rough is that y'all stay letting other witches get schooled. I mean, why? If there's danger, just tell the girl. If Annie already knows, so what? She already knows. Big deal."

"Because you can't just go assuming somebody you're not related to is a witch," Dee said, her Vacherie accent coming through. "How messed up would it be for somebody to walk into your house and just tell you you're a witch before you even know it yourself?"

I winced again, raising my hand. "That's what happened to me," I said.

"And what happened to you was messed up," Dee responded. "Why you think I made sure you had a real room at camp? I didn't even know you yet. I was just trying to make your situation a little less messed up. That's something you should have gotten to tell people if you wanted to. Otherwise, it's not their business."

Mine your business, sha.

I never heard Grandmé Annette say those exact words, but Grandmé Annette's voice popped into my head just like that when Dee said "business."

"Dee's right," Angelique said. "It's kind of like walking up to somebody and telling them they're gay. They can tell you they're gay, but you can't tell them. It's rude."

"Exactly." Dee nodded.

"However . . ." Angelique added, "I do think this is an extenuating circumstance. I mean, first of all, we did watch her blossom. That's already pretty intimate. Second of all, between the capture and LaToya getting her to squeeze her magic, Annie is in real danger of burning out. And the only thing worse than a promising witch is a burned-out witch."

"Well, I vote we talk to her and at least make sure she's OK," Luz said. Dee gave her a look, but Luz gave the look right back. "What? I might not be in the coven, but I still get a vote. Annie's my friend, too."

Angelique raised her hand. "I agree with Luz," she said.

Dee flopped back against my bed. "I can't stop y'all, but I wish I could. When you don't know everything that's going on, nine times out of ten, you'll make things worse by getting in someone's business, not better. And I promise you, unless Annie comes to us asking for help, we will not know everything that's going on."

They all looked at me. I guess I was the only one who hadn't voted.

"I don't know," I said. "I need some time to think."

"Well, while you're thinking, I'm gonna go check on Miguel," Luz said. "Apparently his class is full of 'terrible' people."

"Yeah. He probably needs to vent," I said. "They did the locker lesson today."

Luz chuckled, putting her shoes on. "I remember that group locker session. I was so embarrassed about not being able to open my lock in front of Jason Anderson that I literally wanted to die. You remember that, Hasani?"

I nodded. Who could forget?

"Well, have fun with your coven meeting without me!" Luz said, heading out the door.

I was laughing with Luz, but when I looked back at Dee and Angelique, the mood had shifted to serious.

"I have to go in a few minutes," Angelique said, "but there's something I wanted to tell you in person before I do. I'm going to leave Riverbend Middle."

"Why?" I said. It had been only one day. Public school couldn't be that bad.

"After what I found out today about the capture, I just can't risk it. My parents must not know about it, or they never would have let me go in the first place. I'm going to tell them at dinner tonight. They're both in town, so it's perfect."

"Dangerous? Are you serious?" I said. "Ms. Coulon only said not to do magic. Do you think Ms. Coulon would stay if she thought it was dangerous?"

"Ms. Coulon is in the talented tenth," Angelique said calmly. "So are you. And Dee is extra-talented, so she may as well be, too. If one of you loses some magic, it won't mean the end for you. But if I lose any magic at all, it might be the end of me."

"You think you might burn out?" I asked.

Angelique nodded, still managing to hold her chin up.

"Even if you do, you'll still be a first daughter of a first daughter," I said.

"We both know that won't be the same. Everyone will look at me differently. I won't even be able to show my face at 3Thirteen, let alone build up more credits. They might even revoke my membership."

Dee looked at her, surprised. "Not being magic enough for 3Thirteen would really bother you?"

"Of course. I don't mind the way it is now. I can't do very much, but at least I can do something. Like Daddy always says: People get rich by sticking to budgets."

"Seriously?" I asked.

"Of course! It doesn't matter how much money you make. If you spend everything you have, you'll never be wealthy in the end. Conversely, if you make a budget that includes saving and investing and stick to it, you may not get rich fast, but you'll get rich eventually.

That's why I've always been so careful with my magic. There's no point in wasting it, even if I had a lot. But it turns out, I don't. I can't risk it."

I was more thinking, *Rich people talk about money so much that they have sayings about it?* but I got what she was saying. I just really, really didn't want her to leave Riverbend Middle. Mathletes needed her. I needed her.

"Or," I said, "and hear me out. Staying at Riverbend Middle is the best thing you could do to boost your magic. It's on a riverbend! Aren't those supposed to make everybody crazy powerful? You stay, let the riverbend do its thing, loop it through the dolphin, and store it in the fleur-de-lis. Boom. Dividends."

Angelique sighed. "That's not dividends, but I do get your point. I just don't want to risk it without knowing more."

"You have a library card, right?" Dee asked. Angelique nodded. "Well, let's know more."

Angelique sighed again. "The two of you are fine. More than fine. But, Dee, you should have heard the way Ms. Coulon talked about promising witches."

"And green witches," I said.

Angelique nodded. "I was so embarrassed, but honestly, she was right. Promising witches probably burned out all the time at that capture. How foolish would I be to stay there when I know the capture could absorb my magic before I could blink?"

"I guess you should talk to your mom about it," I said. "Make sure she knows so she can get you checked out."

"Oh, I'm not telling my mom about the capture. She'll definitely want to get my magic levels checked afterward, and there's no way I'm doing that. She'd find out I'm only promising. She doesn't even know I joined 3Thirteen." Angelique looked at the floor. "She'd be so disappointed."

"Your mom doesn't know you're—" Dee cut herself off, inhaling like, *Oh! Right!*

Angelique was adopted. Her mom couldn't see her magic any more than mine could.

"And you think being promising would make a difference to your mom?" Dee asked.

Angelique shrugged. She didn't look like herself. I wanted to pick her first daughter of a first daughter up off the floor and wrap it around her shoulders. Only I couldn't be the one to do that.

"I know that's why she's been trying to get her hands on the sixth pair of rose-colored glasses all these years. She wants to be able to size me up."

"She said that?" Dee asked.

"No. She didn't have to. It just makes sense."

"You're already a charmed girl. The top of our class. How could she possibly be disappointed?"

"You've met my mom," Angelique said. "Her standards are high."

True dat. "And now that she's getting all buddy-buddy with Ms. Coulon, she's going to get a pair of rose-colored glasses. It's only a matter of time. My best bet is to be in either Dakar or Geneva when she does."

"You're leaving the country?" I exclaimed. "Whoa. Wait. What do rose-colored glasses have to do with Ms. Coulon?"

"She made 'em," Dee said.

I blinked. "You knew that?" Did everybody know that?

"Nah. I didn't know. But she's a belle demoiselle who makes glass, right? I just put two and two together."

Maybe Dee should have joined the Mathletes.

"I also know Angelique might be overreacting," Dee said matter-of-factly.

Angelique looked at Dee. "How so?"

"You say you're *promising*, but your magic might not even be that low."

Angelique rolled her eyes. "Do you need me to show you my 3Thirteen card?"

Dee shook her head. "Your flow isn't that strong, but how long you been wearing those earrings?"

Angelique touched one of the tiny gold hoops she always wore. "I don't know. I've never taken them off. They're from my birth mom, I think. My mom never took them off me so I'd have some connection to her. I don't know if I want to have a connection to her or not, but I'm glad I have them. They're how Grandmé Annette found me."

Dee nodded like that clinched it. "I'm guessing you don't know about confinements?"

Angelique and I were all eyebrows.

"Nowadays people call them custodies?"

Angelique and I both shook our heads.

"It might be a Vacherie thing, but where I'm from, people get their babies' ears pierced as soon as they can leave the house. Like two weeks old. Everybody does it because the babies are too young to mess with the piercings while they heal, but the witches started it. It technically doesn't trap your magic completely or anything. It just kind of holds it in so you can't accidentally waste it when you're really young."

"Like a trust fund?" Angelique asked.

"Or a prison?" I added. It was sounding more like a capture than something that gave free money to me.

"Not like a prison," Dee said. "You're still free to use your magic. Like, it's yours, they're just making sure you don't mess it up before you can handle it."

I was not hearing the huge difference in that, but I let it go.

"All I'm saying is, when I first saw your magic, I assumed your mom hadn't released yours yet."

"I mean, you just said that your mom's super controlling," I said. "Maybe Dee's right. Maybe your mom hasn't released your confinement yet."

"Custodies," Dee corrected. "They call them custodies now."

"I honestly don't think that makes it any better, but OK. Custodies."

"That could be why you only tested promising. If you're wearing a custody, that's slowing your flow."

Angelique's eyes brightened. "So, do I just take them off, or—"

"Hold up," Dee said. "Slow your roll. Taking them off won't stop the custody. The only thing that might happen is you end up losing the earring that has the custody in it. If that happens, you won't be able to get it released."

"So how do I know if my magic is being custodied or not?"

"Maybe ask your mom?" Dee said, like, *Duh.*

"No." Angelique put her chin back up. She was looking more first daughter of a first daughter every second. "If my mom is doing this on purpose, she's just going to say no. I think this is one of those times it's better to ask forgiveness than permission. People, prepare for a slumber party. I think we need a night trip to 3Thirteen."

LATOYA

USE, NOT USED

*A*untie Regina and I never fought about anything until she tried to throw out my cup of unicorn tea.

"It's spent," she said. "You can't reheat it. After the steam is gone, the water that's left is no use."

"I want to save it," I said. "Like a souvenir of everything you've been teaching me."

That wasn't exactly true, but it didn't work, anyway.

"What you look like keeping a cup of used water for a souvenir? Get your daddy to buy you some more unicorn hairs and make it again. Or better yet, tell him to get you a scope or a fancy pair of glasses. They last longer and they're less mess."

I didn't want to tell her I couldn't do any of that, so I didn't say anything.

She scowled like I said something rude, but there was nothing I could do about Auntie Regina getting mad at me. She was a witch. I couldn't influence her with perfumes and sprays the way I did with my teachers at the Academy. She was fussing at me, and I just had to let her.

"All I know is I bet' not find a cup of old water sitting around my house to spill over and call mold and every creature in creation."

"Yes, ma'am," I said, carefully lifting the cup of cold unicorn tea so I wouldn't spill a drop and heading to the front door. I think she thought I was going to dump it outside, but there was no way I was doing that. She wasn't the only person who could help me. I had Kaitlynn, too.

The entrance to 3Thirteen was less than a mile from Auntie Regina's house, but walking there holding an open cup of unicorn tea made it feel like a marathon. I made it, though. I always do. Once I was inside, no one paid any attention to my cup. There were way more interesting things to look at, so I made it to Kaitlynn's retail experience with absolutely no problem.

Kaitlynn's white monkey, Jasper, wrinkled his nose at me from the top of a shiny fiddle-leaf fig, but I didn't let him bother me. I kept all my focus on Kaitlynn and her white linen jumpsuit.

"Of course!" Kaitlynn said, clasping her hands together and bowing her head when I told her what I needed. "These homebrews are truly precious. Do you have a spellbook, or is this a genius creation of your very own?"

"I have a spellbook," I replied, wishing I had thought to just say I'd made it up myself. I probably sounded smarter that way.

But then Kaitlynn said, "You know I collect old recipe books, don't you? It's a little hobby of mine. No pressure, but if you're ever thinking about giving yours up, let me know. I'll give you a great price. In the meantime, Jasper!" Kaitlynn clapped her hands, making the sleeves on her jumpsuit flutter. "Bring our friend a key to one of our practice rooms. They're on the fourth floor. You can't miss them."

I grinned and nodded more times than I should have when Jasper dropped the triangular key in my hand. I thought Kaitlynn would let me take up a little space in the warehouse. I never dreamed she'd offer me a practice room. She must have known I was on my way up.

CHAPTER SEVEN

SHIELDS AND DUTY

*A*ngelique's parents gave "sleepover on a school night" a hard no. Honestly, I was glad. My mom might have been cool with just Luz because Luz half lived at our house anyway, but she would have even side-eyed Luz sleeping over during the first week of school. Instead, we practiced something I'd never heard of called shielding.

Apparently shielding was like a ziplock baggie for magic: The seal didn't last forever, but while it did, no magic would leak out. Angelique kept saying how we didn't have to do it just to cover her, I kept telling her that of course we did and of course we would because that's what covens are for, and after saying it was cool one time, Dee would not dignify Angelique's unnecessary apologies with a response.

Shielding was probably the easiest magic thing I ever learned, maybe because I could see what was happening the whole time. Apparently, shielding is a lot harder to do without a Belles Demoiselles charm, but with one, we basically just had to hold out a big drop of magic, maneuver it so it was right next to Angelique's charm, then move it up really fast to put a little coating of magic around Angelique's fleur-de-lis. It was kind of like dunking an Oreo, but instead of bringing the cookie to the milk, you brought the milk to the cookie.

Angelique kept warning us that shielding uses a ton of magic until you get good at it, but there was only so much we could practice it before Angelique had to go, so we focused on shoring up the duty schedule instead. Dee would shield Angelique on the way to school in the morning and check in with her between classes until lunch. Both of us were on duty at lunch, and it was me for the rest of the day. If Angelique's fleur-de-lis charm started looking dry at any time, we'd slip out the back gate and either run toward my house or to the block with the coffee shop. Our school was almost on Tulane's campus, so there were always lots of college students walking around, and Angelique figured that at least two of us were sophisticated enough to blend in with them. I didn't ask which two. I could figure it out, but I didn't want to know.

And for added protection, Dee temporarily linked our phones. She said it would wear off in a couple of days, but in the meantime, if Angelique put her ring finger on the phone screen, it was basically the same as sending up the bat signal. We'd know instantly, and whichever one of us was on duty would rush to her rescue. I know Angelique was grateful that we wanted her to stay with us that much, but I don't know if she fully appreciated how much of a sacrifice Dee was making. The coding stuff Dee could do in her sleep, but this alarm was basically the same as Dee turning on the notifications on her phone. If that wasn't love, I don't know what is.

Despite our precautions or, as Angelique said, maybe because of them, absolutely nothing happened at school the next day. OK, maybe not nothing, but nothing bad. For one thing, Angelique showed up wearing her hair in a high puff. I think I'd seen Angelique with her hair up maybe one time before. Usually she wore it out no matter how hot it was, even though it was way thicker than mine and hung halfway down her back. I guess if she couldn't use charm, even Angelique couldn't survive the heat.

For another thing, Annie showed up wearing a plastic Mardi Gras bead necklace like it was actual jewelry. No. Not just jewelry. Like jewelry given to her by actual royalty. We tried to talk to her. I tried. Luz tried. Angelique tried. But in the end all Annie did was say something weird about "witching lesson seventeen" and cancel her snowball date with Angelique.

Since everybody was going to be free right after school, I was going to text Sandy again about having everybody over for tea, but Angelique said it was rude and Dee and Luz both agreed, so I figured maybe I better not. Besides, Angelique and Dee made plans to show Luz the vending machine for 3Thirteen and try their luck at setting up an appointment with somebody who knew something about custodies. There wasn't really a directory at 3Thirteen, so the vending machine was the best way to search how to get started.

Annie had a seat of honor at LaToya's lunch table—right next to LaToya's seat with actual flowers and placemats at both. I had to hand it to LaToya: The setup she had at their table was way better than the leftover cornbread we had at ours. We ate all that cornbread, though. It was a day old, but it was still good.

With Ms. Coulon there sipping on a perfectly cold cup of iced coffee through all of seventh period, LaToya was Angel-LaToya through the end of Geometry and, honestly, it was like Sandy's spell was working again without any re-upping. I felt free. Plus, I was really looking forward to hanging out with Sandy. I was looking forward to it so much that when Jenny tried to catch me again after school, it didn't even feel like an excuse to say that my stepmother's little car was already parked out front.

"What's up, girlie?" Sandy smiled. Her little white sports car was cool, inside and out. Especially inside. Sandy had the A/C cranking, and I was there for it.

"Your school doesn't look like it was hit with Hurricane Hasani." She winked.

"Yeah, well, my dad said you always ride with the top down," I said, teasing her back.

Sandy laughed. "Somebody should tell your father what it's like to have all this hair in all this heat. Believe me, I have been living for this A/C."

"Really? You don't use charm for that?" I asked, wondering how else Sandy always looked like she was walking through a perfect ocean breeze.

"Well, I'm actually on a little diet right now."

I looked at Sandy. "You trying to gain weight?" Seriously, she did not have room to lose any.

"Yes!" she said, brightly. "I'm kind of looking forward to it. But what I actually meant is that I'm going on a magic diet. I'm trying to restrict myself to just the basic needs, which, let's be honest, is not much. I mean, people live without magic all the time, right?"

"True," I said, but something didn't sit right. "Did Ms. Coulon tell you to stop doing magic?"

"Oh, honey. Witches don't tell each other what to do. Not even the ones in your circle of friends. They do make suggestions, though."

"OK, did Ms. Coulon suggest you stop doing magic? Because if she did, she shouldn't have. Your spell was great. It made me feel so much better. And even if we don't know exactly how it works, so what? Why does that mean you should stop doing magic?"

Sandy was looking like she might burst if she didn't give somebody a hug, preferably me. I didn't mind, so I leaned over in her direction to let her know it was OK, and she threw her arms around me and squeezed me tighter than I knew she could.

"Hasani!" she squealed. "You're defending me!"

"I am?"

"You are! You're trying to protect me! But, chica, you don't have to. Beverlyn Coulon is the dearest person in my circle of friends. You don't have to protect me from her. She's on our side!"

It had sounded like "Beverlyn" was talking trash about Sandy to me, but I decided to let it go. Sandy was too happy.

"Cool," I said, settling into the front seat. Really. It was. The vent felt amazing. I didn't remember the seat being that comfortable when Sandy drove me to Vacherie. Or maybe I had been just too stressed to notice. "You mind if I check my YouTube comments?"

"Go right ahead, chica," Sandy said, putting the car in gear.

We pulled out and I leaned back and pulled up my latest video, the one about cat looks. I honestly meant for it to be a crossover video for Othello's Instagram. Maybe launch a YouTube channel for him. Not all his followers would port from IG, but he'd been on my channel before, and those videos got lots of love, so I figured enough people would follow him to give his channel a good launch. Othello had other ideas. He was kind of in the cat looks video, but only cat bombing. A tail here. Knocking brushes off the table there. It wasn't good for a channel launch, but it was crazy cute, and the comments section showed it.

It had been so long since I had fun reading comments that I kind of didn't know what to do with myself. The bitbot Dee made me was perfection digitized. It didn't block bad comments or remove them. It trolled them. Trolling trolls is genius and hilarious, especially since the bitbot would stop whenever they did, but people can't resist trying to have the last word. Unfortunately for them, the bitbot had time—infinite time—and only one job to do: serve serves. I was so wrapped up in the hilarity that I didn't realize we were driving to my dad's house until we were already on St. Claude.

"Is there an entrance to 3Thirteen over here?" I asked. There was always hope.

"No. The closest one is a tiny one on Canal Street. There used to be a big one down there, but I guess once they built the aquarium, too many tourists wandered in by accident and they closed it. There is a vending machine in Araby. That sounds far, but it's really right there."

"No. That's OK. I just thought we were going to get tea."

"We are. Just at the house. I'm just trying to take a little break from magic, remember?"

"Full stop?"

"Maybe? It wouldn't be long. Six or seven months? A year, tops."

"A year?" I said. Sandy kept her eyes on the road, but I knew she felt me staring. "Because Ms. Coulon told you not to?"

"It's not exactly that. I'll tell you more later, but please, if you can, cut Beverlyn some slack? She's a lot like you, actually. Always prepared. Always with her little checklists." *What's wrong with a checklist?*

"But I have to be at the Freret entrance to 3Thirteen at six o'clock."

"I'll drive you back in time. Does that work?"

"I guess." I sighed.

I thought we were going somewhere magical. Even if it wasn't 3Thirteen, Sandy's regular people had a quirky-and-free thing going, too. At least the ones who came to the wedding did. The only one who didn't was Ms. Coulon. I was still debating telling Sandy how Ms. Coulon had been talking about her. It wasn't exactly bad, but it wasn't good, either. And friends, especially your "circle of friends," which is what Sandy called her coven, are supposed to lift you up, not bring you down. Maybe it was better that we were going to my dad's house. It'd give Sandy some space to be sad or angry or whatever she felt about Ms. Coulon talking about her without having to put on a show. Plus, the back porch on that house was pretty magical. A mixture of furniture I picked out and touches by Sandy had turned it into a full-blown oasis. And Sandy's iced tea was actually really good. Not as good as my mom's, but good. I didn't panic until I saw my dad's convertible charging under the carport.

"Dad's home?" I said. So much for talking witchy with Sandy. Sandy may have told him she was a witch, but he didn't need to know about me.

"Hasani, your dad misses you."

"Yeah, right," I mumbled. "He misses me so much that he sends all his messages through you and Mom."

"He's been busy lately, but he talks about you all the time. Every day."

About me, but not *to* me? Seriously, she could miss me with all that.

"I know it's kind of an ambush. I'm sorry. But will you come inside? I know Bobby wants to see you. And we have some news we wanted to tell you in person. Together."

Great. The last time my dad had news, I ended up blossoming in full view of a Belles Demoiselles satellite and ruining my summer.

What was it? Were they getting a divorce? Not surprising, with my dad involved. At the beginning of the summer, that was my literal plan, but I kind of didn't want that anymore. Not because of my dad, though, or my mom. Because of Sandy. For whatever reason, she really seemed to love him and, after everything we'd been through, I didn't want her to get hurt, not if she didn't have to.

"All right," I said. "I'll talk to him if you want me to."

"I do." Sandy smiled.

I smiled, too, but I didn't throw any charm in it. I wasn't feeling it.

My dad's house had changed a lot. Now there were tons of plants. Sandy loved plants the way my mom loved tea. I once heard my dad telling my mom that when Sandy moved in, she brought more monstera and calathea than clothes. Sounded like a dig to me. Like Sandy was too shallow to know what was important. But my mom just said, "Ooh! I love calathea. I'll ask her for a cutting," and left it right there.

Knowing my mom, she meant what she said, but I liked to think of it as her checking my dad. You know. Trolling the troll. Putting him back in his place. I get that my mom's not mad at him, and I'm not, either. Not really. But that doesn't mean I had to go chasing him down. When people really want to be in your life, they are. He wasn't. And it wasn't my job to do it for him. Especially when he literally greeted me by saying, "Hey, stranger."

Not "I've been talking about you, but not to you, and that must stink"?

Or "I've been literally chained up without my phone!"

Or even just "Hello."

Of all the things he could have said, he went with calling his only child a stranger.

I rolled my eyes so hard that it probably looked like a blank stare.

"Well," Sandy said. Without using charm, I'm sure it sounded way more strained than she meant it to. "Does anyone want tea? Hasani, it's actually one of your mom's blends. Her newest."

"The blueberry ginger sunrise?" I said, ignoring the look my dad was giving me. "Yes, please."

"Great!" Sandy said. "And the cantaloupe smelled so delectable when I passed it in the farmer's market, that I have some of that, too. Pre-chilled. And sliced," she added. "Should we eat outside or in?"

Meanwhile, my dad sat on the sofa with his mouth hanging open while Sandy and I got the pitcher and trays from the refrigerator and brought them out on the back porch.

"It's cool out here," I said when Sandy and I stepped outside. I lowered my voice, adding, "I thought you said you were on a 'diet.'"

Sandy laughed. "Oh, I did this ages ago. I got inspired when we visited your camp."

The whole Belles Demoiselles campus was surrounded by an enormous curtain of intentions that, among other things, kept the air at Belles Demoiselles cooler and drier than it ever would be outside. Sandy's was doing something similar. It wasn't quite on that level because I could definitely still feel the heat, but at least there was something cool in the breeze.

"The fans!" I said. "You didn't do the whole porch, you just did the ceiling fans. That was smart."

Sandy grinned. "It was kind of an accident, but I also kind of love it. Do you love it?"

"Yeah, I love it," I said, just in time for my dad to finally make it to the porch.

"You called me 'it'?" he said, using his jokey-jokey voice. "That's not nice. I'm not a thing, I'm a person."

I looked at him.

"You said you love 'it.' I'm 'it,' right? But if you love me, you have to know," and here he broke into song, "*I'm not just a plaything. I'm flesh and blood, just like a man.*"

The fact that Sandy was smiling didn't erase any of the awkward.

"You *are* a man, Dad."

He took off his silly face. I was glad. It felt like a mask. "I know," he said. "I was just being funny."

No. You weren't.

I looked at Sandy. "Should I pour us some tea before the ice cubes melt?" I asked.

Sandy nodded and sat on my dad's side of the table. That was cool. They were married, at least for now. It kind of left me alone on my side, but whatever. My side had the cantaloupe, so . . . more for me. I picked one up and took a big bite. It tasted just as good as it smelled.

Sandy put her hand in my dad's. He squeezed it, but then he just sat there. Sandy had to elbow him for him to realize that he was supposed to talk.

"Hasani," he said. "Sandy and I are having a baby."

I looked up from the cantaloupe. "You're having another kid?" I asked.

Sandy cut in. "Really, *we're* having a baby. Our whole family. The baby will be a part of this family, and this family wouldn't be a family without you."

"No. He said it the way he meant it," I said. "Congratulations."

"We know you might be having feelings about it, some good, some bad," Sandy said. My dad just sat there. "We thought about taking you out to dinner, but then we thought maybe it was better to talk to you in a space where you'd be able to show, like, a full range of feelings. Happy. Sad. Nervous. I know I am. How are you feeling?"

"I'm fine," I said.

"Are you sure?" Sandy asked.

I nodded.

My fingers weren't buzzing. Magic was not sloshing under my skin trying to break free. I felt . . . nothing. And right then, feeling nothing seemed a whole lot better than feeling something. But somewhere in the back of my head, I could hear my mom saying that I was taking out on Sandy what I wanted to take out on my dad. I tried to focus on that, let it fill me up. None of this was Sandy's fault. Sandy was just being Sandy. And Sandy was having a baby.

"I'm sure," I said. "Babies are great. Who doesn't like babies? I'm happy for you."

The next thing I knew, Sandy was on my side of the table hugging me and answering a bunch of questions I didn't ask.

"The baby's due in February. We are having a baby shower, but we are not having a gender reveal. The cakes and glitterfetti look really good on the gram, but no matter how cute the cake inside is, it doesn't stop making a public announcement about your kid's genitals from being weird. We'd love to hear your thoughts about it, but we're thinking maybe Bobbi for a name because it's kind of gender neutral and we're hoping that this tiny person will embrace the full spectrum of masculine and feminine that makes all of us human. Am I right? Am I . . . . right? Hasani?"

I wasn't really paying attention, but I did hear my name.

"Yeah. That sounds good."

OK. Maybe I was feeling some type of way. Or maybe I was just a glutton for punishment.

"I guess I just wanted to hear what Dad has to say."

Pause.

"Nothing," he said. "That's it. I'm happy. I know I wasn't always perfect with you and your mom, but I figured it doesn't hurt to try again."

Wow.

"Right," I said. "Well, OK, then. What time is it, Sandy? I think we need to go. Traffic."

"OK," Sandy said, "but is there anything you wanted to say while we're all together?"

"No," I said. I couldn't think of anything else to say. "Good luck with your replacement kid" didn't seem like it would end the conversation, and honestly, I just wanted out. Even if I had thought of something else, I wouldn't have said it because what was the point?

CHAPTER EIGHT

NETWORKS AND SPORES

The ride back Uptown with Sandy was OK. Sandy kept talking at me about how she had been wanting to tell me, but she didn't find out for sure until yesterday and she had to wait so she and my dad could tell me together. And how she thought I'd be an amazing big sister and, if I wanted her to, she could ask Beverlyn, aka Ms. Coulon, to keep helping me with the spells in the spellbook she gave me while she was on her magic diet.

"I'm not supposed to do magic until the baby is born," Sandy said. "I think it's just an old superstition, but everyone always says that if you do magic while you're pregnant, you might use up your kid's magic and, as much as I don't really believe in all that stuff, at the same time, who wants to be the mom who uses up their kid's magic because she thought she knew better than everyone? Right? But I still want you to be learning magic. I don't want this baby to slow you down in any way. Honestly, I probably should have had Beverlyn teach you, anyway. They may be my spells, but Beverlyn's probably a better teacher. What am I saying? She is a teacher. Of course she's a better teacher. I could book you guys a practice room in 3Thirteen if you want. One with magic return. Maybe she could meet you over there tonight."

"Not right now," I said. "But thanks."

"Text me when you're ready, OK?"

I nodded, but by the time she dropped me off, I didn't know if I would.

There was a girl who didn't look much older than me at the entrance to 3Thirteen. She was wearing a St. Mary's uniform and reading a magazine. They were always reading magazines. "Good evening," she said, glancing up as I passed. Then she kind of did a double take. She didn't jump up or smile really big or even put down the magazine, but she did give me the upchin and say, "Hasani, right? I follow your channel."

Jenny could take lessons from this girl. I liked her. She was chill.

"Thanks," I said, waving my black card over her magazine to open the way in.

The girl nodded. "Othello is cute. He should have his own channel."

I smiled. "Working on it," I said.

She nodded again and went back to reading as I went through the door.

Once you got inside, it was kind of a long walk to the Rivyèmarché where I was meeting Luz, Angelique, and Dee, especially if you let the moving walkways do all the work carrying you to the entrance like I did. The whole ride I tried to figure out how to tell my friends about my dad and Sandy's baby. It's not like they didn't know my dad and Sandy were together, or that they thought my mom would be sad about it. Plus, all of them liked Sandy. They'd be happy. Like, all the way happy. And I was happy, too, but only partly. I didn't feel like being the monster who was hatin' on a baby, but I also didn't want to lie to them by leaving stuff out.

In the end, I just spilled the whole thing as soon as I saw them. For some reason, Luz was wearing a Halloween witch's hat, but I didn't let that stop me from telling the whole thing, warts and all.

"You want us to talk about it?" Dee asked. "Or is this more of a listening moment?"

"Listening moment," I said.

"Would a hug help?" Luz asked.

I nodded.

They all got up and hugged me. Nobody called me a monster, but I did end our movie moment by asking Luz what was up with that hat.

"The hat check!" Luz said, instantly flipping to full whine mode. "I was wronged!"

"They said they had to mark her as an unanchored guest because she came without her host," Angelique explained.

"Why the hat, though?"

"I guess because no witch would be caught dead in one? It stands out."

Understatement.

"It's so embarrassing," Luz whined. "We couldn't even order chai. No one would serve us. The stupid hat scares them off. And on top of it, they were gonna leave me to go to the mushroom room."

"We were not going to leave you," Dee said. "Worst-case scenario, Angelique would have gone to the second level by herself."

"Can you please allow me my melodrama, Dee?" Luz said, flopping her arms around. "It's the only dignity I have left."

Dee laughed. "My bad. Continue."

"Anyway, as I was saying before I was so lovingly interrupted with non-hyperbolic facts, thank goodness you made it! They were gonna make me sit here by myself while they go talk to mushrooms."

"Oh, right!" I said. Even with their hosts, guests are only allowed on the first level. There's a lot of cool stuff on the first level, so that's usually good enough, but, to translate from the Luz, Angelique must have said something about going to the library. That was on the second level.

"Were you gonna use the Interweb to find somebody to help with your earrings? The vending machine didn't help?"

"The vending machine was helpful, but not as helpful as we hoped it would be," Angelique began. "We did locate some people who said they work with custodies. All of them said they could identify them with no problem, but only one of them has a stall on the first floor. So we figured we'd go check her out. We did."

"And?"

"It seemed like her business practices might be a little suspect—"

"She was shady," Dee cut in.

"Well . . . I wouldn't have said that, but now that Dee did, fair trade or not, that lady was shady. And we couldn't afford her, anyway."

"Even without Luz? No offense, Luz. I can see why that hat might scare people off."

Angelique shook her head. "I went by myself. She looked right at me and said, 'Don't bother, honey. You can't afford it.' Can you imagine?"

"She probably scanned your card," I said. "Do you know how much she wanted?"

"More than two credits, apparently," Angelique said.

"More than nine," Dee added. "I went with her, too. No dice."

"I still have some credits," I said. Thanks to Sandy. Without her I would have had less than zero. "Let's go straight to the best one we can afford. That's got to be better."

"I told you they left me and now you're leaving me, too?" Luz said, but before Dee could sigh and explain, she added, "You know I'm messing with you! I told them go. Just like I'm telling you now. The only thing keeping you from the higher floors is me." Technically, the higher number floors were actually lower, but I didn't interrupt. "I'm gonna go start working on that Louisiana Studies project while y'all go to the extra-witchy floors."

"No!" I said. "I'll stay with you while Angelique and Dee go check it out, and then—"

"Hasani. It's cool. I promise. I'll be fine. They need you. Just do me a favor?"

"Of course!"

"Come with me to hat check? I don't want them to make me wear this thing again the next time I come."

I don't think she wanted it, but the hat check let Luz keep the hat.

Angelique was super pressed about hitting up the library and would not stop talking about her punch card, so Dee and I walked Luz out and agreed to meet Angelique at the library afterward.

The library was only one level down, so when the elevator didn't come right away, we took the stairs. Dee moved like she knew where she was going, so I just followed her, but it turned out she was just following the signs.

At first, the library was kind of disappointing. It wasn't that big, and the books were in rainbow order. You do you, but putting books in rainbow order is like the golden tools in *Animal Crossing*: cute, but useless in real life.

"I hate to say this," I said, "but this place looks like it'd go viral on Instagram, and I'm not feeling it. It's like, the books are fake. They don't even have anything printed on the spines."

"That's because these books *are* fake," said a woman with green glasses and the wildest, whitest hair I have ever seen. Somewhere in the world there was a picture of her with the hashtag #LibrarianChic. "This is just the lobby. Card holders only after this point. Are either of you looking to apply for a library card, or are you waiting for a friend?"

I didn't have a chance to answer before Angelique swung open a wall of books and stepped out grinning, clutching a bag of sawdust like it was gold. Not *Animal Crossing* gold. Real gold.

"That was fast," I said.

"Well, I would have been faster, but I ended up reading a whole article. I started out looking up custodies, but it said, 'see also, confinement,' and somehow I fell down a rabbit hole that ended with me reading about the capture at the riverbend. Do not recommend. But anyway, I'm ready. Were you waiting long?"

Chic Librarian answered for me. "They just got here, Angelique. And congratulations."

"Thank you, Miss T," Angelique said, squeezing her bag of sawdust again excitedly. "I'm really ecstatic about the mushrooms!"

"Just so you know, after seven consecutive visits within the first fourteen days of membership, library patrons are given the opportunity to be the caretaker of a developing section of the Interweb," Miss T said.

"I get to grow mushroom spores!" Angelique squealed. How she made that sound like a prize was beyond me. "Once the mushrooms establish mycelium, they connect to the mycelial network and, voilà! We're on the Interweb. Hopefully very soon, we'll be able to do research from the comfort of your home."

"Why?" I asked.

"The chairs inside are all mushrooms," Angelique began.

"Makes the connections easier to establish," Miss T explained.

"Mushrooms are spongy, but they're not nearly as comfortable to sit on as you would think."

"No. I meant why did you say from the comfort of *my* home?"

"Oh. Right. I apologize. I should have asked you first, but you know how my mom is about her garden"—*and you not having access to the Interweb*—"and Dee doesn't have a garden at her dad's house, so I was hoping we could do it at yours?"

I literally laughed out loud. What was I gonna say? No? My house was getting witchier by the minute.

126

"It's cool," I said.

"Thanks, Hasani! Thirty-five consecutive days and I can get the app on my phone." She grinned. Dee looked impressed.

"Let's not get ahead of ourselves," Miss T said, her fluffy 'fro floating like a cloud. "Network spores need proper care and attention, so I'd concentrate on nurturing those first if I were you. If those don't take, next time you'll need forty-nine consecutive days before we can give you a new starter."

Dee's eyebrows said, *Dag!* "How many punches fit on that card?"

"Three hundred forty-three," Angelique and Miss T said together.

Miss T smiled. "Let's make sure you don't need them. Now, how do you young people plan to spend the rest of your evening? Homework?"

"Not yet," Angelique said. "We're looking for someone who works with custodies. We were thinking about going to Svetlana on the fourth level."

Miss T looked at Angelique's earrings before looking at her again. "Svetlana's good," she said. "But who you really want is Thelma Louise."

CHAPTER NINE

PRISMS AND PROTECTION

Supposedly, in 3Thirteen, the lower you went, the more special the items got. Miss Thelma Louise was on the third floor. Specialty items. Only one level down from the library, so how special could she be?

"We sure about this?" Dee said as we stepped out of the stairwell onto the third level. "Because once we spend these credits, that's it. We don't get 'em back."

Miss Thelma Louise's shop was the first one on the left. REFINED CONFINEMENTS: CUSTODIES AND CARES FOR THE PEOPLE WHO MATTER MOST. Compared to Kaitlynn's "retail experience," Refined Confinement looked like a Claire's.

"I'm sure," Angelique said.

"I don't know," I said. "Thelma Louise sounds like a fake name, but OK."

"Fake name my behind. This is the name I was born with and it's the name I'm gon' die with, too." I heard the fussing way before

I could see the person doing it. "Young people these days don't have a lick of manners. And now I bet you gon' have nerve to ask me for something after insulting the name my mama gave me and questioning the integrity of my shop."

I was not prepared for the woman who poked her head out of the shop. Bright red hair the same texture as mine, dressed head to toe in black and gold. I'm talking nails, a cowgirl hat, and black boots trimmed with gold fur. She only came up to my shoulder but, trust me, she did not seem small.

"Well, what do you want?"

This was Angelique's time to shine. Charming adults, even witchy adults (which was technically impossible), was her specialty.

"We apologize, Miss Thelma Louise. My friend thought she was being humorous, but clearly poking fun at someone's name crosses a line. If you're still willing to help us, we'd really appreciate it. You were highly recommended by Miss T, but I understand if you'd rather we just go."

"Miss T?" Miss T's name must have been magic because, in an instant, Thelma Louise's whole tone changed. "I love Miss T! Come in and tell me why she sent you."

"Thank you, Miss Thelma Louise. I really do apologize," I said as we stepped into her shop. It still looked like a Claire's, but that was no shade. Half of what makes places like that cool is that they have fun things that you might be able to afford. Kind of like the dollar store. At least I wouldn't have to spend a bunch of credits.

"Y'all can just call me Thelma Louise," she said. "I'm not that old, and if Miss T sent you, you're not that bad."

"I actually like your name. Were you named after the movie?"

Dee nudged me.

"Sorry! Was that wrong?"

Thelma Louise shook her head at us and laughed. "I was," she said. "But imagine being named after a famous movie while that famous movie is still a really famous movie. I've heard that joke a lot of times."

True. My bad.

"But y'all didn't come here about all of that. And since none of you is carrying a baby, I'm assuming that you're coming to me about this young person's creole earrings. Seven credits to start. I might charge less when I get in there, but I'll let you know if it's more. That work for you, or do you need to make some kind of arrangement?"

That was Thelma Louise's polite way of saying that she had already scanned Angelique's card and knew she couldn't afford it.

"I'm covering it," I said.

Thelma Louise turned to me. "OK, then. Does that work for you?"

"Yes," I said.

Thelma Louise nodded and turned back to Angelique. "Which one is the confinement? Do you know?"

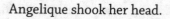

Angelique shook her head.

"Well, step over into my office and let's have a look."

Thelma Louise pointed Angelique toward a chair with a pump pedal at the bottom. She did one long step on the pedal until the chair was as low as it could go, then pumped it twice so that Angelique's earrings were exactly at her eye level.

"These are beautiful," she said. "Look at the craftsmanship."

Thelma Louise pulled a huge magnifying glass on a stretchy arm out from the wall and angled it so we could get a look at Angelique's left earring. They were so small. Without the magnifying glass, they just looked like hoops. But up close, calling them just hoop earrings seemed like an insult. They were more of a teardrop than a circle, and the surface was covered with diamond faces hammered in with geometric precision.

"Are they gold?" I asked.

"Probably," Thelma said, adjusting the magnifier, "but with a little silver and copper mixed in. That helps hold the magic."

"They're beautiful," I said. "I've never seen earrings like that before."

Thelma smiled over at me. "Well, you must not be from Vacherie," she said. "Creole earrings are still pretty common around there. Although these days they just come from the store. Machine crafted. Meant for one-time use. You don't see ones like these much anymore. Handcrafted to last generations."

"Wait," Dee said. "I thought custodies were just a one-time thing."

"Most charms are. They bond with the user and are worthless to anyone else. But confinements are different. I know people don't like to hear this, but a mother's love is confining. It restricts you. It holds you in. It keeps you safe. Because deep down, even if she doesn't know it, when her child is hurt, mothers can't breathe." Thelma Louise tapped her boot on the floor twice, and a little cart of supplies rolled itself over to her. She grabbed a tiny pink bottle and squeezed a drop of something into her eye before turning back to the earring. "Nowadays," she said, "people call that codependence. That's why people started calling them 'custodies,' trying to make them sound less restrictive. But the love that holds these together is restrictive. And the day you put them on a child you love, you're already imagining the day you're going to have to take them off. That child will be free to get hurt and make every mistake you didn't want them to, but you don't want them to throw out the kind of love that you put into them. You do everything you can to make sure it gets saved and passed down to the child that child will love someday. That way their love doesn't have to stand alone. It carries your love, and the love that was given to you along with it. So, no. Not one-time use. Anything but. You've been wearing these since you were, what? Two weeks old?"

"I'm not sure," Angelique said. "We don't know either of my birth parents. But my mother says I was wearing them the first time she held me, and that was when I was around three months old."

Thelma Louise made a noise like she heard that all the time.

"Well, let's have a better look."

I didn't know how much better the look could get than the magnifying glass, but Thelma Louise did not disappoint. She turned the glass over and, suddenly, the earrings were fractals of color.

"It's like a brass glass scope!" I said.

"You know the glassworks, huh? I used to have one of those squinty little jewelers eyes, but I hate squinting. When my business took off, the glassworks made this one for me custom. Didn't even charge me. I asked them why they wouldn't take my credits. All they said was, 'It's not for you. It's for the culture.'"

Prisms of color shimmered underneath a thin, clear coat of magic.

"Is that a shield?" I asked. It looked like the shields Dee and I were practicing on Angelique's fleur-de-lis charm, but thinner and not as gloppy.

"Yes, indeed. They must have taken to teaching the charmed girls more than manners these days. That's good know."

I didn't want to throw Belles Demoiselles under the bus, but I didn't learn any of that at charm school.

Thelma Louise made a face. "Wait a minute," she said, switching over to Angelique's other earring. "Both of these are custodies. And they're double shielded."

Double shielded?

"Oh!" I said. "No, that's just us! Dee and I shielded Angelique's fleur-de-lis charm earlier today, but we haven't done it a lot, so maybe we got some on her earrings. It should have worn off by now, but I guess we're better than we thought? How do we take it off?"

"Listen, the customer is always right and all that, but you are dead wrong. Do you think I'd get enough credits to use this space on the third level of 3Thirteen if I couldn't tell the difference between real shields and something a couple of thirteen-year-olds slapped together? Talented tenth or not, you blossomed, what? Three years ago?"

"Three months ago," I said. *Almost.*

"Yeah. There's no way you did this. The earrings are both confinements and they're both shielded. Maybe one shielding from each parent. Having two talented parents has always been rare, but ever since colonialism took off, it's almost unheard of. If they weren't shielded, I'd be able to take them off for you. We'd just do a little incantation of mine to tell the magic inside you that you know you might get hurt, but you're ready to be free and—BAM. You'd be free. But this shielding complicates things. I'd need a key to at least one of them, but from what you've been saying, I'm guessing you don't have the key to either one, huh?"

Angelique shook her head. "I don't even know if my biological parents are alive," she said.

I blinked. I guess it was just facts, but it was weird to hear Angelique say something like that so casually.

Thelma Louise sighed. "You can try someone else. Melisse on the fourth level would be my suggestion, but I doubt anyone will touch it without the key. Too dangerous. I guess you could also try working on the crows to get the key out of S-Crow. They've been known to do that if the term of the contract is over, which would be the case if your biological parents are no longer with us. The good news is that you can never get burned out, not as long as you have these babies. The bad news is that your friends here are gonna have to keep paying for you. Unless you want to start racking up service hours. I have a few saved. Want to work here?"

"I understand," Angelique said, standing up from the chair. "Thank you for your time and thank you for the offer. It was a pleasure to meet you."

"Good luck, honey. If you don't figure it out, just focus on the good news."

When we left Thelma Louise's shop, none of us were in the mood to explore the third level, even though the shop right next door was called Pig Mint, and according to the glamorous pig on the signs, their sweet-smelling herbs made pigment for all kinds of applications from face tint to paint tint. Clearly at least Dee and I needed to check that out at some point, but Angelique was sad and I was confused as anything. Pig Mint could wait.

Angelique kind of walked ahead of us, but that just gave me a chance to pull Dee to the side. "What's supposed to be the good news? Because all I'm hearing is that the only way we're gonna get rid of those custodies is if her parents are dead."

I must have not been whispering as well as I wanted to, because before Dee finished saying, "Not getting burned out sounds pretty good to me," Angelique said, "And my parents are not dead."

I froze.

"My DNA donors might be dead," she said without looking back, "but my parents are alive and well."

"Got it," I said. "So, should we go to S-Crow next?"

"No," she said. "Let's go to your house. I want to plant the spores."

CHAPTER TEN

GOLD AND EGGS

The next day, Angelique was in a way better mood than I thought she would be, and I guess it kind of rubbed off on the rest of us. Angelique stopped at my house in the morning to check on the spores. We had helped her put them in a piece of broken tree branch we found in my backyard.

Well, "help" is a loose term. We were more like moral support. Angelique wouldn't let us touch anything. She said it was because she had only one pair of gloves, which sounded bogus at first because Dee and I didn't mind getting our hands dirty.

"I'm not worried about your hands getting germs on them," Angelique said. "I'm worried about your germs getting on the spores. They're very delicate at the beginning. Contamination could ruin everything."

I didn't think the ground in my backyard could possibly be any more sterile than my hands, but since I didn't know anything about mushrooms, I let Angelique handle her business.

Turned out minding my business was a good idea, because after Angelique checked on her spores, she couldn't stop herself from grinning ear to ear. Plus she gave Luz, Miguel, and me a ride to school with her and Dee.

"Whoa! Is this a limo?" Miguel said. He looked like he was scared to climb in. I put my hand out. He grabbed it and pulled himself inside.

"This isn't a limo," Angelique said as Miguel settled in between me and Luz, "but it does have limo seating. It's not fancy. It just makes it easier to talk to people face-to-face."

Miguel nodded, but I could tell he was really impressed.

"Are you gonna get a limo, too, Hasani?"

I gave Miguel a look. "Not all witches have limos," I said. "Just Angelique."

Miguel nudged me with his shoulder. "Not the witch thing," he said. He had been surprisingly chill when we told him about that. "Your channel's almost at two million subscribers!"

"It is?" I guess I hadn't been focusing on my subscriber stats as much as I used to.

Miguel pulled out his phone and showed me.

1.89M subscribers

"Wow," I said. Seriously, hadn't I just crossed over a million?

"'Faux Freckles on the Cheap Cheap' is still your most popular video.'" Miguel grinned. His perfect freckles were grinning, too.

"He has a counter," Luz said.

"Luz!!" Miguel whined.

"Whaaaat? It's true. He used like a month of allowance to buy one when you were at camp. I thought he was about to start a channel of his own, but nope. He connected it to yours."

Did I say Annie was my first fan? Correction: Miguel was my first fan.

"You know the freckle pattern in that video is based on yours, right?"

"For real?"

"For real."

Miguel sat back and smiled for the rest of the ride. It was only another block or so, but still. Miss Nancy let us all out at the sixth-grader gate. Miguel waved and ran inside, but Luz kept looking at him until the door finished swinging closed.

"What's wrong?" I asked.

"Nothing," she said, but I could tell she was worried. "I was just trying to see if Miguel was talking to somebody from his class this year, but that's Amy and Tayshon. They were in his class last year. Apparently his class this year is 'the worst ever.'"

She was trying to say it like it was no big deal, but Luz never had been good at hiding her feelings, at least not from me.

"No, *we* had the worst sixth-grade class ever," I said, more to distract her than anything else. "Remember Dave kept announcing that he was taking off his shoes?"

"He didn't have to say it. We could smell it. How could I forget?"

"*That* was the worst."

"Glad I wasn't here, then," Dee said. "My sense of smell is crazy good."

I mouthed, *Miguel's gonna be OK*, to Luz while Angelique and Dee laughed. Dee didn't laugh often, but when she did more than chuckle, it was enough to cover everything.

Luz nodded, then turned to the group to add in the part about Dave not being able to get his shoes back on in time for a fire drill, which only made Dee crack up so much that the rest of us started laughing again from the joy of her laughing. So all of us were laughing as we walked through the main gate, and the little Miguel worry was gone from Luz's eyes.

The bead tree felt naked without the aqua beads looking down at me, but I looked at the spot where it should have been anyway when we passed underneath it. There were still lots of beads in the trees, but all the ones on the ground were long gone, and I was pretty sure I knew where they went. Annie walked through the gate laughing and talking with a whole group of people. Honestly, it was nice to see, even though it gave "mini-entourage" more than "group of friends," and Annie was still wearing the glorified Mardi Gras necklace LaToya had given her. At least she looked happy.

Jenny was in Annie's group. She smiled in my direction when they came in. I smiled back, but the way she looked away really fast made me know she didn't want other people to know she had been talking to me. Three days in and LaToya was officially queen bee. And, from the looks of it, Annie was her second-in-command. All the people in their little group flocked over to her as soon as she made it into the front yard, and when LaToya arrived, her suitcase of water bottles in tow, Annie was the one giving out the orders.

"You can hand them out today," she said to a kid with a red skirt and matching red headband. "Kenyatta, you can help. But don't give one to Vic. She still hasn't returned her bottle from yesterday, and she knows we're supposed to recycle."

Oh. Eco-friendly.

I didn't say anything. I just smiled at Annie in a way that hopefully said I was still willing to be friends if she was and went back to my own group. Apparently there was some new reality TV show that Angelique, of all people, was watching. I got so caught up in the discussion that I didn't notice the flurry of activity until it was really in motion. LaToya was there, but it wasn't about LaToya. A kid with short blonde hair and a rainbow T-shirt had bluebonnets growing right from her hands. Right in the middle of the front yard. Half the yard rushed over to see, but when the bell rang, Angelique, Luz, Dee, and I walked inside without giving them a second look.

The bluebonnet girl, Becky, was there at lunch, rocking her own set of stepped-up beads. It was her turn to sit right next to LaToya, but she didn't keep her spot long because, ten minutes into lunch, another kid was blossoming. Tulips.

"This place is gettin' wild," Dee said. "It would never go down like this in Vacherie. Maybe I was wrong. Maybe it is that water." Dee looked at Luz.

"You don't have to worry. I'm not gonna drink the Kool-Aid just to become a witch," Luz said. "It wouldn't work, anyway. After you said that the other day, I asked Angelique to look it up for me. Put all that library time to good use."

Angelique nodded. "The water from the Mississippi contains powerful magic. I mean, none of it survives the filtration and purification process for tap water, but if you filter it the right way, it's potable and magical. And the stuff from the sharpest corner of the sharpest bend is supposed to be an off-the-charts magic booster. At least it is for witches. For other people it's supposed to be really hydrating, though."

Angelique added that last part on for Luz. I don't think Luz cared that much about being hydrated.

Jenny looked over at me again but just as quickly looked back at her table.

"That water must not be that strong," I said.

"Why?"

"Because if LaToya is using it to influence Jenny, it's not working. She keeps trying to talk to me."

Luz looked confused. "Why don't you talk to her, then?"

"I don't know," I said. "Something about it just feels weird. She likes the channel and she acts all weird around me, but it's not like she's only ever watched me on her phone and then I suddenly appeared in real life. I'd get it if that's what happened. But we're both Riverbend lifers. We were in the same first-grade class. We've been square-dancing partners. She knows me. That's why it's so weird for her to be—"

"Stalkerish?" Luz supplied. "Yeah. That would be weird. You want me to talk to her?"

"Nah," I said. "Let it be."

"Don't poke the hornet's nest. Got it."

"Wait a minute," I gasped. Luz froze. "Did you just make that up?"

"No. It's an expression," she said.

"Whoa. How many ways are there to say that? I've been saying 'Not my circus, not my monkeys' in my head all week. I don't even know where it comes from."

"Poland," Dee said. "And yours sounds Goldilocks-ish, so I'm betting England for yours, Luz."

We all looked at Dee.

"What?" she said. "I read. And I'm guessing there's at least one for every culture."

"What do y'all say in Vacherie?" I asked.

"Min' ya business," Dee said.

I laughed. Maybe the varieties were endless.

"I'm not trying to get your hopes up," Dee said, "but we could always have you tested, Luz. I mean, you already have a guest pass to 3Thirteen, and it might be better to know than to wonder."

"Nah," Luz said, but by her inflection, it was the kind of "Nah" that meant, "I'm thinking about it." She didn't think long.

"I don't want to have to wear that hat again," she said. "OK. Let's do it."

So the plan was set. It was Dee's turn to cook for her and her dad, but after she did that, Miss Nancy would scoop her up and drop her off at my house, where presumably Angelique would check her mushrooms, then we'd head over to 3Thirteen on foot for Luz's testing. The chances that Luz was a witch were slim, but they weren't none. After all, Luz was already pretty magical in my book. And, just to give us the best chance at having this amazing, witchy energy carry over, all of us spent the rest of the day minding our business.

Dee seemed satisfied.

"'Bout time y'all listened to me," she said with a chuckle.

In seventh period, LaToya was weirdly normal even when Ms. Coulon stepped out of the room. It felt like she was up to something, but minding my business was batting a thousand, so I forced myself to keep it going.

Not my circus, not my monkeys.

Whatever LaToya had going on with Mardi Gras beads and water bottles was on her.

I think Ms. Coulon must have noticed our new, chill leadership vibes and even asked if we wanted anything from the coffee shop when she went on her coffee run like we were adults.

"I have to warn you: I'm only getting coffee with chicory," she said.

Oh! Right! That explained why Ms. Coulon had been double-fisting the coffee lately. Everybody knows that chicory helps keep your magic in check, and I guess I was glad she was following the advice she gave us.

"Yes, please!" I said when I realized the offer still stood if I got a double mocha chiller instead of a café au lait. Angelique declined.

"You don't like frozen coffee?" I asked when we had the room to ourselves. "Don't think of the potion-y part. It's not squeezing, it's reverse squeezing. Delicious reverse squeezing."

Angelique shook her head. "I don't need it, remember?"

"Right," I said, not sure what to say next.

"It's a relief, actually," Angelique said. "It shouldn't really matter, but all this time I've been wondering if my biological mom ever really loved me. I may not know who she is, but after talking to Thelma Louise, I think maybe she did love me. At least a little. It doesn't really change anything with my real mom, though."

"Why do you say that?" I asked. "You love your mom and your mom loves you. Maybe she didn't birth you, but she chose you, right? She chose you to be the first daughter of a first daughter. And I bet for years before you were born she couldn't wait to hold you." The sudden thought of baby Angelique not being held by her mom for three months washed over me. I couldn't imagine going that long without my mom holding me.

Angelique shook her head again. "Her choosing a dud would only make me more of a disappointment."

"You? A disappointment? Seriously, what are you talking about? The first time I saw you, I thought you were an actual goddess!"

"Tell my mom that. I think she's hard on me to make sure I'm prepared in case one day I unleash this great magic. And I used to think that, too. Then you and Dee saw my magic. I already knew the flow of my magic probably wasn't as strong as yours. When you did magic, I could see the way Dee looked at you."

"Like I was a wild person," I said.

Angelique smiled, but only half. "Yes, but more like 'Wow!' I don't blame her. That's how I felt when I could finally see your magic, too. Like you had enough for all of us and then some. So at first, when Dee didn't look at me the same, I didn't think anything about it. I figured I was extra-talented or something, but that would look like nothing standing next to you.

"Then I got tested and I had to get used to the idea that I was just promising. Barely magic at all. I was so scared my mother would find out. And when Dee said the thing about my earrings being custodies, I thought, she must be wrong. No way would my mother have known something like that about me and just never said anything."

"Maybe she didn't know what they are."

"Oh, she knows what they are. She said so much, but she never told me that. I had to hear about it from a stranger. It makes me nervous about what else I don't know. Like maybe she's hiding something from me, and whatever she's hiding might be the reason she's never totally loved me."

"That's not true," I said. "Of course your mom loves you. And you have no idea how strong you are. I mean you literally do not know. What if those custodies get released and you find out you're in, like, the talented twentieth?!"

Angelique shook her head. "What if I find out that my mother loves me like a Kinder Egg or an abandoned gold mine? It's all good

147

now. It's all perfection and charm and bright futures. But what happens when she finds out for sure there's no prize inside?"

Whoa.

It took me a few seconds to realize I was holding my breath. That was so heavy that I had to tell my body to exhale.

"Do you really feel that way?" I asked.

Angelique shrugged. "Whoever gave me these earrings saw my magic. They saw the whole me. No one else has, not even you and Dee. They saw me and they loved me enough to keep my magic safe. They just . . . didn't love me enough to stay. What if my mom sees me and does the same thing? So, no. I'm not sure how I feel about it. I just know it's better this way."

I wished I could look at her and say she was being ridiculous. That parents never leave. But I couldn't.

CHAPTER ELEVEN

SCHEMES AND CREAM

When Ms. Coulon got back to the room with my mocha chiller, I didn't want it anymore. Angelique ended up drinking it for me. And when the rest of the team members got there, she was in full Mathletes mode, like she didn't just pour all the pain of her soul out in front of me while I was scrambling around looking for a bucket. I was the one zoning out and missing a step in a calculation.

LaToya corrected my mistake. Ms. Coulon was in the room, but still, LaToya didn't roll her eyes or snicker or make one of her faces. And after Mathletes, LaToya stayed again to help put the desks back. She didn't talk to us or anything. She just put the desks back and left.

When we were alone again, I tried to get Angelique to talk more about her mom, but she just waved me away and asked if I wanted a ride home before she and Miss Nancy went to pick up Dee. If I thought she would talk to me in the car, I would have said yes, but I didn't.

"I'm gonna walk home."

"You sure? It's hot."

"Yeah. I'm sure," I said.

Angelique shrugged like it was my funeral, and she rolled up the window to her not-limousine as Miss Nancy pulled away.

I really did want to walk home alone. Of course Jenny came running out of the yard as soon as Angelique was down the street.

"Hey!" Jenny said jogging toward me.

"Were you just hiding behind one of the trees?" I asked. "I swear I didn't see you and I was just looking that way."

Jenny shook her head no, but then she changed it. "Actually, yes. Sorry. That was weird. And I just realized how weird it was just now. I just wanted you to know that I saved you one of these. Don't tell anybody. I could only save one and I don't want anybody to be mad at me."

It was one of LaToya's water bottles. Correction. It was one of Kaitlynn's water bottles. Jenny was holding it out to me and, without thinking about it, I took it. For a second, I expected something to happen. Lights to flash. Flowers to explode. My life force to drain out of me. Something. But it just felt like a bottle. The surface had a cool texture. The green was mesmerizing. But it was just a bottle with a fancy design on the label.

"No, thanks," I said, handing it back to her. "I've got water in my bag."

"You sure?"

"Yeah. I'm sure. Thanks, though."

I turned to walk away, hoping that would be enough for Jenny to get it without hurting her feelings too much.

"Hasani?" she called after me. "I just want you to know that I don't believe what LaToya's saying about you."

If that was supposed to bait me, it didn't work. I kept walking.

I felt a little better when I made it to my house. Not much better, but a little. Luz was waiting on my doorstep.

"Why didn't you go inside?" I asked. "It's hot."

"I just got here," she said. "I didn't have a chance to knock yet. But look what my dad and Miguel gave me!" She held up a colorful piece of paper that said:

Congratulations on Being a Witch!

We love you, Lucita!

Luz turned it over.

Congratulations on Not Being a Witch!

We love you, Lucita!

"Isn't it just the sweetest? I told Miguel he still can't come to 3Thirteen, so they want you to hold up this sign. Miguel and my dad worked on it together. See all the parts that are colored outside of the lines? That means my dad helped. He's terrible at coloring."

"The right side!" Miguel yelled. I hadn't noticed, but he was out-side, too, standing on their porch two doors down.

"They want you to hold up the right side of this sign since Miguel can't come with me," Luz repeated louder so Miguel could definitely hear.

"You told your dad?" I asked, giving Miguel a thumbs-up so he knew I'd do it. He gave me a thumbs-up back and went inside.

"Of course. I wasn't supposed to?" Luz asked, looking genuinely confused. Then she lowered her voice. "Is this like that camp?"

"Oh. No," I said. "Nothing like that. You can if you want." It was my turn to be confused, but I guess back in the days of Stevie Wonder and pancakes, before everything fell apart, I would have wanted to tell my dad, too.

"Cool," Luz said. "So . . . are we going inside? Like you said, it's hot out here."

Luz took pics of Othello for his Instagram while we waited for Angelique and Dee. I meant to open YouTube to see what was up with me having 1.89M subscribers but, honestly, Othello was way cuter than a subscriber count could ever be, especially the way Luz had him wrestling with a pair of socks like he was an anime hero battling a demon. So. Cute. How could I not watch that photo shoot?

"Seriously, you should have Miguel do this next time. All of these setups were his idea."

"Dag. Those are good shots," Dee said. How she saw them from across the room and partway into the hallway, I do not know, but after Dee and I spent a few minutes ooh-ing over Othello to give Angelique time to check on her mushrooms, the four of us headed out to 3Thirteen.

Miguel and Mr. Jose were standing on the porch waving like they were watching Luz walk across the stage at graduation. They were whooping. Clapping. They had everything but an air horn. Luz smiled and did her parade wave until we got to the end of the block, then she turned to us, suddenly all business.

"Level with me," she said. "What do I have to do?"

"What do you mean?" I asked.

"For this test? Is it combat? Battle of wits? Do they draw blood? I hate when they draw blood. Please say it's not blood."

"You put your hands on some grass," I said.

Luz blinked. "That's it?"

Dee tried not to chuckle but didn't quite make it. "Nah, bruh. That's it."

Luz looked a little disappointed, but she was back to hype again before we got to 3Thirteen. The girl in the St. Mary's uniform was there again.

"Hey! I remember you!" I said.

She smiled. "I remember you, too. I see you still didn't make Othello his own YouTube channel, though."

"My bad," I said. "I'll get on it."

"I'm waiting," she said.

The St. Mary's girl, whose name was Zayvion, talked Luz through the whole thing about getting tested. "The thing is," she said, "if you qualify for membership, there's no fee, but if you don't, the person who referred you gets charged two credits. It's supposed to deter people from burned-out lines from testing everybody and their uncle. It's like, boo-boo, just face the music. This not for you."

I don't think what she was saying was funny, but we all laughed anyway. It wasn't what she said so much as the way she said it. Everything always sounds better in a New Orleans accent, and listening to Zayvion talk, I wished mine stuck out more. Unless I was saying "baby" just the right way, I sounded like I was from somewhere in Ohio. I blame my parents for always playing NPR.

"We laughing, but I'm serious, yeah," Zayvion said. "So which one of y'all is referring Luz?"

"I am," I said.

"Cool," Zayvion said. Then the chair came out, Luz hopped in, the chair went down, and part of the wall opened in front of Luz's face at the perfect height for her to put her hand in.

She hesitated, but before she could stretch it out too long, I channeled my best Mr. Jose, and whooped and clapped and said stuff like, "You got this, baby girl!" Angelique and Dee did, too. I could almost feel Luz smiling as she reached her hand in and carefully placed it on the grass.

One second. Two seconds. Three seconds. Nothing.

Zayvion moved like she was going to bring the chair back up, but—

"Wait!" I said. "The grass! I saw a blade of grass move. Maybe her flower is grass?"

"Nope!" Luz said. "That was me trying to stop a sneeze. Nothing happening down here. You can bring me up. My dad said if I didn't get it, he'd take us all out to ice cream."

"What would he have done if you did get it?" Dee asked.

"Take us out to ice cream," Luz said. "It's kind of his thing."

"That's what's up," Dee said.

Zayvion raised the chair, I waved the CONGRATULATIONS ON NOT BEING A WITCH sign, and all of us, including Zayvion, cheered Luz on.

When Miss T from the library showed up in a giraffe-print caftan and her awesome green glasses, she got in line and applauded, too.

"Right on time for orientation," Miss T said to Angelique. "And by on time, I mean five minutes early. Well done. And I'm so happy to see that you have such a beautiful team supporting your decision. Brava!"

Angelique beamed.

"Orientation?" Luz asked at the same time as I said, "Decision?"

"Yeah, bruh," Dee added. "You've already been to the library a bunch. Why are you just now getting oriented?"

Angelique stood up straighter. "I'm getting oriented because I'm going to work there."

We all looked at her. Every one of our mouths was hanging open. Well, not Zayvion. She didn't really know Angelique like that.

"What?" Angelique said. "I want to be able to carry my own weight. And, as Daddy always says, 'If you want to control your outcome, start by increasing your income.'"

How many rich people sayings were there?

"Cool," I said. *I mean, you could also talk to your mom, get those custodies released, and then you'd probably get a billion credits automatically just for being a member of the talented tenth, but cool.*

"So . . ." Luz said, "are we waiting for you for ice cream, or . . ."

"No. Thanks, though. You can go without me. But I am getting picked up from Hasani's house, so I might see y'all later."

Angelique disappeared with Miss T through a life-sized portrait of Billie Holiday, and when Luz tried to talk to Zayvion on our way out, Zayvion gave only a half wave and said, "Good evening. See y'all later."

"Was that untalented discrimination?" Luz asked.

"I don't think so," Dee said. "She was really caught up in that magazine."

"Well, her loss," Luz said. "I hope whatever's in that magazine is better than ice cream."

"You were gonna invite her to ice cream?" I asked. "I mean, we just met her. Your dad would be cool with that?"

Of course Mr. Jose would have been cool with that. It seemed like he had already invited everyone we knew, apologizing to Luz that, on such short notice, he could only get two of her cousins to attend. The way he apologized, you would have thought Luz had turned fifteen, not taken a totally voluntary witch exam. He ordered the twenty-five-scoop, twenty-five-flavor sundae for people to share. That thing was as big as our dining room table. In fact, that's why he had the ice cream delivered to my house instead of theirs. That and something Luz said made him think that we could only talk about magic inside the "webs" at my house. I didn't correct him, though. The last thing I wanted was a million of Luz's cousins telling everybody about witches on the street. I don't think anyone would really believe them, and witches were really good about hiding right where you should be able to see them . . . but still. Otherwise, the more the merrier, right? Even if we had to shut it down by 7 P.M. because it was a school night, it was still a party. Sandy was even there.

Actually, that last part kind of threw me.

"Mom?" I asked as she set out another round of blueberry ginger sunset. It was going like hotcakes. "I'm not trying to be rude, but why did you invite Sandy? I mean, she doesn't know Luz that well."

"I didn't invite Sandy," my mom said. "Jose did. Why?"

"No reason."

But as soon as I got a second with Luz I asked, "How did Sandy make friends with your dad?"

Luz shrugged. "Sandy makes friends with everybody."

True dat.

I wasn't exactly avoiding Sandy, but I wasn't ready to talk, either. And it was hard to be around Sandy without talking. Eventually, she pinned me down. I thought she would be all babybabybabybaby, feelingsfeelingsfeeelingsfeelings, but instead she said, "Angelique got a job?"

Dag. So much for witches keeping to themselves. That news traveled fast!

"I'm so proud of her! We're gonna be work buddies. I thought about taking time off. I mean, I do have enough credits saved. But then I thought, *Why should I stop?* It's not like it's dangerous. I don't even do magic on shift. Plus, I'd hate to miss out on the perks. If you go more than a month or two without working you don't lose your credits or anything, but you do lose your employee perks. You should consider doing it. I know you have a lot of credits, but it couldn't hurt to build up a few more."

"Sandy," I asked, "is there a reason you went out of your way not to say 'maternity leave' or 'baby' just now?"

Legit, Sandy looked guilty. "You were just so upset when we told you. You said you were OK, but then you didn't call me and you left my last message on read. I was worried. Are you mad at me?"

"No," I said. "Well, maybe a little, but I know it's not fair. I guess I just wonder how much longer you're gonna be texting me about Girls' Night and Self-Care Sunday. I don't think you'll do it on purpose, but I guess it kind of feels like I should get used to it now."

"Oh, Hasani. This baby can't replace you."

"I know," I said.

"And I can't promise you that I won't make any mistakes or do anything that will make you feel left out because, Hasani, this is my first time doing this. Freedom is my thing, but this feels more like flying by the seat of my pants. I have no idea what I'm doing. If I do something that hurts you, it would really help me out if you could tell me. I might not be able to just fix it, but I bet between the two of us we'll be able to figure something out. Deal?"

"Deal," I said. I felt my shoulders relax a little.

"OK." Sandy bumped my shoulder with hers. "We didn't exchange flowers or put it on the blockchain or anything, but I consider that binding."

"I'm glad you came." I smiled.

"Me, too," she said.

"What about Dad? Did Mr. Jose invite him, too?" At least they used to be neighbors.

"It was last minute," Sandy said. "He had something."

I could tell by the way Sandy looked at the floor that "had something" was code for "didn't want to come."

"It's probably for the best, though. Jose only said 'to celebrate Luz's test results,' but there's a lot of witchy talk at this party. Your dad might have started to ask questions."

Yeah. Then I was doubly glad he didn't come.

As quick as Mr. Jose was to start a party, he was even quicker to shut it down. We had to practically drag Miguel and the two little cousins away from my YouTube backdrop, but honestly, they weren't any trouble even though Luz used cleaning up after them as an excuse to stay a little extra. I'm glad she did. If she hadn't, she would have missed Angelique's big discovery.

"Yay! You're all still here!" Angelique said.

"Of course I'm still here," Dee said. "You're my ride."

"Right. To that end, Miss Nancy will be here in ten minutes. Which gives me exactly enough time to tell you about the most amazing thing ever. It's like reality TV for witches."

"Ooh, that does sound good," Luz said. "Spill."

"OK. So you know I'm not usually one for schadenfreude, but this just got under my skin too much not to share it."

We were all literally sitting on the edge of our seats. Then Angelique started telling us about a database.

"Wait a minute, wait a minute, waitaminute," Luz said fast enough for it to be one word. "Did you get us all hyped up and then start talking about a spreadsheet? I love that all my people are math people, but I think this might be too much."

"No. Listen. Yes, it's like a spreadsheet. Well, more of a ledger since you can't put formulas in it. It only records things. But anyway, every transaction in 3Thirteen is automatically recorded in a ledger entry on the blockchain. Which means, technically, every transaction in 3Thirteen is public information. Like, any member of 3Thirteen can go and look it up just to make sure that everything happening is fair. It's actually showing at all times on a wall in the Rivyèmarché, but it's in code."

"Computer code?" Suddenly Dee looked more interested.

"The zeros and ones wall!" Luz chimed in. "I've seen that."

Dee gave her a look like, *Wow. Without me, bruh?*

"You shouldn't have left me," Luz said. "Anyway. Continue. And this better get juicier than zeros and ones."

"Believe me. It does. Anyway, that string of code is called the main view. But when you're working at 3Thirteen, you can just hold your finger down on an entry to see the refracted view, which, apparently, is changed by your eyes, so it ends up being in whatever language is easiest for you to understand. And you don't have to go to the Rivyèmarché. It's all in a magazine!"

"OK. Now I'm really glad I'm not a witch," Luz said. "I definitely could never get this hype about reading list of receipts."

"Well, let us see," Dee said. "Code" had her all in.

"Oh, I don't have it with me. I barely went through the orientation. You don't get your own magazine until you hit one hundred hours of service, and then to keep it you have to do at least ten hours in each month. Miss T was only showing me hers, but while we were watching, I saw something good."

We didn't literally shout "spill!" but the way we were staring did the work for us.

"LaToya . . . is in debt."

Crickets.

"Angelique. Bruh. I know your dad is like, a finance guru or whatever, but come on, man. LaToya owing somebody money is not the same as reality TV."

"OK. Maybe the magazine is losing something in translation, but in person, I promise you it's as addictive as WeBop. But that's not the point. Oh! Right! Wait. I'll show you on WeBop."

"The blockchain is on WeBop?" I was even more confused.

"No! LaToya, who clearly has very poor financial skills, has racked up a bunch of debt and is trying to pay it off by peddling water bottles. Look."

Angelique had opened her WeBop and, sure enough, the very first was from LaToya. There were so many water bottles in the shot that the caption should have said #ad, #sponsored, not #witchschool.

"Hashtag witch school? Wow," I said. "She is bold."

Dee just sucked her teeth and shook her head.

"Who cares if she wants to out herself? She's basically running an MLM," Angelique said, sounding actually grossed out. "That's . . . awful! I can't believe she ever asked me to join her coven."

"LaToya asked you to join her coven?" Luz said.

"What's an MLM?" I asked.

Angelique blinked. "Y'all really don't talk about money at your houses, do you? OK. An MLM is anything that uses multilevel marketing. Like, OK. Here's an example. Say I give you ten water bottles, and I tell you that if you sell them, I'll give you a credit. But if you bring me more salespeople, I'll give you half a credit for every bottle they sell, too. Then if the people you bring in bring in even more salespeople, I'll give you a quarter of a credit for every bottle those people sell. What would you do?"

"I'd try to convince all of y'all to sell water bottles because I don't have any credits in 3Thirteen."

"Exactly," Angelique said.

"What's wrong with that?" I asked.

"In theory, nothing. In practice, a lot. Those first ten bottles aren't free. The salespeople either have to pay for them out of pocket or go into debt to get them. That's probably just fine for the first person. They can probably find a lot of people who want to sell water bottles. But in a closed community, it eventually gets to the point where there are no more people to bring in. The people at the top are doing just fine, but the last salespeople recruited are stuck with a bunch of product they can't sell and the debt it took to get them."

"Wait a minute," Luz said. "That's a pyramid scheme. Why didn't you just say 'pyramid scheme' in the first place?"

"So you think LaToya is running a pyramid scheme and getting rich off—who? The kids at Riverbend Middle?" Dee asked. "So, she's been, what? Recruiting an army of salespeople? This reality show is about LaToya starting a business?"

"I don't think that's it, y'all," I said. "Angelique said people at the top of pyramid schemes make money, but LaToya isn't making money.

She's in debt. And if those water bottles are involved, she's probably not in debt to just anybody. She's probably in debt to Kaitlynn."

"Kaitlynn?" Dee asked.

"You remember her. Fake Marie Laveau? From the French Market?"

"Oh, right," Dee said.

"Trust me. Kaitlynn is bad news. If Sandy hadn't jumped in, I'd probably have to be doing what LaToya's doing right now."

"Sorry, but I don't see what the big deal is," Luz said. "I mean, they're not supposed to, but people sell snacks at school all the time. LaToya's selling water. OK, maybe it's magic water, but with everything happening in her family, she probably needs the come up. If the water isn't, like, secretly turning people into witches against their will, so . . . what? She creates a secret army of witch recruits who sell her products for her? She's Madam C. J. Walker. Or Mary Kay. It's just business."

"Is she even selling them?" Dee asked. "Seems like she keeps giving them away."

"That's worse!" Angelique was practically shrieking.

"How is that worse?" Luz asked.

Angelique shook her head like she couldn't believe we weren't getting it. "If they aren't selling you a product . . ." she started, then left it dangling like we could finish it. The thing was, we could.

". . . you *are* the product," we finished.

165

"Favors are worth more than LaToya could ever get selling water. Especially if she's secretly recruiting a bunch of new witches who don't know how any of this works."

"Oh, she is trying to recruit new witches," Dee said, scrolling through LaToya's feed on Angelique's phone. "But it's not a secret. Look."

Witch Life Lesson #1: How to Spot a Fake Witch from a Mile Away

Witch Life Lesson #3: Charm vs. Magic

Witch Life Lesson #4: Florals Are More Than a Vibe

Witch Life Lesson #7: Wildseed or a green witch? Who can say the W-word?

Witch Life Lesson #10: How to Spot a Sanlavi

Witch Life Lesson #15: Avoiding Captures

Witch Life Lesson #17: Trust but Verify

There were a bunch of them and, I'm not gonna lie, for a new witch, the series looked really useful. I mean, if Belles Demoiselles had shown videos like that, my summer would have been way better. Too bad LaToya was the one making them.

Every video had the water bottle in the thumbnail, including one where the thumbnail was LaToya with one hand on the side of her face and her mouth wide open in fake shock while she looked at the water bottle in her other hand.

"Why don't those bottles have words on the labels?"

"Aesthetic?" Dee offered.

I was too busy reading the caption.

New to Witch Life? Here's how to get started. #MagicWater #CashIsQueen #NotNotSponsored #TeamLaToya

I know I've said it before, but I was being funny then. Was LaToya seriously using #TeamLaToya unironically?

Angelique was looking at something different.

"See?" she said. "Hashtag cash is flash but credit is queen? LaToya's scamming kids who probably haven't had a proper financial education, especially not where magic is concerned. It's totally unethical."

I knew Angelique had money, but I didn't know she was into money like that. When she started talking about this LaToya thing, I thought it was gonna be funny, but at that point, she was really getting heated.

I, on the other hand, was getting nervous. Othello rubbed his head against my arm. It helped, but it wasn't enough.

Dee sighed. "Look, Hasani said she doesn't care about LaToya calling her out, so what LaToya does is not our business. What would we do anyway? Walk around telling everybody not to trade anything for the water? Tell her mom?"

"She's not talking to her mom," Angelique and Luz said at the same time. "Or her dad," Luz added. "They're fighting."

A blank message popped up on Angelique's phone.

"Miss Nancy's here," she said. "We have to go."

"Go," I said. "I got it."

"What are you gonna do?" Dee asked.

"Nothing magic," I said. "I'm gonna call Thuy."

"Smart move," Dee said, grabbing her backpack.

Honestly, calling somebody from LaToya's coven was the least bold thing I could think of. If LaToya's parents weren't going to jump in to save her, her coven was the next best thing.

CHAPTER TWELVE

RINGS AND LEADERS

I was feeling all *not my circus, not my monkeys* until everybody left and I started pulling up LaToya's videos. I figured before I called Thuy, I should at least know what I was talking about.

LaToya didn't tag me in her WeBop videos, but between the people she did tag and the people tagged in the comments, the rest of the school was, so her videos were easy to find.

They were basically skits where LaToya played all the characters. I'd seen that style of video before, but it's amazing how much LaToya fit into seventeen seconds. Her scripts were great. Artful, really. And you know they had to be good for me to say that, especially since when LaToya wasn't playing LaToya, the only other character she played was me.

In the videos, I was "Sani," but, I mean, same difference. Nobody called me that, but it was obviously just a part of my name. She was trying to get a rise out of me, and Dee was right: The longer I watched, the more I wanted to get back at her. The matted afro wig she wore when she played me did not help. Neither did the withered morning glory she stuck in the wig, or the derpy look she always had on her face. So what if her parents were having trouble or whatever. Lots of people's parents have trouble. My parents had trouble. That didn't give LaToya permission to take her problems out on me.

I don't know how long I had been swiping through videos, but before I realized it I had slunk underneath the covers on my bed, Othello had curled against my chest, and I was just about to swipe for another when my phone pulsed with a video call. It was Thuy. And it was much later than I realized.

"I was just gonna call you," I said, keeping my voice low.

"Why are you whispering?"

"It's ten o'clock at night. If my mom hears me on the phone, I'm not gonna have a phone."

"It's only eight in California. Put your headphones on." *Good point.* "I'll do the talking."

I grabbed my earbuds and got back under the covers.

"Listen," Thuy said. "I just wanted to give you a heads-up about LaToya. She's really doing the most right now. I don't know everything that's happening, and I'm not on WeBop that much, but when I saw the content she's posting over there I was like, WOW. That is a choice. I know you're like me and spend most of your time on YouTube, but seriously, you should *not* go over to WeBop and watch them."

"Too late," I said.

"Dude! No! They're awful! And I promise you that you look nothing like that."

"Well, you knew it was supposed to be me," I whispered. "It couldn't have been that far off."

"Girl, please. The character's name is Sani! Who else is it supposed to be? I was trying to save you some drama, but it looks like I didn't catch you in time. You want me to let you go to sleep?"

"Yeah, but wait. What are y'all gonna do about LaToya?"

"Y'all?" Thuy asked, her long, black hair falling to one side when she tipped her head.

"Y'all. You guys. Whatever." This was not the time for Thuy to act like she didn't understand just because I wasn't speaking Californian.

"Oh!" she said. "You don't know. Yeah. Dude. LaToya isn't in my coven anymore. I don't know if she has a coven at all."

Whaaaat?

I let my eyebrows do the talking.

"Yeah. A couple weeks ago LaToya started calling all of us, asking us to ask our parents for money. Like, actual money. Not credits or anything."

My eyebrows probably looked like exclamation points.

"Wait. That's making it sound worse than it was. She wasn't asking us to give her money directly. She was asking for our parents to pay her private school tuition and to tell her dad she got a scholarship. I guess they couldn't afford to pay for her after this semester."

"That's sad," I said.

"I know, right? Really sad."

I think Thuy and I meant two different kinds of sad. My family wasn't rich, but I couldn't imagine having to ask somebody else's parents to help you go to school. I know it was LaToya, but I felt bad for her. I honestly didn't know things were so tough for her.

"That wasn't even the worst part. After that, she wanted us to all join 3Thirteen and give our credits to her to so she could buy into some business."

"So y'all ditched her?" I whispered. "She's in your coven. How can you even do that?" What I was asking was more How could you do that to a friend? but what Thuy answered was more logistics.

"It's not like we had an organic connection or anything. My mom gave her some money, LaToya and I wove our signatures into a contract, and that was it. Kalani and I found each other organically, though, so we reconnected even though she's all the way in Hawaii."

"Congrats," I said.

"Thanks! My mom's really happy about it. She keeps reminding me that she paid for the first mistake, but after that, it's on me, so I'm just gonna go organic from here on out. Everybody else pretty much did the same as far as LaToya goes, so, yeah. As of a couple days ago, the Cool Kids officially broke up."

The Cool Kids broke up. I didn't know how to take that. When LaToya made that coven without me and Dee, I was hurt. But looking back on it, I couldn't even remember exactly what I was upset over. I didn't even really know what a coven was. Now I couldn't imagine living without one.

"So what are you going to do?"

"About what?" Thuy asked.

"About LaToya!"

Thuy laughed. "I'm not worried about LaToya. If she wants to ruin her life, that is not on me."

Unfortunately, the more I knew, the more it felt like it was on me.

Thuy was shocked that we were already in school. Apparently in California they don't start until September. After we got off, I did what I could to fall asleep, but when I got up in the morning, I felt like I never did. I picked up my phone to text that we needed another group meeting, but Angelique beat me to it.

She had messaged all four of us. Dee never responded, but we still kept her in the group chat.

Angelique:

Can we videochat before
school? I have news.

Same

Luz:

Can't. Miguel is frying
sick
FAKING sick
He doesn't want to go
to school

He's not rlly sick?

Luz:

Nah
This kid named Margeaux
Won't leave him alone
Classic diva bully.

Need help?

Luz:

Nah. Giving him the
speech about not letting
terrorists win

That should work.

Luz:

Ye. She sounds like a
nightmare though

When it was time to go, Miguel still wasn't budging, so Luz texted that I should walk by myself so I wouldn't be late. When I got there, it was like a flower free-for-all. There were three different kids in different parts of the front yard just sprinkling flowers on the ground in full view of the street. The way crowds of kids had circled around them, it looked like an actual three-ring circus.

"That is so weird," I mumbled to myself. "Why aren't they freaking out?" But I should have known I wasn't by myself because ever since my YouTube channel blew up, whenever I thought I was alone . . . nope! Jenny was there.

"They're used to it," Jenny said. "They all follow LaToya. I manage her WeBop. Or at least I used to."

I sighed. "Congratulations," I said. But then something clicked. "No, not congratulations," I said. "I mean, I'm not hating or anything. If you want to be friends with LaToya, that's on you. But you know she doesn't like me. You know she's been saying horrible things about me. You're clearly her friend, and yet every time I turn around, there you are talking about how much you like my channel. What gives? Are you a spy or something? Because otherwise I don't get your point."

Jenny blinked. She looked surprised. Maybe I was yelling more than I thought I was.

"I guess I deserved that," Jenny said. "Here."

Jenny held out her hand, and draped across her fingers was the aqua bead.

"I saw the way you were looking at it, and when I realized it was the only glass one left, I put it on the side for you. Do you want it?"

I looked around the yard. The kids sprinkling flowers were all wearing Mardi Gras beads pulled apart and twisted together to make patterns that kind of mimicked the intentions woven through the tops of the trees. I wondered if that was on purpose. I wondered if LaToya had seen the intentions with a brass glass scope just like I had,

but I didn't say any of that. I stared at my aqua bead and then looked up at Jenny. "Why are you giving this to me?"

"Because we're friends?"

"We're not friends."

"But we used to be, right? We've never been close like you and Luz, but I thought we were friends."

"We couldn't be," I said. "If we were friends, you wouldn't just hang around with people saying awful things about me. Actually, you're not friends with them, either. If you were, you'd tell them when they're doing something that's not right, not sneak around trying to make nice with the enemy."

"You're right," Jenny said, looking too embarrassed to look me in the eye. "I'm not their friend, but I'm trying to be yours. And I know that this is going to sound really sketchy when I say it right now, but it's probably going to sound even sketchier later, but . . . I need help. Specifically, I need your help. I know you're a witch." She said that last part so fast, I almost didn't catch it.

I shook my head, instinctively looking around to see who might have heard her. No one did. There was too much magic going on.

"I don't know what you're talking about," I said.

"I saw you," she said. "At orientation. The termites? Everybody else ran out of the gym with termites all over them. Not you. You're an influencer, right?"

"You know I'm an influencer on YouTube," I said, even though we both knew that wasn't what she meant. "Do you want tips for starting your YouTube channel?"

"No—magic. LaToya said she would help me. That's why I've been hanging out with her. See, Riverbend Middle is sitting on the world's strongest capture. A capture is—"

"I know what a capture is," I said.

Jenny looked a little relieved. "Well, LaToya said that all the magic holding the capture in is what was holding my magic in. You know. Stopping it from getting out where I can see it and feel it. She said if I helped her fix the capture, she would fix me."

"Fix you? Jenny, you're a whole human being. Just because you don't have magic doesn't mean you need fixing."

"Would you still think that if I told you I'm a witch?"

I stopped and looked at her. Really looked at her. Her hair was just as blonde now as it was when we were little, minus the curl. I searched her face, looking for some sign that she was messing with me. All I could see was the cat-eye makeup.

"No you're not," I said finally.

"I am," she said. "Or I was. When I was little, everybody loved it when I smiled. I called it 'the sparkle.' It was my mom's idea to put me in the commercials. When they turned the camera on, for take after take I poured everything I had into that smile. I was little. I didn't know how to control it. So when my grandparents sold so many cars and everybody was so happy, I kept pouring out the sparkle. Then, one day I just couldn't anymore. And everything felt wrong. Like part of me is missing."

"You were . . . burned out?" I could hardly say the words.

Jenny nodded, ashamed.

"Did your mom know?"

Jenny nodded.

"And she let you keep making those commercials?"

She nodded again. "I don't think she thought I could run out so fast, but yeah. She knew. I'm trying to fix it, though. There's a chance it isn't all gone. The water? That was my idea. I can't get into 3Thirteen on my own, but then LaToya showed up at orientation with a backpack full of them. I thought if she gave me some I could prove to her that I was telling the truth. I thought I would drink it and it would scoop up whatever tiny little droplets of magic I had left and they'd pour out of me like they used to every time I did one of those commercials. LaToya didn't think it would work, but at the time she didn't really have any friends and her coven lives all over, so she let me stick around. She was always a little disgusted by me, though. I'm kind of a cautionary tale."

I just looked at Jenny, those adorable commercials of her kicking tires rolling through my head. I didn't know what to say.

"It's OK," she said. "You don't have to help me. I'll go. But thank you for listening. Oh! And to answer your question from before? The kids watching think LaToya is doing street magic like they do in the French Quarter. They just think she's really good. Annie, Cicily, Jane, and Margeaux know it's real, because now they can do it, too. She made them all leaders. And now that there are four of them, she doesn't need me anymore."

There were kids all around. Annie walked past us carrying a flier that kids were scanning with their phones.

"Sorry to bother you," Jenny said. She was already walking away.

"Wait," I said. "I'm not making any promises, but what's Annie doing? Is she selling those water bottles?"

"No. They're free. LaToya gets credit every time one of them gets returned."

"Returned? That doesn't make sense. Why bother giving them out, then? Why not just get them and immediately return them for credit?"

"The bottles have to be refilled. That's the deal."

"Refilled with what?"

"I don't know. That's just the recycling program. LaToya gets the bottles for free, and she returns them refilled for credit. That's why I suggested we have a party or a festival. You know. Leverage LaToya's followers. Instead of giving water bottles out a few at a time, we could give out a lot all at once. Here. I'll show you. I actually did the design for the invite."

Jenny pulled up an image on her phone:

Fly Fest
Magic and Moonlight on the Mississippi
Invitation Only

I shook my head. That's what Annie was getting everybody to scan. The whole thing made me nervous, and it wasn't just because of the way scanning witchy things tended to take over your phone. It was because I was trying to get one plus one to make two, but it just wouldn't add up. And I am very good at math. Unfortunately, so was LaToya.

LATOYA

MIST, NOT SPRAY

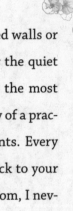

The beauty of a practice room wasn't in the upholstered walls or the variable climate control in every work station or the quiet atmosphere, or even the fact that the rolling chairs were the most comfortable things you could ever hope to sit in. The beauty of a practice room was that it would never let you waste ingredients. Every potion you make could be undone, rewound all the way back to your fresh ingredients. If Kaitlynn hadn't given me a practice room, I never would have figured out how to atomize unicorn tea into a fine mist without a hint of spray. The mist was so fine, it would pass for water vapor any day. I couldn't see through it quite as clearly as I could when it was hot, but that didn't matter much when I could do it over and over again until the glass beads you got from the trees finally showed you what they were all about. Turned out, they were boosters. Luckily, I had spells I wanted to boost, too.

The bad part of a practice room is that, eventually, you had to leave. And sometimes, when you did, you overheard two of your dad's cousins in Sunday church hats who supposedly never step foot in 3Thirteen talking about you in the food court.

"Was that LaToya?" the one in the bright pink hat lined with flamingo feathers asked when she thought I was out of earshot.

"Not with that hair," the one in the tiger-striped hat replied. Both of them laughed.

I didn't have any credits to spend, but I got in the boba line a few feet away from them anyway. I'd duck out before I got to the front, but I just had to listen.

"LaToya's in Paris," the tiger-striped hat added. "I know because her father begged me to pay."

"Really? I heard she's been selling trinkets in the French Quarter. Dressed up like Marie Laveau."

More laughter.

"Her mother ought to take time with that girl. She gets less presentable by the day."

"What else could we expect, letting that bumpkin into the family?"

"Shameful."

"Just shameful."

New plan. When I made it to the top, the Charbonnet cousins were not coming with me.

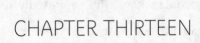

CHAPTER THIRTEEN

BOTTLES AND BEADS

Jenny didn't try to sit with us at lunch. Or LaToya. Nobody in LaToya's crew seemed to notice that she was sitting in a corner eating by herself. Maybe it's because _AnnieOaky_, who had clearly been promoted to Gold-level sales rep, was handing out water bottles to a curated list of people while LaToya talked to everyone who came to the table like she was running for governor or something, except instead of shaking hands, she broke into WeBop dances whenever a kid who came up started one. Then she'd give them a bead, and the wildest part is they wore it. Trust me, the first week of school is not Mardi Gras bead season.

Dee half winked. "You not gon' go up there and get yours?" she asked Angelique. Dee was just trying to make everybody laugh, but Angelique answered her seriously.

"I told you already. I don't want to have anything to do with LaToya now. I feel bad about everything her family's going through, but that doesn't mean I have to get dragged down with her. So, no, I will not be accepting her invitation to 'hang out.'"

That's why Angelique had been trying to call a meeting this morning, but between Jenny and Thuy, there was a whole lot on the table. The end of the Cool Kids coven was not as surprising, at least not to Angelique and Dee. But the fact that LaToya was trying to talk to Angelique again was.

Dee shrugged and shook her head, saying, "Groups break up when you force stuff. In a working group everybody has to be committed and want the same things. I doubt LaToya ever asked any of them what they wanted. She probably just promised them a bunch of stuff and assumed they'd be on her side. You still gotta build trust, even in a circle of friends."

"Well, it sounds like they shouldn't have trusted her," Angelique said. "Did you know that when you're in a circle of friends, your linked sisters are responsible for your debts in the market? I learned that in orientation and I was shocked. The linked sister doesn't even need to be a member of 3Thirteen. One sister's signature obligates them all. Same for mentors and guardians. They can be responsible for stuff they didn't even sign up for. That's all the more reason to make sure you two get a proper financial education. I mean, I would have wanted you to have it just because it's good for you, but I also want to make sure y'all don't tank our credits. Daddy says he'll give us private classes if we want."

"Uh . . . thanks?" I said. "But maybe that can wait a bit? We still don't know what LaToya's up to."

"We should just ask her," Luz said, swallowing a bite of cafeteria grilled cheese.

"Which her?" Dee asked.

"Jenny. We should ask her to just tell us."

"You think she would tell us the truth?"

"Come on, talented people. Y'all don't have truth serum or anything?"

Dee shook her head. "Even if we did, are you gonna be the one to force her to take it?"

"True," Luz said. "My bad. I'm not ready to start my supervillain arc right now. Probably not ever."

"I looked up the car commercial," Angelique said. "It was incredibly popular when it aired on television despite the poor production quality. That part of her story checks out. She wouldn't be the first early bloomer to burn out as a child star."

"Wait. You had to look it up?" I said. "You're from here. You don't remember it?"

"I'm not from here, but even I remember it," Dee said.

None of us was cold enough to imitate the commercial that may or may not have burned someone out while they were sitting friendless in the same room, but from the length of the silence at the table and the way Luz, Dee, and I were trying not to smile, I knew that in our minds we were all saying, "That's a good car, Mawmaw!" Probably in sync.

Angelique shook her head. "My family doesn't really watch TV," she said.

Of course they didn't.

"Is there, like, a test for being . . . burned out?" Luz asked. She kind of whispered the last part. I think she could tell that talk of being burned out made us nervous.

"Kind of," Dee said. "And she already passed it."

"What's the test?" I asked. "Being awkward?" If so, Jenny had aced it.

"Awkward is sort of right, but it's more like uncanny. Like if you were to see a ghost."

Luz perked up. "There are ghosts?" she asked.

"It's a metaphor," Angelique said calmly. "Supposedly, when you're with someone who is burned out, there's this overwhelming feeling like something is wrong. Like the part of them that's missing is what's looking at you. And you can feel it looking at you, you just can't see it."

"Grandmé Annette says it's life longing for itself. I think she might've got that from a song, but it still works."

I sighed. Awkward vibes was not exactly perfect proof that Jenny used to be a witch, but there wasn't much else to go on.

"I guess we could find out what she has to say and see if we can trust her." Then I remembered Witch Life Lesson #17. "Trust but Verify," I said aloud. At least LaToya's WeBop was good for something.

If Jenny was telling the truth, we'd be able to see proof of LaToya's transactions on the blockchain. If LaToya returned bottles and it showed up for credit, then that would mean at least part of her story was true.

Luz told Jenny at least three times that if she wrote everything down and gave it to us, it meant we had written evidence we could hold over her head at any time, so maybe she should just tell us out loud. But Jenny delivered a note through a vent in my locker, anyway. It had everything we needed inside. Everything Jenny knew about LaToya's operation. Plus my aqua beads.

Luz flipped into mom mode and wouldn't let me touch the beads until Angelique and Dee both used the brass glass scope to examine it for traps. There was nothing on the outside, but seeing the glow of Dee's and Angelique's magic through one of those tiny beads was incredible. No wonder I'd always looked for it. My heart was attracted to the magic. Othello's was, too. Every time he saw them, I couldn't stop him from pouncing.

We were in my room because we were always in my room, but even more than that, I had the whiteboard, and we needed a checklist.

The Facts

According to Jenny, the witches in LaToya's crew collected the bottles and brought them to LaToya right after seventh period. Annie counted them and checked to make sure they were all there, then everybody had to go home while LaToya refilled them and brought them to 3Thirteen for recycling. There was more than that in Jenny's note, but there was no point in going all in before we could verify the basics.

The Steps

Step 1: Get a 3Thirteen magazine.

If Angelique was on library duty and Miss T let her stare at the magazine for her whole shift and we could make sure Angelique's shift was aligned with whenever LaToya would supposedly be returning the bottles, then that could have been the plan, but there were too many ifs in it. We also thought about asking Zayvion, the girl who did Luz's test, if we could use hers, but we didn't know if she was on duty or not, and more importantly, we didn't know her like that. That left Sandy.

Sandy insisted on coming over to show us how to use it, even though Angelique assured her that she already did. Turned out Angelique did know how to use it, but Sandy knew it better.

"When you hold any finger on a corner of the page, you get the refracted view. But when you put a finger like this and hold it"—Sandy tapped and held a block of code flying down the screen—"you can pause it in refracted view. You can't take a screenshot or anything, but it'll pause long enough for you to read longer if you see something really juicy. The first line is the date. Then comes the person who initiated the trade, their signature, and their coven order. Then the person who accepted the trade and their info. After that is the status, like pending, final, or nested, which is like if you take an old agreement and add it to a new agreement. The old trade is final, but all those terms still stand in the next agreement. This one doesn't have it because it still says 'pending,' but if the trade is complete it gives the date it was completed."

"What happens when you pick your finger up?" I asked.

"All the trades that were happening in the meantime go flying across the screen so fast that you just let it happen and hope you didn't miss anything really good." Sandy laughed. "Now, I'm going to let you borrow my magazine for a few days under the following conditions. First, please keep the magazine inside the house. It's hard to damage it, but I would get a serious penalty if it were lost or stolen."

"We're not gonna lose it," I said.

"You're not going to mean to lose it. That's not the same as being able to guarantee that you won't lose it. You might even lose it in this house, but if that happened I'd know where to concentrate the search efforts." Wow. Sandy was sounding more like a mom every day.

"Second, I'm not going to ask what you're doing with it. I like teen bonding as much as the next person, and I wouldn't want to hinder your freedom, but"—I knew there would be a but—"please keep in mind that the people doing these transactions are real people. Even if you can figure out who is doing a transaction, do your best to give the person privacy. Yes, it's a public ledger, but that doesn't mean we shouldn't specialize in kindness. And, as your 3Thirteen guardian, I feel compelled to remind you that your actions don't happen in a bubble. As far as 3Thirteen is concerned, your debts are my debts. Oh! And have fun!"

"Wait. My debts are your debts?"

"And Dee's and Angelique's. All of us would be encumbered." Sandy smiled like she was totally cool with being the team mom.

Angelique gave me a look like *told you*.

"Why do you ask?" Sandy winked. "Got your eye on something expensive? You're not borrowing my magazine so you can stalk the movement of dragon scales, are you? Because I promise you none of us can afford it." Sandy put her hand on her belly and laughed. "If this little one ever blossoms, THEY would probably still be paying for it. Dragon scales are out of our league."

"So if me or anyone in my coven buys something we can't afford in 3Thirteen, they might charge you AND the baby for it?" I was horrified. "Remind me: Why did you want to be my guardian again?"

"I trust you," Sandy said. "And, honestly, you guys are doing me a favor by taking the magazine off my hands for a few days. Following the ingredients posts just makes me want to experiment, and you know I'm trying to hold off on magic for a little while."

"Baby Burnout." Dee nodded sagely.

Sandy squealed. "You believe in it?"

Dee shrugged. "I don't not believe in it. But, like, why take chances, right?"

"Agreed!" Sandy held her hand up for a high five. Dee looked like she didn't know what they were high-fiving about, but she high-fived Sandy anyway.

Step 2: Follow LaToya until she makes a trade.

Since it turned out we did not live in a movie where stuff like spying on people is always incredibly easy to do, step 2 was the hardest part of all. The best we could come up with was having people stationed in a bunch of different places and sending text messages back and forth. Picking duty locations at school was easy.

Angelique watched out of a third-floor window, Luz took the cafeteria, I took the main stairwell, and Dee kept watch on the outer gates since at the end of the day she'd be coming from Tulane anyway. Sending text messages if we saw anything was easy. The hard part was waiting.

They don't tell you this in the spy movies, but waiting with nothing to do is the most boring thing ever. I'd think I'd been standing there for like five minutes, but every time I looked down at my phone, zero minutes had passed. It felt like time was moving backward.

I almost blinked back tears of joy when I could finally text:

Headed downstairs.

I was on the third floor and LaToya was coming from the second floor, pulling her flowered suitcase behind her. I don't think she saw me, and it felt like it took forever for her to get down the stairs, but the bag must not have been too heavy because she carried it instead of wheeling it step by step. When she was far enough away, I texted

1st floor and finally stepped out of my hiding place.

Luz was next, texting that LaToya had entered the cafeteria. Annie was already there waiting for her.

Luz:

Annie's gone

What felt like three hours later but was more like five minutes, Luz texted that LaToya was leaving the building.

That was Angelique's cue. She was watching from a corner window on the third floor to see which way LaToya went, which would be Dee's cue to go set up near that gate.

Angelique:

She's not leaving!

Seriously. She's not leaving.

I think she's waiting for everyone else to go.

No. Maybe she's waiting for a ride?

She's reading a book.

She is never going to leave!

Wait. No. Some kids just left.

She got up.

No! She's opening her suitcase. I swear it's like she's setting up camp.

She is literally methodically opening every bottle in her bag and lining them up on a bench. I mean, I like a pattern, too, but this is torture.

Hold on.

Long pause.

Luz:

What?

Dee:

What?

What?

Angelique:

She is laying every bottle on
its side in a patch of flowers.
I promise you, I am not
making this up.

Luz:

Flowers?

Dee:

Which flowers?

Flowers? I thought. In a flash, I could see the world like Othello sees it, like I could see it through the brass glass scope. But I was only seeing it in my head. I needed to see it in person.

I abandoned my post, noisily digging in my backpack for the brass glass scope as I ran to the room next door to Ms. Coulon's. Unlike Ms. Coulon, Ms. Gower always left her door open.

The view from Ms. Gower's window was basically the same as the one from Ms. Coulon's, just one room to the right. The lights woven through the trees were waiting for me, but I looked straight down at the ground. Without the scope, the front yard was a patchy sea of signature flowers. With the scope, the flowers were gone. There were only puddles of magic there, just like there had been before. I froze. That didn't make sense. Kids had been wasting magic left and right. How were the puddles of magic *exactly* like they had been before? There should have been puddles everywhere. Then it hit me. This brass glass scope couldn't see wasted magic. That's what made rose-colored glasses so special. These brass glass scopes only showed intentions. Which meant those puddles on the ground couldn't be wasted magic. They had to be intentions. And LaToya knew where to find each and every one.

One by one, LaToya picked the bottles up. Every time she did, a patch of flowers shrank back and disappeared as an intention on the bottle sprang to life. Then she put all the bottles in her suitcase and rolled toward the side gate. I couldn't see it, but I knew there was a different-colored magic sloshing in every one.

LaToya wasn't collecting credits.

LaToya was collecting signatures.

CHAPTER FOURTEEN

CREDITS AND PLANS

"Those intention puddles could have fooled me," Dee said. "They look almost exactly like what you keep dropping for Othello. You sure she's collecting signatures, though?"

"I guess it works like an extender," I said. "You should have seen the intentions all over those bottles. They were woven so tight, she could have trapped a genie in there. I couldn't see the magic, but yeah. I'm sure."

"Signatures are no joke. If somebody gets yours . . ." Dee trailed off. She was mostly talking to herself, but after the whole thing with Kaitlynn almost getting my signature, I did not need reminding.

We were in my room on step 3: Read the magazine, but it was hard to pay attention. It felt like it didn't matter if LaToya sold those signatures to Kaitlynn or kept them for herself. Any way it went, collecting people's signature magic was no good.

"It's your literal signature," I said for like the eighth time. Nobody complained, though. I was glad. I needed to say it. I needed to get it out. "That's so scary. She could literally sign anything with it and you'd be responsible."

Luz was the only one not stressed out. I think because she was over there being the live version of a Twitter feed, reading aloud every post on the blockchain that she could catch before it swam past.

"Casey traded rainbow glitter for rainbow powder."

"Eliza traded rainbow powder for three credits. Dag. I hope she got a deal."

Angelique was outside with her mushrooms, so Dee was basically doing the same thing on WeBop, scrolling and making announcements about who blossomed, only Dee sounded more like, "Dag. Another one. What's Charliese make? Number eight? No wonder you saw so many colors." And "Nine?" Sucks teeth. "Nah. Some of these gotta be made up."

That left me with Jenny's note. I like details, but unfortunately Jenny left a bunch of stuff out. Maybe she didn't do it on purpose. It's hard to write every single thing down, especially when you were writing by hand. By the time you finish one sentence, your brain is already six sentences past that. But I did have questions, and having questions meant needing to talk to Jenny, and to be completely honest, I didn't want to talk to Jenny. The more I thought about her, the more I was convinced she really was a burned-out witch. Then, whenever I thought that, I was instantly bouncing back and forth between feeling bad for her and being so, so glad it wasn't me. Then I felt guilty. It was wild.

"Everybody is talking about Fly Fest. What's up with that?" Dee said.

"Donna traded Hoa for a dragon scale future. Do we think that tracks dragon weights in the future, or gives you a future with dragon scales in it?"

"Oops. Missed one."

"Oops. Missed another one."

"This *is* like reality TV. So addictive. Ooh! Somebody traded for the best boba flavor."

"Joyful joyful?" I asked.

"That's the one!"

At least Luz was happy.

Angelique came in from the garden, looking more worried than a person who loves growing fungi should.

"Are the mushrooms ready?" I asked.

Angelique shook head. "Did LaToya do a trade?"

I shook my head.

"So, this is bad, right?" Angelique said.

I nodded. This was definitely bad.

"Well, I think we're a little bit past the *plucky group of kids doing stuff on our own* level," Angelique said. "We need to tell somebody. Somebody who could help."

"Well, that rules out my mom," I said. "She'd want to help, but the whole kismet thing makes her hit or miss."

"What about Sandy?" Angelique asked.

"No way. Magic is too dangerous for her right now," I said.

I didn't mind risking my dad. He wasn't doing anything, anyway. But since he wasn't magic, he wouldn't be any help.

Angelique made a face at me. "You're saying that because Sandy's pregnant? Pregnant people are perfectly capable human beings."

"Right," I said, "and that perfectly capable human being said she's taking a break from magic, which means taking a break from stuff like this."

"Fine," Angelique said. "What about Miss Lafleur?"

"What about your mom?" I countered.

"No," Angelique said. "That would mean I'd have to speak to her, and I am currently not speaking to her, not that she's noticed. My mom's not here, anyway. Miss Nancy texted a few minutes ago to say they're driving to something in Amite. Dee, my dad's gonna pick us up."

Dee nodded but kept scrolling WeBop. "Another one about Fly Fest," she said.

"Ms. Coulon?" I suggested. "Supposedly Sandy has her on standby as my substitute freedom spell instructor."

Angelique made a face. "What do you think is going to happen if we go to her, our *Math* teacher, without proof? Especially since we'd basically be outing LaToya in the process?"

"I think we past that," Dee said. "There's kids posting their blossoming all over WeBop. They're tagging LaToya. Giving her credit for their transformations. Hashtag WitchLife is trending. Locally, but still."

I leaned over to take a look. All the kids Dee showed me were wearing the twisted Mardi Gras beads.

I know there was bigger stuff going on, but I couldn't stop myself from rolling my eyes. "If LaToya starts a trend of people wearing Mardi Gras beads all year, I swear I will never forgive her," I said. "What's next? King cakes at Christmas? And with all the witches in the world, why are we the ones looking into all this? Shouldn't Belles Demoiselles be doing something?"

Dee wrinkled her forehead. "Bruh," she said. "You know that's not what Belles Demoiselles is, right?"

We both looked at Luz. She was staring at the magazine, but she must have felt us staring. "Deleted from the Internet. Blah, blah, blah. I'm not gonna say anything. I swear," she said. It wasn't our first time. She knew the drill.

"Belles Demoiselles is out there running the world, but stealthily," I said. "They should stop LaToya, if only to stop her from giving

Belles Demoiselles a bad name. Actually, come to think of it, they should be taking care of the whole capture thing, too. Why do they even exist if they're not going to handle stuff like that?"

"Who is 'they'?"

"The Belles Demoiselles."

"You mean you? And me? And Angelique? *We're* belles demoiselles. And we are doing something."

"You know what I mean. Like, the organization. 'The Belles Demoiselles,'" I said, putting the name in quotation marks with my hands.

"You mean the rotating group of volunteers that comes together to help uplift some members of the next generation? Or do you just mean my mentor? Because she's the only one who lives in that building all year."

"So there's only one witch in central command?" I asked.

Dee laughed. "Hasani, you know good and well there's no such thing as 'central command.' Witches don't have a prime minister or a queen or anything like that. We never have. How you gon' live and let live if somebody is ruling over you? Or, say we do get a ruler, right? And she seems fair and cool and all that. How do you know she'll stay that way once she gets all that power?"

"Belles Demoiselles must have a central command. How else do they get so much done?"

"Consensus," Dee said. "When a hundred belles demoiselles agree, it changes things for all of us."

"Just a hundred?"

Dee laughed. "That's just for belles demoiselles. It's like three hundred if you want to change something for witches everywhere. Somebody always wants to change this or add that or scrap the whole thing and start again. Why you think witches don't have to follow that many rules? It's almost impossible to make them. 3Thirteen is the last thing that ever got passed, and it only exists because it's a co-op and it's built on the only two witch rules I know."

"What's that?"

Dee held up one finger. "Contracts are binding." Dee put up a second finger. "And no witch can be forced into a contract. That's it."

"And those were made by a Conseil des Demoiselles like the one they called when they couldn't agree on whether or not I earned a fleur-de-lis?"

"That's just at Belles Demoiselles. Outside, it's called a conseils des sorcières."

"So if I call a hundred witches together and get them to agree on something, I could make a rule that everybody has to come fix the capture at Riverbend and LaToya would have to permanently stop doing the most?"

That really made Dee laugh. "It's exactly three hundred thirteen if you want to make a rule for everybody. And yes. Please do call a conseils des sorcières. That's gon' be hilarious. Good luck getting three hundred thirteen witches to agree to be in the same room, let alone agree to the same thing. I think it took them like six hundred years to get a consensus for 3Thirteen. You'll be there 'til you're eighty and you still won't make that change."

"LaToya!" Luz shouted.

It took me a second to realize that she wasn't talking about the changes my nonexistent council of witches would make. LaToya's name had popped up on the blockchain.

"Tap and hold!" I shouted, not that I needed to. Luz was already on it.

> 5780.333.1616
>
> _LaToyaNull_black_gladiolas palustris_1_1/1
>
> _KaitlynnSkye_orange_bellis perennis_3_1/1
>
> 13 glass bottle type 2 refills, ordinary magic, to Kaitlynn Skye
> from LaToya in consideration of .13 credits applied to
> nested balance. Remaining balance 43.4 credits and
> one future favor TI.
>
> Nest Alpha_Beta_Gamma_Delta_Epsilon_Zeta_Eta_Theta_
> Iota_Kappa_Lambda_Mu_Nu_Xi_Omicron_Pi_Rho_
> Sigma_Tau_Pending

I was writing it down on the whiteboard. Angelique was tapping it into her phone. She said "got it" a few seconds before me, but we both said, "Read it back?" at the same time.

We did have it. Luz lifted her finger and that entry on the block-chain slid up the magazine and into oblivion.

For a minute we all smiled and whooped and yessed with relief, but after the hype of spotting and recording the entry passed, we had to figure out what it meant.

"OK," I said. "So this is definitely a trade between LaToya and Kaitlynn, right?"

Everybody agreed.

Dee tapped her teeth. "It says bottles, so she sold them, right? Does that mean Jenny was telling the truth?"

"Yeah," I said, "but it doesn't say anything about signatures."

"What's ordinary magic?" Luz asked. She was still scanning the magazine.

Dee shrugged. "Ordinary magic? Like stuff nobody can claim. Like the river and stuff. You know. Regular."

"Of course," Luz said. "Regular. Got it." Luz was rolling her eyes with her tone because her regular eyes stayed locked on the magazine.

"If the bottles she just returned are the ones she filled with signatures, that would mean she's only getting a hundredth of a credit for each one," Angelique said. "I'm not condoning selling signatures, but they have got to be worth more than that. That is a horrible return on investment."

"Yeah," Dee agreed. "That math ain't math-ing."

"LaToya!" Luz shouted again. Angelique and I ran to our posts. Luz dictated.

> 5780.333.1618
>
> _LaToyaNull_black_gladiolas palustris_1_1/1
>
> _KaitlynnSkye_orange_bellis perennis_3_1/1
>
> 1 globe sunk, rooted, removed, and returned as specified, by LaToya and two (2) or more linked sisters at specified location in peak moonlight to be completed within forty-eight (48) hours of this agreement and before the start of the waning gibbous in consideration of 43.4 credits and the refund of one future favor TI upon completion or 86.8 credits and the addition of one future favor TI upon failure.
>
> Nest Alpha_Beta_Gamma_Delta_Epsilon_Zeta_Eta_Theta_ Iota_Kappa_Lambda_Mu_Nu_Xi_Omicron_Pi_Rho_ Sigma_Tau_Upsilon Pending

"I thought she didn't have a coven," Dee said.

"Yeah. And what's with all the Greek letters?" Luz asked. "That's almost the whole alphabet."

"That's how it shows that you rolled one contract into another one. Like taking out a loan to pay off a loan. That's awful. She's just digging a deeper hole every time she nests," Angelique said. "That's twenty times by my count."

"Yeah," I said. "And it looks like she just went double or nothing."

Angelique shook her head. "What is she betting on?"

"Fly Fest," I said. "Jenny said something about doing a bunch of bottles at once."

"She'd have to at the price she's getting for them," Angelique said. "A hundred bottles to get just one credit and she apparently owes 43.4?"

"She's about to owe 86.8," Dee said.

"Right. So that's not four hundred thirty-four bottles she'd have to refill. It's eight hundred sixty-eight. Even if every kid in our school blossomed right at that festival, there still wouldn't be enough."

"Unless that's not what she's betting on," Luz said. "She might be betting on sinking this orb, whatever that is."

For a second, we all went silent.

"I think we have to talk to Jenny again," I said.

Dee looked a little reluctant, but Angelique looked exactly as uncomfortable as I felt. It wasn't just that it felt weird to be around someone who had been burned out. Or that it felt weird to feel weird about being around someone just because they burned out. Now that I knew it, that part was on me, and I could handle it. What I couldn't handle was that I was pretty sure I knew the favor Jenny wanted to ask. She wanted me to help her get her magic back, but in this case I was more like the Wiz than Glinda. I didn't think I could.

"Is that Ms.—" Luz jammed her finger down on the magazine page.

"What?" I said.

Luz looked like she was trying to calm herself down. Like she was trying not to bring the hype, even though she desperately wanted to bring the hype. "Isn't Ms. Coulon's first name Beverlyn? I mean, there can't be that many Beverlyns in the world, right? I mean, maybe there might be a few Beverlys, but BeverLYN?"

"What's happening?" I asked. I appreciated that Luz was trying to slow down her hype train, but at that moment, I needed her to speed it up.

"I think Ms. Coulon is doing something right now at 3Thirteen. Her name just showed up on the blockchain."

Angelique whipped out her teacher voice. "Technically, any witches entering a contract anywhere can put it on the blockchain if they want it to be automatically enforced. The magazine has a filter to only show what's happening in 3Thirteen. You can toggle it on and off. The default is on."

We all looked at her.

"What? I was just saying that the Beverlyn person might not be in 3Thirteen. She could be signing a contract right now in England or The Gambia for all we know."

The looks continued.

Angelique rolled her eyes. "Well, excuse me for sharing knowledge."

"Sorry, Angelique," Luz said. "I'm not an enemy of knowledge. I just want to know if we should read it or not. Remember what Sandy said? It might be personal."

We all looked at each other again. On the one hand, I never want to know anything personal about my teachers ever. They are robots that activate when I enter school and deactivate when I leave school. On the other hand, I want to know everything.

"Just read it," Dee said.

"'Beverlyn Marie—'" she started.

I waved hand for her to stop. "Never mind," I said. Knowing me and Ms. Coulon might have the same middle name was already too much.

Luz started to move her finger to let it go.

"Wait!" Dee said, sounding way more hype than usual. "You started. You might as well finish, right?"

We all looked at her like, *Dee? Is that you?*

Luz grinned her *welcome to the dark side* grin. "It's better than WeBop, right? Once you get started, you just don't want to stop. OK." She returned to the magazine. "So it looks like Beverlyn Marie and Angela Elise—"

"What?" Angelique jumped up and ran over to Luz. "Did you say Angela Elise? That's my mom."

"I thought your mom was Angela Hebert," Luz said.

"Elise is her middle name. Angela Elise Bourgeois Hebert, but she stopped using the Bourgeois when she got married."

"It might not be her," Dee said.

Angelique looked unconvinced. She read over Luz's shoulder, then plopped down on my bed. "It's middle names," she said. "The identifier isn't first and last name. It's first and middle. That's my mom."

"You want me to let it go?" Luz asked, ready to pull her finger off the screen and let the entry fly off to wherever blockchain entries go.

"No. Read it," Angelique said.

Luz looked like she didn't want to be the one to read it aloud, so Dee and I read over her shoulder instead.

5780.333.1631

_AngelaElise_unknown_primula zebra blue_3_1/3

_BeverlynMarie_black_rosa halfeti_1_3/13

1 pair of glass lenses composed of proprietary glass 1
according to specifications provided in consideration
of 6,666 credits to be held in S-Crow and released
upon completion.

Pending

"They're not at 3Thirteen," Angelique said.

"You don't know that," Dee said.

"I do. They're in Amite at Ms. Coulon's glass factory."

Dee and I froze.

A light flashed on Luz's phone. She grabbed it, and the entry flew off the screen, replaced by an endless sea of others none of us could read.

"It's Miguel," she said. "That Margeaux kid will just not leave him alone. I gotta go."

Luz grabbed her bag and ran out the door. I heard my front door click. I wanted to go check on Miguel, too, but it was hard to leave with Angelique in front of me looking like she did. Her hair was perfect. It always was. She couldn't help it. Her outfit was perfect. White top with just a touch of ruffle. Denim skirt—casual, but classy. Black ankle boots with no frills, just an elegant line that showed off the leather. Not a lick of makeup. Just the charms to set it all off. And the earrings, of course. Looking at her, she was perfectly put together and I could have kicked myself. I was her friend. I should have known that even when she looked perfectly put together, inside she might be falling apart.

"What do you want to do?" I asked as gently as I could.

Angelique shook her head. "There's nothing to do. Ms. Coulon is making my mom a pair of rose-colored glasses so she can see my magic. Now she can do the one thing she could never do before, and my life is over."

"It might be that," Dee said, "but it might not. Maybe we should ask them."

"You're right. We should ask them," I said, running over to my door before anyone could stop me. "Mom!" I shouted. "Is Lucy charged? Will you drive us to Amite?"

CHAPTER FIFTEEN

MOMS AND MISTAKES

My mom was game to drive us to Amite, but our electric car, Lucy, was not.

"Lucy is more of a city girl. You know that," my mom said. Honestly, using magic I could get my mom's car to full charge in like twenty minutes, but for some reason she kept blocking that fact out, so I stopped bringing it up. "Do you want me to call Sandy? All five of us would be a squeeze in her car, but I bet she'd do it. I actually just got off the phone with her. She was asking if I'd make her a special blend of mother's milk tea."

My mom was beaming. Her friendship with Sandy—aka, her ex-husband's new wife—was still a little weird to me, but I was getting used to it. Plus, any excuse my mom had to develop a new kind of tea was a good day for her. She lived for that stuff.

I gave her a hug, so, so, so relieved to be able to hug her again whenever I wanted. "Thanks, Mom," I said. "Don't call Sandy, though. She's on a magic diet for the baby." *And you know how we do.*

"And I know how y'all do." My mom smiled and shook her head at the same time. "You can't take the magic out of the girls and you can't keep the girls out of the magic. Well, let me call about renting a car."

"Don't," I said. "I think I know how we can get there."

Twenty minutes later we were riding the moving walkway in 3Thirteen, trying not to miss our fork.

"I think it's the first one," I said. "I'm not sure, though."

"Relax, sweet pea," my mom said. "We'll read the signs. It'll be fine."

I pointed. "That's it. That's the sign!"

"North Africa?" my mom said, puzzled.

"No! Local Destinations! The tiny one with the oysters and the sugarcane?"

"Oh! I see it. That's the fork farthest on the right, right?"

If you were going to the Rivyèmarché, the walkway did the work for you, but if you wanted to go in any other direction, you had to put a little hustle in it. All of us jogged forward and jumped to the right just as the walkway began to split. We all made it, but my mom insisted on counting heads, anyway. We had to make a jump again at Northshore and another jump away from Mississippi, but eventually all our heads were counted one last time and we exited our walkway right where it ended, underneath a sign that read:

SUBSOL

HAMMOND

INDEPENDENCE

AMITE

KENTWOOD

FOLSOM/BOGALUSA EXCHANGE

"Who knew there would be so many stops in Louisiana," my mom said. Honestly, she sounded kind of proud.

"It's more than that, baaaybay," said a woman behind a counter just inside. She said "baby" the New Orleans way, and I loved her instantly. "You should see the one for Acadiana and the River Parishes."

We couldn't really see her from where we were standing in the entrance, but once we stepped inside, I literally gasped. First of all, there were plants hanging everywhere, including the places to sit and, on closer look, some of the plants actually were places to sit, growing from vines in the ceiling. Second of all, the woman selling tickets behind the counter was a vision. I don't care what anybody says. That deep blue eyeshadow was perfection against her dark brown skin. And who rocks a gold lip to work? Fabulous people, that's who. Fabulous people with salt-and-pepper cornrows.

"Y'all look like you from Vacherie–Edgar way," she said, looking between me and my mom. "You, too," she said to Dee. Dee lifted her chin in agreement. "Y'all kin to Jeffery 'nem?"

I looked at my mom.

"I'm not sure," she said. "Our family's from Vacherie, but we honestly haven't spent much time there. We're planning to change that very soon. And my daughter actually just spent the summer there."

Stretch. Belles Demoiselles was there, but it wasn't *really* there. I had been to Vacherie, though. And gotten lost, which is how my dad says you know you've really been to a place.

"That's all right, my baby. Where y'all going?"

"Amite," I said.

"Glass factory, hunh? They know you comin'?"

"Not exactly," I said.

"You sure you wanna go? It's summer. The oysters not even good right now. What you gon' do if the glass factory don't let you in?" She froze. Then she shook her head. "Earnestine, you know better than to get in these people's business," she said to herself. "I apologize," she then said, her voice turning buttery smooth, traces of her New Orleans accent all but gone. "I can offer you five tickets to Amite. Is that what you'd like?"

I nodded. I'm sure the shock from her having a completely different voice was right on my face.

Miss Earnestine laughed. "I don't code switch much, but I do it every once in a while at work—just to get my mind right."

I laughed, relieved to hear her regular voice.

"They two credits each, nah? You still want 'em?" she said like she either wasn't sure we could pay or wasn't sure we wanted to pay.

"I got it," I said.

She smiled. "All right, nah. I heard that."

I grinned. I didn't really care about having so many credits, but it did feel good to be able to treat everyone to this ride.

"We'll have the subsol ready for you in about a minute."

"Excuse me," I said. "What's a subsol?" I knew there were gondolas and submarines in the 3Thirteen travel section, but I'd never heard of subsols. As Miss Earnestine had just said, I wanted to get my mind right.

"It's kind of like a train, but it's small and it travels underground."

I'm not gonna lie. I was a little disappointed.

Dee sucked her teeth. "Man . . . that's just a subway," she said under her breath. I guess she was disappointed, too.

"There isn't a gondola or a submarine we could take, is there?" I asked.

Miss Earnestine smiled. "No, my baby. Local destinations are all subsol. You been to Dakar yet?"

I shook my head.

"That's all right. You young. Start with this subsol first. You'll get there."

Miss Earnestine told us to grab headsets and wait for her to call us. They were something like the ones we used for the VR games at Luz's house, except they were super soft and fit your head as soon as you put them on. I could still see the plants and the counter and Miss Earnestine, but I could also see that what I'd thought was a wall behind the giant, potted birds of paradise was actually a tiny train car sitting on the end of an extremely twisted train track.

"Is that a double helix?" Dee asked. Now she was sounding impressed.

"Yes, my baby, it is. Just give me one more second."

When people say that they never mean one second, but Miss Earnestine literally meant one second, because before I even thought to count off seconds in my head, the train car plumped up and got clearer, and so did the DNA train track. I don't know if they got bigger or got closer or what, but it didn't matter. Either way, it was cool.

"Leave the goggles at your arrival station and enjoy the ride." Miss Earnestine smiled at us as the birds of paradise moved to each side to make a path for us to walk through.

My mom took my hand. All of us walked through and grabbed seats on the subsol. My mom did one last head count, then she gave Miss Earnestine a thumbs-up, the doors closed, and we were off.

The seats on the subsol were a plush blue velvet and the chandelier was gold, but everything else was bright white and elegant.

Exactly Angelique's aesthetic. I would have told her that. I would have geeked out with her about using limits to perfectly calculate the area of the curved, marble ceiling. I would have teased her about sitting up so perfectly straight even when there was no one around to say it wasn't "proper." But the Angelique on that subsol couldn't take any teasing. Not even from a friend. This Angelique needed a hug. Or a mama. Luckily, we had one.

There weren't many seats. Eight in all. Just enough for each of us to have a bag chair if we wanted one. My mom and I sat right next to each other. Dee sat one seat away, but Angelique had chosen a spot the farthest away with all those empty seats between.

My mom went over to Angelique's side of the car. "Can I sit here?" she asked.

Angelique nodded. My mom sat down, but she still left one seat between them. I guess she was trying to let Angelique have a little space.

My mom didn't say anything at first. She was only a kismet, but she had this magic of her own that she could use whenever she wanted to. Just her sitting close made you feel safe enough to start talking. Maybe all moms have that magic. I don't know. But I know my mom did.

It was quiet for a second. Me kind of looking at my phone, Dee pulling out her tiny sketch pad.

"I didn't know my mom's flower," Angelique said eventually.

My mom nodded, leaning in just a little.

"I knew her middle name, but I didn't know her flower. I looked it up." She held up her phone. It was at the wrong angle for me or Dee to see, but my mom nodded again.

"It's beautiful, but she's never shown it to me. I had to read it off some stupid ledger like a stupid stranger. Like any random person who has that magazine."

My mom kept nodding and leaned in just a tiny bit more. Listening. Channeling her breath. I could feel it and slowed my breath, too.

"Why wouldn't she show me this? I'm her daughter, but it's like she doesn't want me to know her."

I thought my mom would say "Of course your mom wants you to know her," but she didn't. Maybe because she didn't know if that was true, and my mom never, ever said things that she wasn't sure were true. Or maybe it was because it was still time to listen.

"My birth mother put these earrings on me when I was born, you know? I knew that part, but no one ever told me what they really were. They're traps, holding my magic in so I can't waste it. My mom told me all kind of things about when I was a baby. Like about how her and my dad raced to the agency as soon as they found out they could adopt me. How the paperwork took weeks and they were so nervous, not knowing who was holding me. How it was a closed adoption and the only thing they knew about my biological parents is that my birth mom is from Vacherie. Am I supposed to think that she didn't know these earrings were some kind of magic trust fund?" Angelique laughed, but not the happy kind. "I guess I am a trust fund baby. People call me that all the time, but I never thought it was true. The thing about trust funds is that they're for people you *don't* trust. Like, you think your kid is too uneducated or too immature to handle the money, so you let someone you trust handle it for them. Or you think whoever takes care of your kid after you die can't be trusted, so you let the bank handle the trust for them. I didn't think I had a trust. My dad always said he'd rather trust me, so he taught me what to do. I guess my mom didn't buy in. Or maybe I'm just not trustworthy."

That's when my mom stepped in. I wasn't surprised. Negative self-talk is not her thing.

"You are trustworthy, but your mother is human, Angelique. She makes mistakes. We all do."

"That's my point. She makes all her mistakes in secret. She hides them. That's why I've never seen her flower. Can you imagine living with a mom so perfect that she never made a single mistake around you? Not a single flower wasted? It's exhausting," she said. "I'll never be that good."

The lights in the car brightened. We all looked around. A calm intercom voice said, "Arriving at your destination: Amite, Louisiana."

"Wait. We're here?" Dee said. "I didn't even think we moved."

"The double helix works like a spring," Angelique said, diving into her phone. "Coil. Load. Uncoil. Unload. I read it in the library."

The lights got even brighter and the voice said, "Uncoiling successful. You have arrived at your destination: Amite, Louisiana. Current affiliation: United States of America. For a list of former affiliations or a brochure of local attractions, please see an attendant at the ticket counter. We know you have a choice in travel, so remember: Car accidents are the leading cause of death for humans under twenty-one years. Thank you for choosing a subsol! Leave headsets on the stands to your right as you exit."

"Wow," Dee said.

Yeah, wow. Way to keep it dark, subsol.

We all got up, but Angelique didn't budge. She was still doing something on her phone. I didn't want to rush her, but I also didn't want to get out of the car without her.

"You looking up the double-helix thing? Oh! Did you already get that library app?"

"No. I had to redownload the Find My Phone app. It'll ping my mom. I want her to know I'm here."

Sounded ominous, but OK. At least Angelique wanted to communicate?

CHAPTER SIXTEEN

BUBBLE AND SEA

There were only four signs in the subsol station in Amite: TICKETS, TOWN, VENDING, and GLASSWORKS. We started following the sign to the glassworks, but the person behind the ticket counter yelled over to us. "Frankie's at lunch. You have to scan your passes over here."

I didn't know who Frankie was, but I did know we didn't have any passes and that Miss Earnestine was right: Maybe I shouldn't have spent eight credits to go to the glassworks before I even knew we could get in.

I pulled out my phone to text Ms. Coulon, which, of course, was ridiculous because why in the world would Ms. Coulon ever have given me her number? I sent her an email instead. Then I called Sandy to ask her to text Ms. Coulon for me, but as soon as Sandy picked up, Miss Nancy appeared.

"Never mind!" I said to Sandy. "I'll call you back."

"Wait!" Sandy said. "Are you in Amite? Where's my magazine?"

"Don't worry," I said. "It's safe at the house. I wouldn't bring it out after you asked me not to."

"Oh, good. Thank you for being responsible. Have fun, girlie!"

Very mom-like, but also very Sandy. I approved.

"Nancy," my mom said. "Thank you for coming to get us. I appreciate it."

"Just doing my job. But I have to admit, I didn't expect four of you. Angela only mentioned Angelique. Let me just message Beverlyn about getting more passes. Ope. Looks like she already knows. It says the passes will be waiting down by the volcano entrance. Follow me."

We followed Miss Nancy past the TO GLASSWORKS sign and down a hall that looked like we could have been in any office building anywhere until we got to a guard stand next to an elevator. I guess that's where Frankie was supposed to be. The elevator had only a down button. I reached out to press it, but Miss Nancy stopped me.

"It won't work for you. Your pass isn't registered. Until then, you're my guest."

Miss Nancy put her thumb on the elevator button and said her name like she was talking to a machine to pay her electric bill over the phone. "Nancy. Wilson. Four guests."

The elevator talked back.

"Thank you, Nancy Wilson. How long will you be responsible for these guests?"

"Until the volcano entrance," she said.

The elevator door slid open. The fact that the elevator was all glass was like, duh, Hasani. It's a glassworks. But y'all: THE ELEVATOR WAS ALL GLASS! Nothing else. No metal. No buttons. Nothing. Just a perfect glass sphere. We were legitimately about to travel by bubble like we were the good witches of the north.

Miss Nancy walked in first, and I got nervous. She was clearly standing on the flattest spot. Traveling in a totally clear sphere is cool, but only if you can figure out how to stand. I had just mentally decided to stand behind Miss Nancy and kind of arch my back to lean against the wall the best I could, but who was I kidding? It was a sphere. There was no wall!

Then Dee just stepped in as cool as you please and stood next to Miss Nancy—and the floor leveled out for her. The rest of us just walked in after that. I did end up behind Miss Nancy, though, so my original plan didn't all go to waste.

"Destination?" the elevator asked.

Miss Nancy used her bill paying voice again. "Volcano. Entrance," she said. And suddenly, we were off. There was a jolt, and then everything was super smooth. The view around us as we drifted was incredible. Traveling by bubble has its privileges. In addition to being the smoothest ride imaginable, it also had three-sixty-degree views. I was hoping for an actual volcano, and the glassworks did not disappoint. It was green and lush like it was made by the heart of Te Fiti, and as we watched, lava spewed from the top and oozed down one side.

"They say it controls the heat," Miss Nancy said. She was watching the volcano, too. "But I'll let Beverlyn tell you all that. It's her place anyway, and I have a feeling I should get the car ready."

Miss Nancy gave Angelique a look, but Angelique didn't notice. She was too busy folding her arms and holding her chin up to make sure Miss Nancy knew she was mad. I didn't want any part of that, so I made sure Miss Nancy saw me going back to the view. It was hard to tell what everything was from this high up. Not that I would have known what it was if we were up close. But I liked the way watching it made you feel. It was kind of like the lights of intention in the trees— if the lights were connected by metal tubes and conveyor belts with a steampunk twist.

The bubble drifted lower. Eventually, the top of the volcano was too high above us to see and we touched down on a platform next to a rolling sea. OK, it probably wasn't big enough to be a sea, but you couldn't see the other side of it, and the waves crashing against the slanted metal shore made it impossible to call it a pit or a pool.

An attendant in a brown uniform that gave me definite *Evilene runs this factory* vibes was standing between us and a large, green metal door right in the side of the volcano.

"You're a kismet?" the attendant asked, looking straight at my mom.

My mom nodded.

"No problem," they said. "You can sign for your pass here." They handed my mom a glass pen and gestured toward a tray of sand.

My mom didn't miss a beat, signing her name in the sand like we did all the time at the beach.

"This'll be a minute," the attendant said, pulling a lever to rotate the tray into something under the table. Then they set a timer for a minute and smiled at us in a way that kind of felt like hold music. The timer dinged, the lever moved itself, and the tray swung back to its original place. Only now my mom's signature was frozen into a piece of glass. My mom was looking at it like it was about to breathe fire.

"Don't worry," the attendant said. "It's safe to touch. The last eighteen seconds is full cooling. Does that work?"

"I have no idea," my mom said.

"I mean, does that work as your signature?"

"Oh!" my mom laughed. "That's the one I use at the bank, so I guess I'll say yes."

The attendant nodded, picked up my mom's name glass, and slid it into a drawer before turning to the rest of us.

"Everyone else can use standard signatures. There's a wall right over there."

Angelique, Dee, and I all wove our signature flowers into a grassy patch next to the door. Louisiana phlox. Miniature rose. Morning glory. They looked good together, but it kind of felt like something was missing. I wanted to weave more vines into it. Maybe make an outline? But then I remembered I wasn't making a thumbnail for my channel. We were about to enter a factory and, if I didn't line up with everyone else, I might get left behind.

The attendant looked at Miss Nancy and said, "Sorry. You need to sign in again. Company policy."

"Oh, no. I'm headed out," Miss Nancy said, pressing the elevator button, which still, confusingly, pointed down.

"Nancy. Wilson," she said.

"Destination?"

"Ground." She stepped in and the bubble lifted off. I wanted to watch her float to wherever she was going, but then I really would have gotten left behind.

CHAPTER SEVENTEEN

VILLAINS AND VOLCANOES

The attendant didn't take us far. Just through a doorway that whooshed air when you walked through it and into what looked like the outer room of the bathroom in a fancy hotel.

"There's a lift on the other side of that door that'll take you there. You have to use it one at a time, though."

"You're sure we won't get lost?" my mom asked. She didn't exactly sound nervous, but she didn't sound not nervous, either.

The attendant smiled. "I'm sure. Ms. Coulon's office is the only room in this building. I think she thought it'd be funny."

My mom's eyebrows said, *Funny how?*

The attendant answered. "You know? The whole supervillain trope? Office in the side of a volcano? Never mind. She's waiting for you."

The lift was cool. Kind of like a bank tube, but it didn't mess up your hair. My mom went first, just to make sure it was safe. Angelique made sure she was last. I think she wanted to make an entrance. When I landed, Ms. Coulon was there, arms crossed, rocking reading glasses on a chain as usual. So was Mrs. Hebert, who somehow always seemed to be wearing gold accents with an all-white suit, standing next to my mom, who was never, ever wearing an all-white suit, and Dee.

The lift ended with me standing perfectly level on a hardwood floor. The only way I knew for sure I didn't imagine the whole ride was the thin circle carved into the floor around me. The others all motioned me to the side. I stepped over and joined them in watching the circle. The circle dropped into the hole, and a few seconds later it popped back up with Angelique on top.

No one motioned Angelique to the side. I mean, I almost did. I thought that's what we were doing. But when no one else moved, I kept my arms still, too.

Angelique had her arms crossed. Her chin was still up. But when she looked at her mom, tears instantly started rolling down her face. I'd never seen Angelique cry before. Honestly, until that moment, it kind of seemed like she couldn't cry. Like no matter what came at her, nothing would ever shake her.

Angelique's mom rushed over to her and wrapped her in a tight hug. After a few seconds, Mrs. Hebert said, "Beverlyn, may I have a few minutes alone with my daughter, please?"

Ms. Coulon nodded, turned to us, and said, "How about a tour?"

I would much rather have stayed to hear what was happening with Angelique, but the look on my mom's face reminded me that I didn't have a choice.

The three of us followed Ms. Coulon through a door on the other side of the room where her desk and fancy couches and coffee tables were, to a room that I actually liked way better. There were a bunch of comfy-looking rolling chairs in front of tables with command screens built right in. No keyboards. Just buttons. *Star Trek* bridge–style. And just like in *Star Trek*, there was a giant, curved screen at the front of the room. It was a whole wall. And the only thing that gave away the fact that it was a screen and not a window to the universe is that the view was of the volcano we were actually standing in.

"The volcano isn't natural, of course," Ms. Coulon said, "but since magic is the most base element of nature, we've taken inspiration from the natural form—in this case, volcanic islands in the pacific— to aid in the magic infusion process."

"Glass fired by volcano. I figured, but . . ." Dee finished with her *I'm impressed* nod.

"Why not just set up shop at a real volcano?" I asked.

"Witches are free to do whatever we want, but over the millennia, we have developed a few rules that all of us must abide."

"A few?" I said. "As in three . . . ?"

Supposedly, witches had zero rules, but I gave Dee a look like, *Bruh. You said two.*

Dee put up her hands and made a face like, *My bad.*

"Not as many rules as you would expect, but one of them is that ordinary magic belongs to all of us."

I raised my hand.

"We are not in class, Miss Schexnayder-Jones. What is it?"

"Somebody said there are two rules." Not naming names, Dee. "Now you're making it sound like three, but you didn't say three. So, how many rules are there exactly? Like, is there a list, or . . . how do I get that?"

"On the Interweb, I suppose, but at the moment it's not important."

Did my Math teacher who made me show my work two ways for every problem just say that a specific number wasn't important? Wow. Speechless.

"My point is that, like all the elements of nature, ordinary magic belongs to all of us," Ms. Coulon said. But all I could think of was *Is she really just gonna keep going and not answer my question?* "You can use ordinary magic. We all can. But you can't sell it because you never actually owned it. Selling ordinary magic would be the same as arriving someplace new, seeing a person there, then selling them the land they already lived on." *Wait. Didn't that happen?* "You cannot sell what you never owned in the first place."

"I get it," Dee said. I was glad somebody did. "A real volcano would have been the best thing, but you didn't want to set up a factory on a natural one and tell a bunch of people they can't use it, so you made one."

"Exactly. And there are some advantages to making our own little volcano, too. We could control the size and choose our location. I wanted to be in an area that already had a high concentration of talented people so most people wouldn't have to commute far to work here. And building our own volcano means that we have more control over its environmental impact. We've done that very well, I'm proud to say, but we still have a ways to go. We can dissipate the heat to a certain extent, but can't erase our heat signature entirely, so we do the most work in summer. That's in part because summer vacation is a convenient time for me to work full throttle, but also partially because the small amount of heat that we are unable to control for is easily absorbed into the environment without interrupting the natural rhythms of the trees and mycelium."

"Amite is hotter than it would be if you weren't here?" I asked.

"Yes. On average it is point-six-eight degrees warmer than it would be if we hadn't installed the volcano. This year we're hoping to get it down to point-six-four. An industrial glass kiln would actually be slightly more efficient if we were making the kinds of glasses you probably have in your homes, but, of course, we aren't making that kind of glass. Ours is more special, and it's made on a seasonal schedule. While I'm at school, every one of these command tables is being used by a talented person who can jump in and help when needed. By magic, of course. We use our heads here, not our legs." Ms. Coulon laughed.

"School started," Dee said. "Where is everybody?"

"Oh, when I realized that I had to come in this afternoon, I let everyone in the command center go home early. No point in keeping them away from their families and personal projects when I'm here to cover it. Have a seat. We'll take the tour," she said, motioning to the leather chairs scattered around the room.

My mom, Dee, and I all sat at different command stations. I kind of thought the chairs might turn into a roller coaster or something, and I must have said that out loud because Ms. Coulon said, "This is a working factory, not the cave of wonders." The chairs were comfy, so I was kind of glad she was showing us the factory on-screen. Her command center wall was better than IMAX, and all the places she showed us looked hot, anyway.

After Ms. Coulon played what was obviously an explainer video on the basics of glass and the differences between glass and crystal, we got to some really cool stuff, like heating sand to thousands of degrees inside what was basically a real volcano, diverting lava flow to use the heat for a bunch of other steps, all of which seemed to involve pairs of people. One person in the pair was shaping, and the other was kind of just standing there, but you could tell by the looks on their faces that they were controlling a flow of magic.

"Are all those people working in this volcano right now? The person outside said your office was the only room in here."

"Yes, that's true. They're not in the building, but they are on the mountain. The feel of being in nature on the side of a mountain assists with magic flow."

Dope. "How come we couldn't see them when we were in the bubble?" I asked.

"A recent addition. There are now intentions woven to deflect the viewing of each individual area. Apparently open concept workspaces are now considered cruel." Ms. Coulon shrugged. "We put up intentions to give each group of workers a more private work area that is usually only observed by the lead support person, or me."

Apparently, everything in the glassworks was made by hand. The conveyor belts were all either crushing untalented glass so it could be recycled, or moving sand salvaged from construction sites to be "remineralized" for use. "Most people think of those things as impurities," she said. "We know that they're magic."

Then Ms. Coulon basically went room by room—or semiprivate outdoor workspace by semiprivate outdoor workspace—giving us the grand tour. I kept my eyes peeled for rose-colored glasses, but I never saw them, maybe because Ms. Coulon skipped some of the rooms, saying those weaves were "proprietary" and we might have "cousins."

After almost three years of being in Ms. Coulson's class, she didn't trust me? I kind of didn't blame her, though. One thing LaToya had right in her little WeBop lessons was the whole trust-but-verify thing. I didn't want to have to sign any more witching secrecy agreements, anyway. I'd done enough of those to last my whole life.

Ms. Coulon had moved us on to glass bricks designed to help the flow of ordinary magic through your house, and car glass that improved the driving range and charging rate of electric cars.

"Ooh. I need that," my mom said.

"Mom—" I started. But I caught myself. I had to remind myself that I did not need to remind my mom *again* that she didn't need any of that because she had me.

"And, of course, crystals don't always have to take their natural form," Ms. Coulon said, showing us the live feed from a cavern full of hand-dripped stalactites and stalagmites in a bunch of different colors that I can only describe as rainbow, but neutral.

"And I also thought you might be interested to see these. They're being used in a product that mysteriously seems to be quite the trend at school lately."

Ms. Coulon clicked the remote. On-screen there were five or six pairs of glass workers moving lumps of glass over a lava flow with a very long pole. They took turns rolling it back and forth along the edge and holding it over the heat again until, at some point, instead of holding it over the lava again, one of them would blow into the pole like it was a bugle announcing the arrival of a king. Then, bam! They smack it on something and it's a bottle. Weirdly, that is not what caught my attention. It was the bottles hovering over the lava on a rack above them. They were deep, matte green with an irresistible gold undertone that jumped out at you even though the screen.

Ms. Coulon zoomed in on the water bottles. The camera must have had a little of whatever was in the brass glass scope in the lens because I could see the pattern of intentions woven into them. I couldn't understand what the intention was doing, but I could see that it was working. Pumping. It was soothing, like watching those videos of people perfectly vaccuming a floor. So normal, yet so satisfying.

"Your friend has been bringing these on campus."

My eyes snapped away from the screen to stare at Ms. Coulon. "LaToya is not my friend," I said. "I used to think she was, but that was a long time ago."

"A month or two?" Ms. Coulon asked.

OK. Maybe it hadn't been that long, but it felt like it.

Luckily, Dee cut in. "Yes, ma'am," Dee said. "Me, Hasani, and LaToya were gonna make a coven, but LaToya decided to go another way."

Understatement.

But Ms. Coulon wasn't satisfied. "I need to be very, very sure. Your friend—"

"She's not our friend," I said again. "We don't even sit together at lunch."

"Your teammate," Ms. Coulon corrected, "has been performing magic openly on the Internet and giving these bottles out all over campus. Ordinarily, I would leave witches be, but this impacts more people than I think you realize, so, please. Tell me about your involvement with those bottles."

"Wait a minute," my mom said. She went from mild-mannered-mom-mesmerized-by-magic to oh-no-you-will-NOT-mess-with-my-baby in less than two seconds. "Let me get this straight. You're the one who makes these bottles, but you're asking Hasani how she's involved like she's the one doing something wrong? Isn't that what we should be asking you?"

For the record, my mom had no idea if I was doing anything wrong or not. I wasn't, but she didn't need to know that to know she was going to bat for me. Also for the record, I was pretty sure Ms. Coulon wasn't going to do anything to us, but in a little part of my

brain Luz's voice was saying, *I have not made you watch enough true crime, because while you're in someone's volcano lair is NOT the time to give that speech.*

Touché, mental Luz. Touché. My mom was handling it, though.

"Yes," Ms. Coulson said. "I designed those bottles and they are made in my glassworks. I am also aware that those bottles are used in Kaitlynn's little 'gift with' scheme. Lazy marketing, if you ask me, but I can't argue with her success. That's all well and fine for Kaitlynn, but now it is my understanding that LaToya is attempting to become Kaitlynn's business partner, and I need to know here and now whether or not Hasani, in particular, is involved."

"Why Hasani?" my mom asked. She wasn't yelling, but her voice could have cut like a knife. "Are you accusing my baby of something?"

"Well, Sandy recently became Hasani's guardian at 3Thirteen."

My mom got a little louder. "Sandy is Hasani's stepmother and my friend. What does that have to do with you accusing Hasani of being involved in some scheme?"

"Sandy is a member of my coven."

"Your coven?" my mom said, her eyebrows shooting straight up. "Does that mean you started it or something? Why is it your coven?"

"I didn't mean it that way. I am the third member in the coven, but it belongs to all of us equally. I only pointed that out because, as a coven, we share responsibility for what the other members do. If, for example, one of us went into debt and couldn't pay it, the rest of us would also be responsible. The same is true when one of us becomes a guardian in 3Thirteen. If Hasani does something ill-advised, Sandy would face the repercussions and, therefore, the rest of us will, too. That is why I want to know how deeply Hasani is involved with anything that traces back to Kaitlynn, including those bottles."

My mom wasn't done. "If those bottles are dangerous, why do you sell them in the first place?"

"Unaltered, the bottles serve a beautiful, useful purpose, but someone has been tampering with them."

I stared at the bottles on the big screen, the intentions glistening softly. Ms. Coulon was right. I couldn't tell exactly what the intentions were doing, but I could tell they were doing something beautiful. The movement was calm. Nothing like the chaos I'd seen on LaToya's bottles through the scope.

Dee and I looked at each other. Dee gave me the nod.

"We saw LaToya collecting signatures at school," I said. "And the intentions on her bottles don't look anything like that one. We think she's done something to them to make them act like extenders so she can collect people's signatures and get out of debt with Kaitlynn."

"I was afraid of that," Ms. Coulon said. "I designed those bottles myself. They are the opposite of extenders. The minerals and intentions woven into the crystal work together to filter all the signature out of whatever magic is collected inside. It's the same thing that happens when magic is released back into nature, only my crystal bottles do it much faster. No matter how it began, after thirty seconds in that bottle, there would be nothing left but ordinary magic. But these"—Ms. Coulon clicked a button and the image switched to one of LaToya's bottles before she zipped her suitcase—"have been tampered with. Full refracted view," she said.

The image on the screen didn't get any bigger, but it went from still to live, and the bottle exploded in colors, like a dot-to-dot puzzle with a zillion dots all moving in different directions. The outline of the bottle was gold, but everything else was . . . a mess.

"The gold is the intention woven into the bottle itself. The other colors are some kind of glaze. I thought nothing could tamper with the perfect order of my crystalized intention, but I was wrong. Something is altering it: chaos."

Chaos? I looked closer. No wonder those bottles were so hard to look at.

"What's it doing?" my mom asked. She was back at attention.

"We're not certain," Ms. Coulon said. "Decoding someone else's intention is a long, tedious, and sometimes impossible process. When it starts off as a potion, which the glaze on this bottle likely did, we stand a slightly better chance, but first we'd need the bottle to determine what ingredients were used in the glaze, then we could go from there. I didn't think that even Kaitlynn had the resources to find a world-class fézur unscrupulous enough to help her. The most likely possibility is that it's the work of a kismet. When luck hits, it hits big."

"What about LaToya?" I asked. "Potions are her thing."

Ms. Coulon gave me the look adults give when they think it's cute that you don't know any better. "I seriously doubt a thirteen-year-old a few weeks out of charm school has reached the level of a world-class fézur," she said.

Ms. Coulon obviously didn't know LaToya.

LATOYA

WISHES, NOT WANTS

*P*ractice rooms are perfect. They're heaven. A genie in a bottle, and not the cheap kind. The grants-you-infinite-wishes-and-turns-back-time kind. No limitations.

I'd started over a million times. More lemon peel. Less lemon peel. Clove? No. Garlic? Yes. Celery, bell pepper, and onions at the start, fresh ginger at the finish. I'd done it so many times that the potion started to brew itself. I wanted to write it down, but I couldn't. When you write things down, someone might get you to share. I had to do it by memory. It wasn't until I powdered the pearls I had gotten for my first communion and added them with the lemon that the potion took shape. A drop of it made a perfect little sphere no bigger than a grape. A puff of mist from unicorn tea, and the spell's intentions pulsed around the surface like the guardians I hoped they'd be. The pulses weren't strong, but they looked enough like the intentions from the one good pair of glass beads that I almost wept with joy.

"So that's what you've been up to?" a voice said.

My heart jumped, but I managed to keep my body still. I wasn't expecting company, but this was Kaitlynn's practice room. She could come whenever she wanted, no matter what I wanted. And right then, I wanted anything but for her to be standing right there.

Jasper jumped onto my left shoulder. His fluffy monkey face reflected in the tiny orb even though his fur was the same pearlescent white.

I nodded so Kaitlynn would know I wasn't afraid of her or her monkey. That I had nothing to hide, just like a good partner.

"I don't think that spell is in the recipe book you gave me, is it? You're not holding back on me, are you?" Kaitlynn asked, her voice sweet, like she was the one who could grant me wishes.

"It's a new one," I said. "I'm not sure what it does yet." That wasn't exactly a lie. I wasn't sure what it would do yet.

CHAPTER EIGHTEEN

LAUNCHES AND LEECHES

Angelique still hadn't come out of Ms. Coulon's office and since, as my mother says, I can't hold ice water in a bucket, I ended up telling Ms. Coulon the biggest reason we came. It wasn't just because of LaToya collecting signatures in bottles. It was because of Ms. Coulon and Mrs. Hebert and a certain pair of rose-colored glasses.

"Ah!" Ms. Coulon said. "That's a good thought, but it isn't correct. I won't tell you exactly what Angela and I traded for, but I can assure you that it was not for a pair of rose-colored glasses. I've tried for decades. I have no idea how to make them."

I blinked. Dee was the one who talked. "The whole glassworks thing? Seriously? You didn't invent rose-colored glasses?"

Ms. Coulon laughed. All the way. I swear I've never heard her laugh like that before. "Exactly how old do the two of you think I am? Never mind. Don't answer that. The Belles Demoiselles have been using satellites with that technology since the 1940s. That is long before I was born. And the witch who made them died before I was born, too. She didn't share her recipe and, so far, none of us have been able to replicate it. I've created a lot of other things, trying, though, so it's not a total loss. But you can bet that if I ever got my hands on a pair of rose-colored glasses, I wouldn't trade them to anyone, not even Angela."

"So what are those?" I asked, nodding toward the reading glasses Ms. Coulon always wore around her neck. They weren't pink, but I guess somewhere in the back of my mind I kind of thought that didn't matter.

"These? The lenses on them are plain glass. I mostly wear them for the chain," Ms. Coulon said, waving the beaded chain so that it glinted in the light.

Fashion? On Ms. Coulon? I was surprised, but the chain was cute. I'd always thought so. Total librarian chic.

"Dag," I said. "So Angelique was freaked out for nothing?"

The door slid open.

"Perfect timing, Angela," Ms. Coulon said. She actually looked relieved.

Mrs. Hebert walked in, her arm still around Angelique, who was puffy-eyed and sniffly like she had just been crying but also leaning on her mom and hugging her, too.

I looked at Angelique like, *You OK?*

Angelique nodded. Not exactly a full thumbs-up, but the way she leaned into her mom made it seem a little better.

"Indeed," Mrs. Hebert said. "Angelique was just telling me that LaToya has been digging herself deeper and deeper into debt at 3Thirteen, and instead of trying to get out of it, she's doubling down on it with this festival we've seen in the works. It's just a crying shame."

"Jenny thinks LaToya's trying to make a new coven," I said.

The adults all nodded sadly, but that was it.

"And probably more kids are going to get caught up in this bottle thing," I added.

"Sadly," Ms. Coulon said. "That is probably true."

"Well, should we tell LaToya that, then?" I asked. "I mean, she's not going to listen to any of us, but she might listen to one of you."

Ms. Coulon and Mrs. Hebert looked at each other like they were flipping a coin to see who would tell us. Mrs. Hebert lost the toss.

"It's admirable that you want to help LaToya better her position. I'm all for that." She turned to Angelique. "That's what Daddy does, and you know how much I believe in his mission. But"—there was always a but—"it is not our place to step in on this."

O.

M.

G.

Was she for real? Weren't adults supposed to spring into action at this point? Especially adults who kept saying how bad it was for children to not be protected?

"Well, whose place is it? The Belles Demoiselles? The con-say day sore-see-air or whoever it is that makes rules for witches? Who makes people do what they're supposed to?"

"Conseils des sorcières are very rare, Hasani." Mrs. Hebert looked concerned, like maybe I was waiting for the all-powerful Oz to show up and fix this, when we all know he doesn't exist. But if he didn't exist, maybe he should have. "They're rare because they are difficult. Consensus isn't easy. It isn't supposed to be."

"So, no one is in charge?"

"Ultimately, no," Mrs. Hebert said. "Personal responsibility is hard, but, ultimately, witches are responsible for ourselves and our families. That's why it's so important to choose your family carefully."

"What about people who don't have any family?"

I was thinking that, but Angelique was the one who said it.

Mrs. Hebert put her hand on Angelique's arm. "They find some," she said.

"Or people like you step in," Ms. Coulon added. "That's how we find our places in this world. We find something that needs to be done, and we do it. It's simple. I'm not saying it's easy, but it is simple."

Shaking my head wasn't enough. Othello wasn't there, so the best I could do was put my hands on my own face and press hard, trying to wipe the frustration away. The next thing I knew, somebody had grabbed my wrist. Ms. Coulon was standing right in my face.

"Hasani, where did you get this?" she said, pushing my sleeve back so the strand of aqua beads around my wrist was easy to see. "Was this out of the trees? Answer me!" she shouted.

My whole body went cold. I wanted to move, but my feet were frozen to the spot. I managed to nod just as something leeched the color from the first aqua bead.

"Don't fight!" Ms. Coulon said, yanking the chain off her neck and smashing it to the ground before jerking at the one on my arm. Dee and Angelique tried to jump in front of me, but it was too late. The strand popped and fell away. I didn't even realize that my wrist hurt until the beads were gone.

Ms. Coulon stood there holding the broken strand in her hands, beads bouncing across the floor like raindrops. Not an aqua bead in sight. Every one of them was pure white.

My whole body tingled. I moved a toe just to see if I could.

"What's happening?" I asked.

"The capture." Ms. Coulon was practically panting. "The capture has come back to life."

"So I didn't fix the capture?" I said it like a question, but I already knew the answer.

Ms. Coulon had herded all of us in the bubble to a different part of the factory. What Ms. Coulon called her private office. It was small compared to the other one. You would have thought it was just a normal office. A desk. A chair. A little fireplace. If it weren't for the mushrooms growing under a glass dome in one corner and the tiny replica of the volcano outside, it would have looked totally normal. Maybe it still could have passed if the tiny volcano wasn't also a tiny glass kiln. I think it could only melt enough sand to make one bead at a time, but no way was that passing as normal.

"I guess it was only a matter of time," Mrs. Hebert said. "You did what you could, Beverlyn. Nancy is upset, too. This was her watch. It's my fault she was out here in Amite."

"Miss Nancy's watch for what?" My mom asked.

"The beads were an alarm system, filled with a faux-magic Beverlyn designed. If the capture activated, it would drain the beads first. There's a group that watches the bead trees for the first signs of Beverlyn's beads going white so we could sound the alarm. Today was Miss Nancy's turn, but I insisted we come out here to get a

gift for Angelique. Honestly, I'm not sure she'll ever forgive herself for listening to me. If Hasani had been burned out, I'm sure she wouldn't have."

"If *I* had been burned out?" I looked from adult to adult in the room. The one who should have had the most answers had her head down on her desk.

"If Beverlyn hadn't gotten those beads off you in time, when the capture was done leeching them, it would have leeched you, too," Mrs. Hebert explained.

You have never seen a room full of brown girls look more bloodless. I swear, every one of us could have passed for vampires.

Ms. Coulon finally raised her head. "That's just it," she said. "I didn't get to her in time. By the time I ripped them off, the beads were completely drained. Completely."

"I could have burned out? From those beads? Why didn't you tell me?" I asked.

"I didn't think there was anything to be alarmed about. The protections on those trees have held for decades. Even after your hurricane they looked like they were perfectly intact. It should have taken a long time for them to drain. That would have been more than enough time to notify everyone. As it was, I barely had time to pull off the ones I was wearing myself. Something has made this capture more powerful than it has ever been."

I wasn't cold anymore, but my voice was still trembling. "LaToya gave beads out to a bunch of kids. What if some of them were like the ones I was wearing? What do we do?"

"Hopefully that's not the case, but what's done is done." Mrs. Hebert's voice was firm. "All you can do now is stay away from the capture and anything LaToya is planning, especially the festival. You haven't let yourselves be dragged into a petty witch war so far, and I hope you can keep it that way. Everything one of you does will affect the others now and forever. You are linked sisters. Organically. There's no turning back."

"Angela," Ms. Coulon said, "do you think you can find them another school to attend?"

Mrs. Hebert nodded. "I'm sure we could get them all in at the Academy. The headmistress owes me several favors."

"That's the school with the uniform?" Dee asked. She sounded straight-up scared. So did my mom.

"Angela," my mom said, "I don't think we can afford to send Hasani to a school like that."

"Nailah, this is an emergency and our daughters are a coven. We're family. Please allow me to cover whatever costs come up for schooling this year. If the girls don't want to go to the Academy, we can homeschool them. I'll hire a cluster of tutors. It'll be fine. It might be better, actually."

"What about Mathletes?" Angelique said.

Forget Mathletes. "What about Luz?" I asked. "She might not be a witch, but we can't just leave her and Miguel there."

"The worst thing that happens to untalented people on a capture is a moderate to severe case of anxiety. Nothing the school counselor can't handle."

I gave Ms. Coulon a look like, *I know you are not downplaying mental health.*

"Besides," she said. "Stabilizing that capture is my project. I'm not just going to let it be, but restabilizing a capture that powerful could take a while. We don't want y'all in danger any longer than you have to be. If I work at it steadily, I should be able to have the protections back in place by August or September next year."

"Next year?" I asked. We couldn't leave the kids at my school to suffer for a whole year. But looking around the room, I saw that no one's face was as upset as it should have been. Then it hit me. I was the only one who had roots at Riverbend Middle. It was my home, but to the rest of them, it was just a school.

"What about the wildseeds?" I asked. "Their parents won't even know they need help."

"Fine," Mrs. Hebert said. "Who's going to this festival? I'll make some phone calls."

The grown-ups huddled, whispering around Ms. Coulon's desk while Angelique and I pulled out our phones. Mine was flooded with notifications, including YouTube notifications in a banner across the top. I had turned those off a long time ago. There were too many of them. As it was, it took a ten count before they disappeared. I jumped on it as soon as they stopped, tapping until I was sure that all the notifications were off so I could get to the real messages. I had notifications from a bunch of people, including a red one from somebody named ZayVEE. Red messages were new for me, so I clicked it. It took me to the comment section of the most recent video on my account: "Five-Minute Full Face for Free-Dress Fridays." My school didn't have free-dress Fridays, but according to the Internet, some schools did, so I went with it. It had a lot of likes and comments, so the Internet wasn't wrong, but I was more concerned with the ZayVEE message bubble that kept popping up. It said inbox. YouTube does not have an inbox. That was my first clue something witchy was happening. I opened it, half expecting it to be some kind of trap from LaToya.

Hey! It's Zayvion, the St. Mary's girl you met at 3Thirteen. Sorry to force an inbox, but we're not friends on IG and I didn't want my message to go to spam. Fly Fest got pushed up, but my cousins and I are still going. Your friend said y'all have roots at Riverbend Middle, so I thought maybe we could meet up and go together. If not, it's cool. We can catch y'all another time.

"LaToya's festival is getting big," Dee said. She was still looking over Angelique's shoulder at her phone.

"Tell me about it," I said. "The girl who tested Luz says she's going, and she's bringing her cousins."

Dee scrunched her eyebrows. "I thought that girl went to St. Mary's?"

"She does," I said. "It's not just Riverbend Middle anymore. It's spreading."

"That's nothing," Dee said, nodding to Angelique. "Show her."

Angelique turned her phone around and turned up the volume. "LaToya is hard launching her coven online," she said.

Hard launching her coven?

Angelique was not the kind of person who would say the phrase "hard launching" about anything, but then the video rolled and I saw why.

"Coven."

[tap-tap, slap clap. Tap-tap, slap clap.]

Latoya snaked her head to the right while Annie slid out from the left.

"Family."

[tap-tap, slap clap. Tap-tap, slap clap.]

Annie and LaToya snaked their heads to the left and Cicily slid out from the right.

"Sisterhood."

[tap-tap, slap clap. Tap-tap, slap clap.]

The three of them snaked their heads in different directions while Jane slid out from the right and Margeaux slid out from the left.

The five of them kept the dance going as words ballooned across the screen.

We're hard launching our coven with the best community service project ever. Anybody with Riverbend roots should come out and join the magic. Who knows? You might be our sister, too.

Then all five of them said, "See you there!"

Green crystal bottles were all over the shot, lined up behind them like a backdrop.

I'm sure it was better without sound. The music was cute, but I could definitely have done without hearing LaToya's voice.

"I guess she got her prime," Dee said. "Covens are always better with prime numbers."

"But if LaToya has five, why is the festival still on?" I asked.

Then a message popped in from Jenny, and I had my answer.

Margeaux burned out!

LaToya is freaking out!

So is Margeaux!

OMG

"How did Margeaux burn out so fast?" Angelique asked softly. "One minute she was in a coven announcement, the next minute: nothing."

"Who is Margeaux?" my mom asked, pulling herself away from the grown-up huddle. The WeBop video playing at full volume didn't catch her attention, but that did.

"A kid who was bullying Miguel," I said.

"And also a sixth grader who recently blossomed on campus," Angelique said.

"And you say she just burned out?" my mom asked.

Ms. Coulon and Mrs. Hebert looked over at us, too.

"Would Riverbend water fix people who, you know, burned out?" I asked.

"No," Mrs. Hebert said. "I'm afraid not. Water in the Riverbend is like a multiplier. If there is even a small amount of magic left, the ordinary magic of the river can temporarily boost it. But if there is nothing . . ."

"Anything times zero is zero," I said. That made sense.

"Exactly. I've known of wealthy witches who spent a fortune on extenders after burning out just to have the illusion of controlling magic again. If there were a cure, one of them would have bought it by now, but none of them has. Maybe someday, but not yet."

"So, that's it?" I said. "We just wait here while everybody gets burned out?"

"I've called in reinforcements. Miss Nancy has gone back to the city. She's alerted her team and, together, they'll do their best to clear the area and warn all the known witches in our networks to steer clear. It doesn't look like a normal containment weave would do much besides be sucked in itself right now. Without any other information, all we can do is steer clear and hope it stabilizes on its own before someone else gets hurt."

"It won't stabilize on its own," I said. "I'm telling you, LaToya is messing with it. She was making a coven right before it happened, the capture gets activated, and a member of her coven gets drained all within minutes? LaToya is involved."

"How many witches were in her coven and what were their levels?" Mrs. Hebert asked.

"Five," I said. "But I don't know what their levels are. How would I?"

"Either they would have told you or you would have read it in a blockchain ledger."

"We have a blockchain ledger!" I said. "We were reading Sandy's magazine, but it only mentions LaToya. She hadn't linked with the others yet. Maybe we could find something now?"

Mrs. Hebert waved my thought away. "It doesn't matter. The only way LaToya's coven would make a difference is if they could somehow get to the roots of the tree without disturbing the capture at all. Otherwise, they'd be drained by it long before they could ever wrap the capture in a containment. And an ordinary containment weave wouldn't be strong enough. It would have to be a containment orb, and—"

"There was an orb!" I said, gesturing at Angelique to pull out her phone. "We told you."

"No one said anything about an orb," Ms. Coulon and Mrs. Hebert said in sync.

Angelique put her phone on Ms. Coulon's desk where everyone could see and opened her notes app to LaToya's last blockchain entry. Then she let them read all the rest for good measure.

Ms. Coulon sat back in her chair, defeated. "That's what the coating on the bottle is," she said. "A containment. I should have thought of it before. The bottles were just for practice. Kaitlynn is making a containment orb to capture the capture. Like dropping the whole thing into an indestructible ziplock bag. That way she could isolate the capture without being exposed to it in the process. It's so simple! Why didn't I see it?"

Mrs. Hebert shook her head. "Containment orbs are almost impossible to make. They require at least a tuft of unicorn hair and—"

"A dragon scale?" I offered.

Mrs. Hebert looked at me hard. "How did you know that?" she asked.

"A couple of weeks ago, Kaitlynn told Sandy the only way she would give back the extender that had my signature in it was if Sandy gave her a dragon scale or unicorn hair. We got her the unicorn hair."

Mrs. Hebert closed her eyes and took two calming breaths before she could say another word. "She can't have a dragon scale," she said, shaking her head. "We have filters. We would have known the second one was listed."

"Unless Kaitlynn went up the mountain and talked to Mamie Seal herself," Ms. Coulon said.

"But Mamie Seal would never—"

"She must have," Ms. Coulon said. "There's no other way. And now that Kaitlynn has the ingredients to make a containment orb, she tricked a child into using it so she wouldn't have to disturb those roots herself."

For the first time ever, Mrs. Hebert looked defeated. "Kaitlynn's going to drain that capture, isn't she?" Mrs. Hebert said, sinking down onto a chair.

My mom looked from Ms. Coulon to Mrs. Hebert. "I don't understand," my mom said.

Ms. Coulon opened her mouth to answer, but I got there before her.

"You remember how Kaitlynn tried to get that extender with my signature in it?"

My mom nodded. "That was awful. Sandy said Kaitlynn could force you to agree to anything and, no matter how horrible or ridiculous it was, you would have had to do it."

"Well take that and multiply it by the signature of every person whose magic ever got sucked into that capture. They're all inside the capture the same way my signature was in that extender. Ms. Coulon said there might be thousands of them in there."

"Even if it isn't quite that many," Ms. Coulon said, rubbing her forehead "it has to be more than three hundred thirteen."

Three hundred thirteen signatures.

Three hundred thirteen people who, if you signed their names, would automatically agree with any rule you made.

"A consensus," I said. "Somebody is going to make herself queen of the world."

CHAPTER NINETEEN

FORCES AND FEELINGS

You think adults are always going to know what to do. They don't. Even smart adults. Adults who love you. Adults with money and power and literal magic can look at something that's going to ruin everything and have absolutely no idea what to do next.

I could already feel my magic sloshing against my skin. "There has to be something we can do that isn't hiding or staying somewhere 'safe,' because none of that is going to stop Kaitlynn from using our signatures to become a one-person conseil des sorcières. Somebody has to do something."

Everybody was looking calm. Too calm. How was I the only one who got how bad this was?

My mom put her hand on my shoulder. It was soothing to feel her there. Like she was something solid to hold on to so I didn't just drift away.

Ms. Coulon waited until my breaths slowed down before she said anything. "We are going to do something, Hasani. None of us wants this. All of us understand that the consequences are too grave to ignore. I know it's scary, and I can't tell you how much your mother, Mrs. Hebert, and I wish we could solve this without any of you ever knowing. But you do know, so now you have a decision to make. A smart choice is to go somewhere that's safe for now and let us handle it. The glassworks has overnight rooms. You're welcome to them. It'd be like staying at a hotel. Say the word and we'll get Luz and her family and you all can stay there and have as many feelings as you would like to until we either solve this problem or don't."

"What's the other choice?" I asked. Magic was pounding in my ears.

"You choose to help us figure it out."

"So either way, we're just supposed to pretend like nothing's scary and everything's OK?" I asked.

"Of course not. The world is not that black and white. Most things are some shade of gray. I'm not telling you to pretend you don't have feelings or to try not to have them. I'm saying that you feel your feelings, but you know that your feelings are just that: feelings. They don't rule you. They don't rule anything. Feel them, then let them go. Because if you stay, we're going to need you."

I looked at Dee. Her magic was pressing against her skin, looping between the charms on her finger and in her ear faster than I'd seen it move before. Angelique's was a gentle glow the way it always was, but now I knew that that was probably her creole earrings as much as it was her. I wondered if she was raging inside like I was. Like Dee seemed to be.

"We're linked sisters," I said. "We have to decide together."

The three of us looked at each other. That time, I noticed the way Angelique kept looking in our eyes as she pulled out the intention she had woven for us and set it up right there in Ms. Coulon's private study. She was so busy watching the intention reflected in our eyes that she didn't see the pride in her mother's as she set to work.

"What do we think?" Angelique asked when the last stitch was in place. "Should we help?"

"We have to, right?" Dee said. "I mean, maybe they've been following Kaitlynn, but they don't know LaToya. They're gonna underestimate her because she's a kid, but the girl is good."

Angelique made a face.

"At what she does," Dee amended. "She's good at what she does. Maybe not at first, but she don't stop until she gets it. It makes her dangerous. We have to stay to make sure they know that."

"Agreed," I said. I didn't even have the urge to say *finally* even though I had been saying that about LaToya ever since we left camp. We were on the same page now and that's what mattered. "And I want to make sure they don't just forget about the wildseed witches. Not everybody is gonna be in their network."

"And the promising witches," Angelique said. "The amount of magic you can access doesn't make you expendable as a witch."

"So you're promising for sure?" Dee asked, looking at Angelique's earrings. "The custodies aren't doing anything?"

"I don't know," Angelique said. "All I know is that one of them came from my biological mother, and one came from my biological father. My mom said she did know about the one from my mom, and her plan was to tell me about it once she tracked down the key to unlock it. She didn't know the one from my biodad existed, but she actually located his key first. His is just a pattern of taps and twists. One-four-three. My biological mom's key is more complicated. My mom got her hands on it after we got our charms. When she couldn't figure out how to use it, though, she put it in S-Crow. But none of that matters because before she found them, she didn't trust them to safeguard my magic, so she wove her own intention of protection over theirs."

"Dag. Triple protection," Dee said.

Angelique smiled softly. "That's why she gave me these."

Angelique pulled a gold eyeglass case from her bag and opened it for us to see the glasses inside.

"They're zebra-blue-primrose glasses," she said like she was launching a brand and we were her first customers.

Ms. Coulon nodded and dove right in. "We don't have much time, but we do have some. The full moon is tomorrow."

"The full moon. Right," my mom said. "Sandy was saying there's something freeing about the river in the moonlight. Is that what you're thinking, Beverlyn?"

"Yes. Captures are difficult to make and hard enough to bury when you're only burying them with a sapling. The trees growing that capture are hundreds of years old. Their taproots are deeper than we can imagine. Right now the signature magic of all people who lost theirs to the capture is actively engaged with the capture. That means it's still signature magic. If Kaitlynn wants to stop it from becoming ordinary magic when she moves it, she'll need it to be a seamless transfer, almost indistinguishable from what is already there."

"So, like, a stealth attack?" I asked. "But how do you sneak up on roots?"

"You send in something the roots will see as themselves. Something that belongs," Ms. Coulon said. "Like having an ant invade its own colony. Every ant in the colony would recognize it as one of them, so there'd be no need to attack."

"Exactly," Mrs. Hebert said. "The timing of this cannot be a mistake. Kaitlynn might not be incredibly powerful in her own right, but she knows about multiplying force. The capture probably was as stable as you thought, Beverlyn, before Kaitlynn started running out of time. Today was her last chance before the full moon to build a containment orb that uses those shared roots. The moon will strengthen the roots in her orb, help her sink it down deep to surround the capture without disturbing it. And, once the capture is contained inside the orb, moonlight on the river will help her free it again."

Ms. Coulon nodded. "Yes. There's no such thing as a capture that's easy to remove. If I were Kaitlynn, I'd want to leverage the moonlight on the river to free it. You need all the power you can get."

"Wait," I said. "Slow down. You're skipping over LaToya. Why would Kaitlynn use her? Why not just sink the capture herself?"

"Kaitlynn's probably not strong enough to do it," Angelique said.

"She's not?" I asked.

"Nah," Dee said. "Look at those blockchain entries again. Kaitlynn is in the third power category. LaToya is top tier."

"LaToya's in the talented tenth?" I asked. Not that I doubted. Dee had called it—the girl was good. "So Kaitlynn is using her just because she's strong? I thought Kaitlynn was out for money?"

"The world is not driven by greed. It's driven by envy," Mrs. Hebert said. "I don't remember who said it, but how often it's true never ceases to amaze me. If Kaitlynn wanted credits, she would have stopped by now. She already has plenty. She wants the power that people like you and Beverlyn have."

"That still doesn't say why it had to be LaToya," I said.

"I don't think it *had* to be," Ms. Coulon said. She was using that voice she used when things were finally coming together. "I think it could have been anyone who could get her connected to some Riverbend lifers. What she really needed was people rooted to the Riverbend."

Eyebrows scrunched and heads tipped all around the room.

"Bear with me. Have you ever felt connected to a place? Like the place itself is home, not just the people in it?"

"Paris," Dee said.

I looked at Dee. "I didn't know you've been to Paris," I said.

"A few times." Dee shrugged. "The first time I went there, I just felt like I was supposed to live there someday."

Ms. Coulon nodded.

"I feel that way about Vacherie," my mom said. "I've never lived there, but it has always felt like it's supposed to be home."

"That's your roots," Ms. Coulon said. "When you're rooted in a place, the magic in you has sunk itself deep into the ground. The connection is as physical as it is spiritual or metaphorical."

"That's how I feel about Riverbend," I said quietly. Compared to Paris or my mom's ancestral home, having that connection with my school felt silly. But silly was just a feeling. I felt it and let it go. "Kaitlynn should have used me," I said finally.

"Apparently she tried," Ms. Coulon said. "But lucky for us, she didn't succeed. You are rooted there. And being rooted in the Riverbend

269

would make it exponentially easier for you to get at the roots of the tree where the capture is and stop whatever Kaitlynn has started."

"A stealth attack," I said again. "I'm not the only one who's rooted, though. So is Annie. So is Cicily. So are Margeaux and Jane. All the members of LaToya's new coven. They're all lifers."

"That makes sense," Dee said. "LaToya's smart. That explains bringing all those water bottles to campus. She was probably hoping to find kids like Annie. Kids already rooted at Riverbend who just didn't know they were magic. She was trying to get at the roots of those trees the whole time."

"Wait! The roots of the trees!" I said, my brain suddenly riding the energy of a really good idea. "That's why the whole thing with the termites happened!"

"The termites?" my mom asked. "The termites that delayed the start of school?"

"Yep!" I nodded. "The ones Miss Lafleur and I saved. Those termites got to the roots, too. If we hadn't rescued the termites, Kaitlynn and LaToya would have had their roots, and they wouldn't have needed Riverbend lifers at all."

"Yo!" Dee said. "That makes sense. Termites stay eating roots, especially if somebody influenced them. And termites are natural, so the trees wouldn't think of them as a disturbance. That's actually a good plan."

!

Should I have been insulted that the termites were Plan A and I was Plan B? Oh, well. At least we were finally putting two and two together.

"Is that why you set a filter looking for people buying dragon scale at 3Thirteen? You wanted to see if Kaitlynn was making a containment?" I asked.

"Looking for dragon scale was more of a side project," Mrs. Hebert said. "Until recently, we thought dragons were fully extinct. They're not the kind of thing you would use for a casual spell. I wish we could say that we knew this was Kaitlynn's plan all along, but we didn't. If we had, we would have done a lot of things differently. We were watching out of curiosity more than anything."

"Like reality TV," Dee said. "I get it."

For half a second, Mrs. Hebert looked embarrassed. But just as quick as the look came, it went, and she was back to her normal self.

"So why don't we just build a containment orb ourselves and beat Kaitlyn to the punch?" Angelique asked.

"Unfortunately, there are no public recipes for containments. The ingredients are only mentioned in old stories, and that's hardly anything to go by. Custodies and containments work on similar principles. In theory, a custody might be strong enough to safely hold a capture, but without extensive testing it's a huge risk," Ms. Coulon said.

"So let me make sure I'm following all of this," my mom said. "This Kaitlynn person got a recipe to make something that can capture a capture, which has people's magical signatures trapped inside it, and she got some Riverbend lifers to bury it for her so she wouldn't break the capture while she was trying to contain it?"

My mom looked dizzy just saying that.

"That's the theory," Mrs. Hebert said.

"Do we have to contain it? Couldn't we just destroy the capture and set the people's magic free?" my mom asked. "I hate to say something simple, but couldn't it be that simple?"

"The simplest solution is usually the best," Ms. Coulon said. "And I've been trying to come up with a simple solution to get rid of this capture since I was a few years older than these girls are now. Unfortunately, trying to destroy it would mean digging it out by force."

"Wouldn't whoever went to dig it up just get burned out?" Dee asked.

Ms. Coulon nodded. "Yes. It may come to that, but we're trying to find solutions around it."

"I have one," Angelique said.

We all looked at her. First daughter of a first daughter was just dripping from her shoulders like the force she was, even though every drop of her magic was being held in.

"I'll go," she said.

CHAPTER TWENTY

ROOTS AND REASONS

All of us froze.

Angelique didn't budge.

After what felt like a million years of silence, Angelique's mom said, "Absolutely not."

Her voice echoed through the room.

I expected Angelique to whine or something, but she didn't. "Mom," she said. "We agreed."

"We agreed that you could decide when to take your protections off. We did not agree that you could volunteer to do something stupid. Do you even know what you're volunteering for?"

"I'm volunteering to do what needs to be done because I'm the one who can do it."

Angelique's mom tried to collect herself. It sort of worked. "Angelique Desirée Hebert"—*not the whole name*—"foolishly putting yourself in danger is not the same as being a hero. Maybe we have to make sacrifices, but not without thinking them through. You don't even know what the plan is yet. How can you possibly know you're the only person who can do it?"

"Because I'm the only one who has these," she said, pointing to her earrings. "Don't these things have to be put on you as a baby? I'm the only one who still has them. There's no way we can stop the capture without getting close to it. I'm the only one of us who won't get burned out."

"You're not rooted there," I said. "I am. I should be the one."

Dee's voice popped in. "Aren't we linked?" she asked. "We're an organic coven."

"What point are you trying to make?" Angelique's mom asked tightly.

"Well, since we've been a coven, we've calmed Hasani's magic down a bunch of times."

The way Angelique nodded, it was like she had been holding that on her chest for a hundred years.

"We've only been a coven for like two months!" I said.

Angelique kept nodding. "We know," she said.

Great. More wild magic jokes. Well, not jokes. Angelique was hardly ever joking.

"Well, if all our magic is connected for that, shouldn't all our magic be connected to Angelique's custodies, too?" Dee asked. "In a way, we're all protected."

"Oh my goodness," Ms. Coulon said. "I've never thought of that."

She was staring at Dee with wonder, like she was surprised Dee came up with something so good, but I could have told her Dee was a genius.

Angelique's mom was a tougher audience. "It might provide you some protection. Might. We can't be sure."

"But we can't be sure it won't, either, Angela," Ms. Coulon said. "I agree, it's probably not worth the risk, but we're doing things out of order. Before we take any concrete steps in that direction, we need a solid plan for dealing with the capture itself."

"What have we been doing this whole time?" my mom asked. I could feel my eyebrows saying, *Yeah. What she said*, when Ms. Coulon tapped something on her desk. The wall behind her turned into a screen, and when she tapped the tip of a pen on her desk, the mark she made was shining up on the wall where everyone could see.

"That was brainstorming but . . . one second." Ms. Coulon tapped something else on her desk and said, "Of course. Send Mariama straight here," before she turned back to us. "But now our expert is here," she said. "And we can all dig in."

"She made it!" Mrs. Hebert looked so relieved that I saw actual tears in the corners of her eyes. Whoever this person was, they had to be good.

Even if I hadn't recognized her, I would have known who it was because she had barely stepped through the door when Angelique jumped up and shouted, "Miss LeBrun!"

"You can call me by my name, Angelique," Miss LeBrun said to her protégé. "I don't care if anyone in here finds me on the blockchain."

"Miss Mbaye!" Angelique ran to give her a hug. "Miss LeBrun" was Miss Mbaye's name at Les Desmoiselles, where all the teachers have code names. She had offered me a spot as one of her protégés, too. Maybe if I had taken her up on it, all three of us would have been in that hug and I would have been calling Miss LeBrun by her real name, too.

"Sorry it took me so long to get here. I had to take a subsol from Paris to Dakar, and you know how slow those are. When I finish my current work, I'm going to set my sights on making sure there is a permanent gondola from Paris to Dakar. Two subsols in one day is more than I can handle. Now, will someone please get me up to speed? I hear we have to rescue a few hundred kids from getting burned out in the moonlight."

The plan looked beautiful shining up on Ms. Coulon's wall. It wasn't just the fact that Ms. Coulon's whiteboard was digital.

It was that I had finally found something better than a checklist: a flowchart.

Tier 1 was our best bet but, ironically, both the simplest and most impossible to do. It involved at least one of us attending LaToya's Fly Fest, so every adult in the room was against it except Miss LeBrun, even when she pointed out that all the steps in it were a perfect cover for tier 2.

Tier 2 was by far all the parents' favorites. It was basically Ms. Coulon's plan. Since I was rooted at Riverbend Middle and had been practicing the freedom spell, she thought maybe having me weave the elements of Sandy's freedom spell into a crystal that we then embedded in the tree roots might permanently balance the site. So it wouldn't remove the capture. It'd be more like adding a yin to the yang.

Tier 3 was the nuclear option. Basically, all hands on deck to destroy the capture as quickly as possible, no matter who got burned out in the process. Hundreds of us getting burned out did not sound good, but it was better than having 313 votes in one person's hands.

The adults, however, refused to choose a plan.

"We'll cross that bridge when we come to it," they kept saying, but there never seemed to be any bridges ahead. Miss LeBrun was on our side, though. She thought Angelique's idea was good, so before we all split up, she convinced the rest of the adults to let Angelique pitch it one last time.

"We make our own capture," Angelique said. "The risks are moderate."

"The risks are recklessly high," Mrs. Hebert interrupted.

"The risks are moderate," Angelique repeated, "but manageable. You said yourselves earlier that custodies are the closest things we have to the recipe for a capture. If we weave those intentions into an orb of our own along with ingredients that would push our containment orb into the tree's existing root structure—"

"I.e., the three of you going on campus and using your magic ON A CAPTURE to dig up roots buried so deep that you're guaranteed to disturb THE CAPTURE," Mrs. Hebert said, sounding like we were getting on her very last nerve.

"What if we used an extender?" Angelique offered.

"That would be something," Mrs. Coulon said. "It wouldn't save you from the impulse to defend yourselves against a capture, which might drain you to nothing, but it would at least be something."

"Absolutely not," Mrs. Hebert said again.

"What if we didn't have to dig up the roots at all?" I asked. "What if we could get the same roots from somewhere else? Then we weave them straight into the containment orb with Sandy's spell!"

"How would you get those exact roots without digging?" Ms. Coulon asked.

"I'd get them from the queen."

CHAPTER TWENTY-ONE

QUEENS AND COMFORTS

How crazy things were didn't totally sink in until after I got off the phone with Sandy.

"My Neptune is white, you're not answering the phone, your mom's not answering her phone, and I am freaking out! What is happening over there?"

"Your Neptune is white?" I asked. Sandy said a lot of weird stuff, but that was beyond a normal Sandy level of weird.

"On the solar system necklace Beverlyn made me. The Neptune is white. That means that the capture is working again and it's literally right where you go to school. Are you OK?"

"The Neptune bead was connected to the capture? Why are you asking me if I'm OK? Are *you* OK?"

"I'm fine," Sandy said. "I wasn't wearing it. It was hanging on my necklace stand. I just always look at it because it's so beautiful, and when I saw it turning white and no one answered I swear I couldn't breathe. You're OK, right? You sound OK."

"We're fine," I said. "Mom, Ms. Coulon, Angelique, Dee. We're all fine. We are trying to stop LaToya from digging up a million magic signatures and giving them to Kaitlynn, but other than that, we're OK."

"Wait, what? Are you serious? Where are you? I'm coming to help. And if you say one word about me being pregnant, I swear I'll—"

I didn't let Sandy finish her threat. "You are helping, Sandy. Ms. Coulon wants me to weave one of your spells into a crystal. Is that OK? She's getting the crystal ready now, but it's not too late to say no because I guess that part takes a while."

"Of course it's OK!" she said.

I don't know if she was crying or not, but it didn't matter. Either way, I could feel the love streaming through the phone.

"And there's one more thing. Would you be willing to give me, Angelique, and Dee a ride to Vacherie? Miss Nancy is . . . busy."

"Are you kidding? That guest house has twenty-four-hour spa service. You had me at hello!"

*G*etting a ride from Sandy was the only way they'd agree to let us go. We were allowed to take a subsol back to the city, but we were expressly forbidden from using our normal exit.

"The Freret Street exit is too close to the capture. Canal Street is safer."

"Canal Street is safer" was not on the list of phrases I ever thought I'd hear my mother say, but if she was letting me go without a fuss, I'd take what I could get. If you consider having Miss LeBrun walk us all the way to the subsol station, through 3Thirteen, and out of the Canal Street exit of 3Thirteen "without a fuss."

"We don't need a babysitter, Miss Mbaye," Angelique said when we finally made it back to the Amite subsol station.

"I know," Miss LeBrun said. "And believe me, I'm not looking forward to taking my third subsol of the day, but I'm going that way, anyway. This is my last chance to see that capture functioning as it did historically. I can't miss the moment."

"You're not afraid?" I asked.

"Of course I'm afraid. I'd be a fool not to be. But you're not the only one with extra protection." Miss LeBrun tipped her head to the side to make her heavy gold hoops shine. "Suffice it to say, our earrings in Senegal have power, too. Plus I'll be smart and I'll be careful, just like the three of you will be when you go off doing whatever it is you haven't told anybody you're going to do."

We all stared. Angelique looked totally stricken.

"Don't give me those looks. Obviously you're up to something.

They had to ask someone to keep an eye on you, but lucky for you, that someone was not me."

Angelique and I turned to look where Miss LeBrun was looking.

"Dee?" I said. "*Dee* is supposed to be our babysitter?"

Dee ran a hand across the side of her fade. "What? It's supposed to be my fault they think I'm responsible?"

Angelique looked actively offended. I'm not sure if it was because they tried to turn one of our own against us or because the one they tried to turn wasn't her.

"Calm down," Dee said. "It's just because my mama's out there. They think my mom will keep an eye on us."

"Will your mom keep an eye on us?" I asked.

No offense to Dee, but after a summer of suffering under Miss LaRose's lessons, I wasn't looking forward to seeing her again.

Dee shook her head. "Since I'm at my dad's this year, she declared this week her first ever 'Turn Down Week.' I'm only supposed to call her if I'm broken, bleeding, or dead."

"How are you supposed to call her if you're dead?" I asked.

Dee shrugged. "But you know I always listen to my mama."

Miss LeBrun tried to act like she wasn't listening. She smiled at that one, though.

And I was glad she walked us all the way to the exit at Canal Street. The walk out was full of riddles and I never would have gotten the one about where the dude got his shoes. Sandy was waiting for us at the bottom of the steps to Spanish Plaza.

"Miss Nancy's OK?" Sandy asked Angelique as soon as we were all buckled in.

We all told her she was, although, to be fair, we hadn't seen her since the afternoon and it was already getting dark. Angelique must have been thinking that, too, because she added, "I'm sure someone would have told us if she weren't." Those ten words kind of killed any road trip vibes there might have been about our ride to Vacherie. We weren't just going to sing songs and trade stories or show each other funny stuff from Instagram. We were on a mission.

"I told your dad that I was worried about the three of you being downtown after dark. That's the truth, though. I was."

"And I guess he wasn't," I said. The words came out before I thought about them, and thinking about them made my skin buzz. I don't know which would have been worse: if he had insisted on coming with Sandy to pick us up, or the fact that he hadn't.

I took a deep breath, trying to press my feelings back into place. They were too big to just feel and let go. I needed to keep the buzzing in.

"Of course your dad is concerned. You're his baby! He talks about you all the time."

Then maybe he should try talking where I can hear him. But I managed to keep that one in.

283

Sandy went on the highway instead of up River Road, so the ride to Vacherie didn't take that long. Angelique and Dee kept giving grim updates from the back seat about all the kids heading to the festival.

I texted Luz again, reminding her that they shouldn't go anywhere near Fly Fest. Reminding them that, if possible, her and Miguel shouldn't even leave the house.

Luz:

This thing is getting bigger. The whole sixth grade is posting about it.

Luz:

LaToya keeps texting me to come and bring Miguel.

DO NOT BRING MIGUEL
DO NOT LET L ANYWHERE
NEAR U OR MIGUEL

Luz:

Duh.

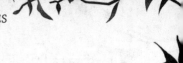

"*L*aToya is messaging me on WeBop, too," Angelique said. "She's desperate."

LaToya's content was friends only, and she's friends with everyone at Riverbend except me. I wasn't going to get any messages from her.

"I felt desperate without a coven, too," Sandy said. "I didn't realize it until they found me, but looking back on it, something was really missing before our magic found each other. I thought I was perfectly happy being a one of one, but I guess people can change, right? Maybe LaToya has changed? That's a part of being free."

I did not want to go into it with Sandy about how much it didn't matter whether LaToya had changed. Especially not when she seemed determined to ruin her life and take the rest of us down with her.

"Let's just get the roots and go back," I said. As long as none of the people going to Fly Fest were named Miguel or Luz, I was cool. But I did ask Dee how to message Zayvion back.

"Uh . . . hit Reply?" she said.

Yep. That totally worked.

There was a little light left in the sky when we pulled up next to the ditch by the sugarcane field where the school was hidden. Miss Lafleur was waiting for us on the porch to the guest house. She wasn't the only lady we passed sitting in a rocking chair on a porch in the evening light, so I was relieved to finally see the right one.

Dee was a little twitchy as we walked through the campus. The Belles Demoiselles grounds were a little overgrown now that the program was done for the summer. Grass that didn't always line up. More petals on the walkways. Swans that swam whichever way they pleased.

"Unicorns are mad judgy," Dee said. "They're loose, right?"

"Oh, the unicorns mostly keep to themselves," Miss Lafleur said. At first I thought she was trying to make Dee feel better, but when she added, "Mostly," I couldn't tell if she was trolling Dee or being legit.

Miss Lafleur led us past the part of the grounds with the main school building to a boat that would take us to the wilder part, where she lived in a tiny little house that always seemed exactly as big as she needed it to be. I didn't realize how much I wanted to go back there until we got close, but Miss Lafleur and a trail of fireflies did exactly what I asked: bring us straight to the queen.

"I'm glad you wanted to check on them," Miss Lafleur said as Dee and Angelique took their turns using Miss Lafleur's special black glasses, the ones that let you see the termite colony we had rescued without disturbing them. "Something has been tugging at them tonight. I think it might be just about time to let them go."

"I didn't come here to see them," I said. It took saying that for me to feel the guilt. It had been more than a week since I checked on the termites, but that wasn't the guilty part. The guilty part was that I hadn't worried about them even once since I started worrying about school and Mathletes and getting videos uploaded and scheduled for my channel. "I'm glad to see them, but that isn't why I came."

I didn't want to look away from what I had done wrong, so I tried to look right at Miss Lafleur when I said that. Once she took off her Belles Demoiselles suit and got into her overalls, it was hard to tell how old Miss Lafleur was. From some angles she looked like an auntie, maybe even a grandma. But sometimes with her two french braids and perfect brown skin, she looked like she could just be another kid in the room.

"I figured as much," she said, sounding almost as much like a kid in the room as she looked in that moment, but that only made her switch back to auntie-grandma that much sharper. "That's why I didn't offer you a formal apprenticeship."

"You knew I'd mess up?"

"No. I knew you needed to be free. You're so talented. You have so many choices. An apprenticeship would have put you under my protection, but it also would have bound you to me. I knew that once you left here, there was every possibility that you would forget all about your affinity for animals, and I wanted to leave you room to do that. If you loved this work, I knew you'd be back."

"I am back," I said. "Does that count?"

"Oh, actions always count, Hasani. People think they are their thoughts. They want credit for every little good thought they've ever had, as if that makes you who you are. But has thinking about feeding the hungry ever fed the hungry? Has thinking about helping a friend ever helped a friend?"

I shook my head.

"Thoughts are only the beginning. What counts is what we do. And the fact that you came does count as doing something."

Miss Lafleur was trying to make me feel better, but I winced anyway. "I didn't really come to check on them. I came here to get something from them. I wasn't even thinking about them before I needed something. That makes me selfish, right?"

"You may be a lot of things, Hasani, but selfish is not one of them. Look at your actions. Your heart is pulling you in the direction you need to go."

"I think right now my heart is telling me I have to protect people. Even my best friend and her little brother, and they're not even witches. It's stressful." If that was how Luz felt all the time, I didn't know if I was ready to be a big sister.

Miss Lafleur nodded. "It sounds like they're your family. It's hard to turn away from family, even when you want to, but from the looks of it, you don't want to. Now, tell me, how is visiting the termites helping keep your family safe?"

I told her everything, even the parts we didn't tell Sandy, the parts we hadn't said to each other yet but all of us knew were coming. We were going to that festival.

"Ah! The time-honored tradition of asking for forgiveness instead of permission. You're becoming more of a witch every day." Miss Lafleur smiled. "Let me guess: No one's warning the green witches that have been popping up around there lately and you want to make sure they're out of harm's way."

"I guess that's kind of it, but"—I shook my head—"it's only a really small part. Like maybe one-thirteenth. Almost half of it is thinking about people I don't even know. It's bad enough that there might have been thousands of witches who got burned out just by being there. Who knows if it was fair or not. But the idea that they don't even get to rest, that somebody might be puppetting their magic, making them say yes to stuff after their bodies have gone away just seems too awful to look away from. It's like, I have to do something."

"That leaves a big chunk of reasoning left," Miss Lafleur said. "What is it?"

"LaToya."

"Revenge plot? Finally ready to make the finishing move in your petty witch war?"

"No," I said. "She doesn't have anyone looking out for her. She might not take our help, but we have to at least try. Nobody deserves to be that alone."

"See," Miss Lafleur said. "I told you your heart would lead you where you needed to go. And apparently that is straight back to your sworn enemy and the strongest capture witches have ever built. No judgment, of course. I've chosen to live openly among animals who might just as well eat me."

"Which ones?" I asked.

"The unicorns!"

Eyebrows. Eyebrows!

"I'm just kidding," she said.

I relaxed a little.

"They don't go after primates much. Rodents, mostly. Stab them right with their little horns."

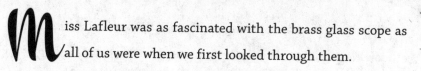

Miss Lafleur was as fascinated with the brass glass scope as all of us were when we first looked through them.

"Supposedly they're one of the glassworks' bestsellers," I said.

Miss Lafleur gave them another appreciative look before handing them back to me. "I've only ever ordered custom things from Beverlyn," Miss Lafleur said. "I guess I should spend some time exploring the racks, too." She stopped abruptly and shook her head. "Actually, no. I won't. I hate shopping too much. I'll stick with my custom orders. They're easy."

I blinked. People hate shopping? That much? Does not compute.

The only reason there was any light in the sky at all was that it was technically still summer. It was late. And we needed to keep moving.

Angelique and I used our brass glass scopes to look through the termite droppings for anything with the look of active magic while Dee kept watch for unicorns. Miss Lafleur said the termites were healing, and from what we saw, that checked out. Most of the droppings just looked like plain sawdust, but when we dug deeper to older layers, we found what we were looking for: termite droppings that danced like faerie lights.

"Careful," Miss Lafleur said. "I kept magic around them to a minimum to allow them to heal, but if I had known there were pieces of a capture in that sawdust, I wouldn't have done any. You should do the same, especially when you get back to that school of yours. These tiny pieces of capture will be pulled to the larger one like metal to a magnet."

"That's what we're counting on," I said. "But we're not going to the school. We're going to the festival. It's close, but not close enough."

Miss Lafleur looked up at the sky the way she does when she's thinking. Then she shook her head. "I was trying to think if there are any evers witches I might be able to call right now to help you. I'm afraid I've lost touch over the years with the few I've known, but an evers witch could bring those droppings as close to the capture as you need."

"What's an evers witch?" I asked. I was looking at Dee and Angelique, but when both of them shook their heads, Miss Lafleur answered.

"Like a human sanlavi," Miss Lafleur said, then covered her mouth with embarrassment. "Oh my. Please forgive the impolite comparison," she said apologetically. "Comparing a witch who has permanently lost her magic to a sanlavi, that's not kind at all."

I caught the part about both of them being places without magic, but I still didn't get it. "Why evers?" I asked.

"Sanlavi are found naturally at the very tops of tall mountains, dear. That's why it was so strange to find something behaving like one where we are below sea level. The most famous one is at the top of Mount Everest. Hence the phrase 'evers witch.' But try not to say that in polite company. Or at least don't mention you got that from me. I don't mind breaking a social rule or two, but there is no excuse for me being that kind of crass."

CHAPTER TWENTY-TWO

MAGIC AND INFLUENCE

Miss Lafleur took us all the way back to the path, but we walked the rest of the way out through the sugarcane by ourselves with pile of termite poop folded in a square of wax paper that Angelique had, thankfully, agreed to put in her bag. None of us had thought to bring a container, and Miss Lafleur didn't believe in throwaway plastics, so that was the best she could do.

"Exactly how much of this internship involves animal excrement?" Angelique asked as we walked to Sandy's car on the other side of the ditch.

"Eighty percent," I said. "And it's still not an internship. Miss Lafleur basically said I should explore other options."

Dee didn't say dag, but, not for the first time, I could tell she was thinking it.

Sandy was already in the car, buckled up in the driver's seat.

"You're ready already? I thought you were getting a mani-pedi?"

"I did," she said, briefly flashing her powder blue nails for me to see.

"Cool," I said. "Look, I didn't think about it before, but the stuff we're carrying is basically a micro-capture, so if anybody has the urge to do even a little bit of magic in the car, I don't know what would happen. Plus, we don't want to make you have to drive all the way downtown for us to take the subsol, or all the way back to Amite, so Dee says she has a cousin who—"

"Ha-ha-ha. Very funny. I'm coming with you." Sandy's face didn't crack.

I didn't know what to say. This was not the plan.

"Hasani, I have ditched more than my share of parents in my day. You're not getting away from me that easily."

"But seriously," I said. "Any magic around this termite excrement and we could all become evers witches just like that."

I know Miss Lafleur said not to say it, but I couldn't help it. Evers witch just sounded cool.

Sandy rolled her eyes. "I'm going with you," she said. "Get in. I can't do magic, anyway."

We looked at each other, but Dee shrugged and got in, so Angelique and I did, too.

"So, which forbidden place are we going to?" Sandy asked. "The school or the festival?"

"Neither," I said. "My house. I need to get my extender."

"Cool," Sandy said. "I'll pick up my magazine while we're there."

"Actually," Angelique said. "I need to make a pit stop at 3Thirteen."

To the surprise of no one, Angelique wanted to go to the library.

"Your home Interweb isn't ready yet?" I asked.

"Probably not," she said. "It usually takes around twenty-one days. But Miss T should be there right now, and talking to her would probably be faster than the Interweb, anyway."

"What's Miss T gonna tell you?" Dee asked.

"How to make a capture."

To Sandy's credit, she didn't say anything. Her mouth popped open and she kept opening and closing it like a fish, though. Honestly, I think it's because she didn't think we could do it. I didn't blame her. If I didn't know Angelique as well as I did, I would have thought the same thing.

The only way we could get Sandy to agree to take us back to 3Thirteen and not immediately drive us back to all our parents in Vacherie and Amite was if we used the Canal Street entrance, which involved parking downtown, which, as Sandy explained at least a million times, was way worse on a Friday night than literally any other day. Except maybe Mardi Gras, but she didn't know that for sure because who would drive anywhere on Mardi Gras?

We finally found our way to the entrance, which was in a little booth by the streetcar tracks halfway to the aquarium. There was a last chance beignet station when you first walked in and a trinket deposit box farther down that was stuffed to the brim with blinky beads and other truly useless things. To my horror, Angelique, of all people, spent at least a minute rummaging through it before we could go in. I would have understood if she came out with cups—I mean, cups are always useful even if we didn't need them right then—but the pack of glowsticks she found hardly seemed worth the time.

It was easier to get to the library from that entrance than the one on Freret, so once we got inside it only took a few minutes to get there. Miss T asked about our mamas, which made Sandy nervous for a second until I quietly reminded her that in New Orleans everybody asks you about your mama even if they don't know that you just ditched yours to do something possibly dangerous. Our plan wasn't dangerous, though. What the adults were doing? Sitting around? *That* was dangerous.

Miss T took Angelique to the mushroom room and left the three of us in the library lobby. Sandy pulled out her phone to "check on your dad," which I decoded as "tell your mom where we are," but I was fine with that because it gave me and Dee a minute to talk.

"Wasn't Miss Lafleur just saying we should message Jenny?" Dee said. "Well, not Jenny-Jenny, but somebody like Jenny? Should we?"

"Nah, I don't think so," I said after a minute. "I know Miss Lafleur said she might be useful, but I don't want to use her like that." Especially since I knew I couldn't give her what she was asking for.

Dee shrugged, that time with eyebrows, and said, "She might surprise you, but your call. That means one of us is gonna have to walk in there."

"That has to be me," Dee and I said at the same time.

"You?" Dee said.

"Yeah. Me," I said. "I'm the one with the Riverbend roots. We literally have a song we sang about it in kindergarten. *Eaaaarth . . .*" I sang, "*dig my roots down deep.*"

Dee blinked. "Are you serious right now?"

My voice wasn't that bad. "It's a real song," I said. "I swear."

"Riverbend is corny like that, so I believe you, but song or no song, it can't be you."

"It has to be me," I said.

"Nah. No offense, but you not accurate enough. You got too much magic. It goes splashing around everywhere. I'm the one with the pinpoint precision."

"I'm the one with the roots."

"Any one of us can have the roots now, remember? That's why we made that whole trip to Vacherie," Dee said. "You did your part. You got us the roots. Now let me do mine."

I didn't like the idea of Dee standing on that capture any more than if she said she was sending my mom.

It was about that time that Angelique came out of the mushroom room looking either like she might cry or she wanted to poke something in the eye.

"Didn't find it?" Dee asked.

"No, I found something. Miss T helped me. It would have taken me at least a week to find it out on my own, and I'm really grateful, but—"

"Librarians. Am I right?" I interrupted. Well, I thought that's where she was going, but that wasn't exactly it.

"Of course librarians are amazing, but first of all, the spell is a spell and, second of all, it needs a hyphal knot," she said, like that was supposed to mean something to either of us.

"I can do the spell for you," I said. "But what's a hyphal knot?"

"Hyphal knots? It's where individual strands of hypha finally come together and—" Blank stares from us. "Never mind. A baby mushroom. It's kind of a baby mushroom." She looked from me to Dee and back to me again.

"I'm gonna have to give up my spores!!" she said finally.

Dee and I looked at each other. That part we got. Angelique loved those mushrooms even more than she loved Snowball. Snowball was cute, too. Not Othello cute, but definitely cuter than a mushroom.

"That's the only containment recipe they had?" Dee asked.

"It's the only public one Miss T could find that might work. It's not like we have time to put out a call in private recipe groups. Sometimes people ignore those groups for centuries."

"Maybe you don't have to use all of your mushrooms?" I offered.

Angelique gave me a sharp look. "ANY of them is a sacrifice. Plus you need a certain mass for the mycelium to get large enough to join the network."

I nodded sympathetically. "Maybe somebody's selling them? Do you want me and Dee to run up to the Rivyèmarché to find some? How much do you need?"

I thought I was doing the right thing, but apparently, that made it worse because I wasn't supposed to buy them, either. I guess all of us were supposed to be sticking to a budget.

I looked at Angelique, truly confused. "So . . . what's happening right now?"

"I have to do this myself, and I'm gonna use the ones I'm growing because we can't keep just buying things from 3Thirteen because eventually we *will* run out of credits, but can I get a second to grieve, please?"

There was so much going on that Dee and I decided to just let Angelique be. Turned out, that was what she needed. After a quick solo run to S-Crow "so she could think," she was pretty much back to her normal self. Maybe even a little bit happy. I wanted to ask her what happened at S-Crow, but Dee gave me a look that said *Sandy was cool, but maybe not cool enough to leave her outside any longer,* so I left that question for later.

Sandy insisted we go back to the car and drive to my house instead of walking there, even though walking from the Freret Street exit would have been way faster. She was correct that going that way would have meant walking right through the capture before we had the extender or before Angelique had a chance to get the potion ready for her spell, but my house was so close to the capture that I didn't think there was a way to get there without at least getting really, really close. Sandy knew one, though. It involved cutting across Oretha Castle Haley Boulevard.

I changed my mind about Jenny when Sandy turned onto Claiborne.

It's not that the closer we got to my house, the more scared I was we wouldn't pull it off or anything like that. It was that, at that point, Jenny had been super helpful, and Dee was right. She could surprise me. But at that point, she was also still the person I trusted the least even though I had technically known her the longest.

Jenny was at my house by the time we got there. I knew she couldn't see the weave of protection Miss Nancy's team had woven around Luz and Miguel's house, but she could see the single strand of beads hanging from it, waving in the wind. The beads didn't go back and forth like beads normally do. They were hovering midair on an invisible hook, that strange wind constantly pulling in the same direction: toward the capture. It felt . . . unnatural.

Sandy pulled into my mom's usual spot and I got out of the car. Jenny stood there like all she could feel was the breeze. Maybe that was all she could feel. Maybe the rest of the dread and heaviness in the air was all magic.

"How'd you get here so fast?" I asked.

The Fly was close, but it was at least twenty minutes if you walked. Maybe ten if you ran, but I didn't know for sure. I never ran that far.

"I live around the corner," she said. "Eight houses away. I counted."

"Oh. I didn't know," I said.

"Yeah, I didn't know, either."

My brain flashed through the bajillions of times from kindergarten to now that I had seen her getting in a car to get a ride home. Or the times she had seen me do the same. It took all of this to make us realize we practically lived in the same place.

"I thought you'd be at the festival," I said.

Jenny shook her head, the paillé edges of her hair standing up even more in the wind. "I was waiting to hear from you."

"I didn't know you would be here so soon," I said. "You have to wait outside. My mom doesn't like me to bring people in the house when she's gone."

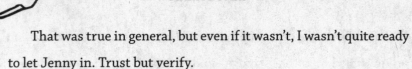

That was true in general, but even if it wasn't, I wasn't quite ready to let Jenny in. Trust but verify.

"I'll wait with her," Sandy said.

I nodded and Dee, Angelique, and I went in.

I thought Dee was gonna lecture me about inviting Jenny over and then leaving her outside, but while Angelique went to check on her mushrooms and get her spell together, Dee sat down at my computer and started typing. A few minutes later, she had pulled up two camera streams: one from the security cameras at the front of our school and the other was grainy footage of what could have been an empty bottle lying on the levee, but I would have known it was the entrance to Fly Fest even if I hadn't seen three kids walk past it and straight-up disappear. My eye kept getting pulled back to the school, though. In that one you could see the outline of the trees. I had forgotten those cameras even existed.

Dee glanced up at me. "I thought you were gonna ask Jenny to tell us what's supposed to be happening inside that tent, but if we're not doing that, we can at least watch the outside of it."

"You think the people in the office at school were watching kids blossom out there all this week? You think they saw me do the freedom spell and just decided not to say anything?"

"Nah. If anything, I think Hurricane Hasani might have taken those cameras out. None of these were functional until just now—I was connecting them."

"You're a genius."

Instead of smiling, she narrowed her eyes at me. "It's your house. You get to decide who comes in. But did you really invite that girl over here for her to stand outside?"

I tried not to look at the window. I didn't want to see Jenny standing out there, but I did pull out my phone to check on Miguel and Luz. Luz was trying to check on me, too, but I said I was fine and asked them again to stay put.

Dee didn't say anything. That's one of the thousand things I loved about her. She didn't say everything was fine when she knew it wasn't.

"You want to go out and check on them?" Dee asked.

"No, I just did," I said, holding out my text messages with Luz for Dee to see.

"No, not them," she said. "Them!"

Dee tipped her forehead toward Jenny and Sandy.

"Oh. Them."

I didn't want to go out. It might have been my imagination, but it felt like the capture was causing that wind. Then I thought of Sandy and future baby, who I hoped they did not name Bobbi, and went to the front door to wave them both inside.

Sandy has never been subtle. Before they came in she said, "Are you sure it's OK for Jenny to come in when your mom's not here?"

"Yeah," I said. "You're here."

Sandy didn't giggle or gush or do any of the things she usually did when I gave even the tiniest sign that I didn't hate her. She just put her hand on Jenny's shoulder and led her to the living room—not my room—for all of us to wait for . . . I didn't even know what we were waiting for.

"Angelique's getting ready," I said when they sat down in front of the coffee table. "Excuse me."

I went to my room to check on Dee. She was still watching the live streams. There was no point in asking her what was happening. We needed to know what was happening inside, and none of us could tell that from here.

I went to my bookcase, the one I could see from almost every angle in my room, and pulled a box off the top shelf. When you opened it, it looked like there was nothing inside, but I knew there was so I grabbed at the air and came up with the invisible bag. I'd gotten it from Kaitlynn's shop when I traded her for Luz's fleur-de-lis. My hand disappeared inside the bag and came out with the extender I'd put there for safekeeping. As soon as I pulled it out, Othello knew what was up. He attention-clawed at my leg, hoping I would drip a little magic onto the floor. I was afraid to do it, though. Something about the weird wind made me believe every warning I'd been given. It was dangerous to do magic right then. At least it was if I ever wanted to do it again. I could feel it.

I shoved the extender in my pocket exactly the way it was— empty—and headed to the kitchen instead. These days, my mom always had a million tea experiments going. Most of them were meant to be hot, but since it was still so hot outside, the refrigerator was filled with iced experiments, too. Most of them were kind of exotic, with turmeric and sage and stuff I'd never heard of. But there was also one labeled Herbal Lemon Mint that, at that moment, sounded normal enough to be good. I pulled out the trays and the glasses and the pitcher and brought some out to Sandy and my guest. My offering didn't look good enough for Instagram, but it was enough to make Jenny smile a little and relax.

"Thanks," she said, taking a glass. "Is this a potion? One sip and I'll be healed?"

I think she was trying to be funny or lift the mood or something, but she did the exact opposite.

"It's just iced tea," I said. "Potions are LaToya's specialty."

"I know," Jenny said. She nodded and took a sip. I knew the tea was good even without the face she made. My mom made it. Of course the tea was good.

Jenny shook her head. "Listen, Hasani. I just want to be helpful. I swear."

The look in Jenny's eyes was the same one Othello had just given me in my room. The giant hope that I would give him even the tiniest sprinkle of magic. From Othello, it was cute. From Jenny it was . . . I don't know. It didn't feel good.

"You can be very helpful," Angelique said from the stairs. "But if you're coming with us to infiltrate the festival, you have to get ready."

When I looked over at Angelique, I literally did a double take. Angelique always looked good, but this was beyond. I wish she had let me record her before, because this was definitely an after. We're talking a real-life, jump-cut transformation video. (Minus the jump cut because that takes forever.)

"Are those my jeans?" I asked, grateful for an excuse to delay that conversation with Jenny another minute or two. Angelique never wore jeans. I didn't even think she had any.

"Yep," she said. "And the hair paint is yours, too. Jeans from the drier. Hair paint from the bottom left cabinet in the bathroom. It's OK, right?"

With some people I would not have been cool with them borrowing my stuff without asking, but with Angelique, it only felt like our relationship had skipped to the next level. From linked sister and good friend to full-on bestie tier. It didn't hurt that the look was so good. Purple tips on all her coils popped against the white shirt she

was already wearing and the hint of sparkle in my jeans. Her earrings even had a little more bling. No, not bling—texture. It looked good.

"Now I get the glowsticks," I said. She had woven them into her hair like a crown.

"I want to look fly at Fly Fest," Angelique said. "It'll help us blend in. Do I look any different?"

Nobody said "fly" anymore, at least not when they were talking about looking good, but I didn't tell Angelique that. She'd totally lifted the mood and I did not want to bring it down.

"You look great. One sec!" I said running to my room to grab a few palettes. I didn't do much. Just a little eyeshadow and blush with a couple of sticky gems. She was already wearing lip gloss. Less than a minute later, she was sheer perfection.

"Y'all can't go like that," Angelique said. "Hurry up and get dressed."

Carefree festival goddess was Sandy's core aesthetic, so she gave a look like, *I got this. Don't worry*, and she whipped the rest of us into shape in no time. We were laughing and posing and Dee said she already looked festival dapper but she wound the rest of the glowsticks through her belt loops anyway and I almost forgot how serious everything was until Angelique suggested I fill the extender right in front of Jenny.

"I know we don't really need the extender until the moon is full, but it's better to see if my custodies stop you from getting trapped by the capture now rather than later, right?"

Jenny looked at me with that Othello look in her eyes. I remembered what Ms. Coulon said about burned-out witches using extenders just to feel magic again.

"Jenny, listen," I said. "You don't have to come with us to stop LaToya. If you came here because you think I can fix you, you should go home right now because I don't know how to fix you," I said. "I'm not sure anyone does, but even if I knew how I honestly might not do it because, from where I'm sitting, there's nothing to be fixed." It felt terrible to say that to somebody who had gone through something so awful, but the more I thought about it, the more I knew it was true. Whatever Jenny had been through, she was still Jenny. And if there was any part of her that needed healing, Jenny had to be the one to do it. Otherwise she'd be in that person's debt forever and then she'd never be free.

"So you called me over here for nothing?" Jenny asked. She sounded more hurt than angry.

"No," I said. "We called you over here because you planned the festival and if there's anybody who knows what's going on inside, it's you. We called you because you're still friends with Annie and Cicily and Margeaux and Jane, so you might know what's going on inside them, too. And being an evers witch is its own kind of power. There probably is something I should ask you to do. Only I'm not going to ask you any of that because if you help us any more, it has to be because you want to. Not because I'm influencing you."

"I'm still a witch," Jenny said. "You can't influence me."

"I can," I said. "Maybe I'm not influencing you with magic, but I know I can get you to do stuff because *of* magic and that's basically the same thing."

"No, you couldn't," Jenny said.

"So, if somebody promised they could get you your magic back right now, you wouldn't immediately turn your back on us? Isn't that what LaToya did to get you to turn on me in the first place?"

Jenny was quiet. I knew she would be after I said that, but it had to be said.

"You're right," Jenny said finally. "I might turn on you. But it wouldn't be because I thought you were a bad person or because I'd be trying to hurt you or anyone else. It'd be because I was trying to save me."

"I get it," I said. "But just because you have a good reason doesn't mean you would have hurt me or anyone else any less. What people do counts way more than what they think. I'm sorry, Jenny. I didn't mean to call you over here just to say this, but I can't get past it. I just don't think I can trust you."

I thought Jenny would storm out the door. Maybe go run tell LaToya everything she heard us say, but she kept sitting right next to Sandy. She didn't look down at the ground. She looked up at me and said, "I may not have come here for all the right reasons, but I'm not just here because I want to get my magic back. Yes, I want to get my magic back, but I want to help, too. The way LaToya talked about you wasn't right. The way she used me and Annie and Cicily and Margeaux and Jane wasn't right, either. Those girls? They just wanted to help, like I did. I mean, thousands of witches being held in a capture? They just want them to be free. It'll be their first great act of witchery. But what you said about LaToya is right. She's not looking out for them. She's using them to pay back her debt to her boss. I think if it weren't for her boss, she wouldn't care about the capture at all. And then when Margeaux got burned out sinking that orb? LaToya acted like it was nothing. Obviously her boss didn't think that was cool. That's why Annie got to be one of three."

"What?" I said.

"One of three, as in Annie is the first member of the coven? I thought that was LaToya," Sandy said. "Where's my magazine?" But Sandy didn't wait for me to answer before she ran into my room to get it.

"LaToya's out of the coven. That's what I thought you wanted to talk about. That's why I came. Annie said LaToya's going wild, saying that all of them are backstabbers and she's better off alone. I think she's probably out there right now trying to do it all herself. But whatever happens is goody for her after all the people she's hurt, including me. But there's still Annie and all the rest of them. The coven might be broken, but they're still bound by the deal LaToya made. They don't deserve to get hurt. I am here because I don't have magic. I can't stop LaToya, but you can."

Perfect is the enemy of done. Grandmé Annette had warned me about trying to be perfect all the time, but I didn't really get what she was saying until right then. There we all were thinking we had time because the perfect time to free the orb was in the full light of the full moon. But not everybody waited for things to be perfect. Some people just got things done.

LaToya got things done. Moon or no moon, LaToya was freeing that capture tonight.

Angelique shook her head. "What are we going to do? She can't do it alone. It's going to take at least five people. Maybe a full thirteen. Do we just go down there and tell everyone what she's up to? Stop anyone from linking with her?"

"No," I said. I was the only one who answered. "I say . . . the only way to stop her is to help her."

CHAPTER TWENTY-THREE

LEMON AND MINT

Jenny didn't come with us. In her world, helping LaToya meant betraying Annie. I understood. I just hoped she wouldn't get in our way.

"You know Jenny's gonna get in our way, right?" Dee said, like she was reading minds or something.

"That actually might work to our advantage," Angelique said. "I mean, if Jenny's down there telling people not to join LaToya's coven, that'll at least make it harder for LaToya to get to five people, let alone thirteen."

Sandy was driving us to the Fly, trying her best to stay quiet. It didn't stop her from making faces, though.

"Who do you think people will listen to more?" I said. "The witch with the dope WeBop, or the girl who claims to have been the mastermind behind all her videos? I hate to say it, but I know who I'd choose."

"If I didn't know any better, I'd choose LaToya, too," Dee said.

"So why are we helping her again?" Angelique asked.

"She needs it," I said. "And we all became charmed girls together. And you know how stubborn she is. If she tries to pull the whole capture out herself without any help at all, even from the moonlight, how do you think that's gonna go?"

"Not well," Angelique said.

"Yeah," Dee said. "If she's that desperate, she won't stop, even if the orb is breaking. Half the city's magic will probably end up in the capture and she'll burn herself out in the process."

They looked at me like I might say "that's goody for her" or something. But I didn't feel like that at all.

"What could be so bad that she'd be willing to get burned out over it?"

"Her family," Angelique said. "I knew it was bad but I didn't think it would get this bad." Who could have guessed anything would get this bad? "She's the last witch in her family," Angelique continued. "She's the youngest of like twelve cousins on her dad's side. None of them are magic except her. At first, everybody was putting this pressure on her to restart the family legacy. The next generation is always better and all that. That's why they poured so much money into making sure her dad and his family looked the part. They thought for sure she'd make good connections at Belles Demoiselles. I think they were hoping that she'd make an organic connection there and get bound by coven to one of the old families, but when that didn't work out, the rest of the family turned their backs on them, saying it was her dad's fault for not marrying better in the first place. But then her parents started fighting all the time and their business was going under."

"I didn't even know funeral homes could go under," I said.

Angelique shrugged. "I don't know. LaToya just wanted to help. That's when she found Kaitlynn. She never said it, but I think she thought if she could make enough money, that would fix everything."

"Even with her family?" I asked. Whose family would ditch them over money?

"Money doesn't change you, it shows you," Dee said. "Getting a bunch of money just makes you more like your real self. So a selfish family with more money is just gonna be a more selfish family."

"That's what my dad says!" Angelique exclaimed.

"I know," Dee said. "That's where I got it from."

I didn't know Dee hung out with Angelique's dad like that, but he did have a point.

"That's basically what happened to Jenny," I said. "Those commercials were cute, but I guess her family just kept pushing her more and more until she didn't have anything left."

"Well, that same thing is about to happen to LaToya."

"No, it's not," I said. "She's gonna accept our help."

"You sure about that?" Dee asked. "I'm pretty sure she hates you for real."

"She does, but that doesn't matter. LaToya doesn't want to be alone. That's why she keeps forcing covens over and over again. Some people are cool with being loners. LaToya isn't."

"I thought that was gon' be me," Dee said. "Being a one of one would have been cool. I'd probably be at my house right now messing with some code while I make a soufflé. Y'all cool, too, though."

"Awww! Dee!" I said.

Dee rolled her eyes, but she was smiling, too.

"I don't know if I'm ready," Angelique said.

"Ready for a coven? Too late for that!"

"No, ready for this fight. What if we can't get LaToya to see we're trying to help? What if Annie tries to stop us? What if our moms find out? No matter what, somebody is going to be against us."

"Well, if people are going to be against us anyway, we might as well do what we think is right."

How I became the voice of reason, I'll never know.

"Guys?" Sandy said. "Before you go there's something you should know. I've told all your moms. I'm sorry. I wasn't going to do it, but then I couldn't not do it. Hasani, I think your mom might have already been around here somewhere, but I'm sure there are less than twenty minutes left before the rest of them show up. I know you're mad and you'll probably hate me forever now and never trust me again, but I still think it was the loving thing to do and I stick by it."

"I'm not mad," I said. "You bought us twenty minutes."

knew exactly where to go. I could have guessed it even if I hadn't seen it on-screen before we left. It's the only place on the Fly that was covered in trees but still had a full view of the river in the moonlight. The water bottle was on the ground in view of the security camera high up on the light pole. As soon as we got near it, the air was saturated in the scent of lemon and mint. If I hadn't smelled it before, I would have guessed it was a giant vat of my mom's tea. But I had smelled it before. It was in the gym the day LaToya drew all those termites.

"Aromatics," I said. "Somebody's boosting their influence."

I put my hand out and felt for somewhere I could push the curtain of intentions aside. It was surprisingly easy to find. It swept open and light and lemon and mint flowed out. And music.

"Keep an eye on each other," Dee said. "Five minutes."

The tent was packed, but of course there was a DJ. At what should have been a hostess stand, there was a little wall of vines with some flowers woven in.

I thought those crystal green bottles would be everywhere, but the only one I saw was the one on the ground outside. Besides the wall of vines and flowers, everything else inside was gold. I looked around for LaToya, but I spotted Annie first. Well, we spotted each other.

"I knew you'd come!" she said excitedly, running over. She was dressed like some kind of flower goddess. Trailing white robes. Headdress. The whole business. "I know you don't like LaToya, and believe me, I get it now. You were right. But I knew that even if you wouldn't come for me, you'd come to Fly Fest as soon as you found out it was for charity. And look! You came!"

Annie gave me a hug. It was weird to not know if she meant it or not. It felt stiff, but it might have just been me.

"What's the charity?" I asked.

"Oh! You don't know. That's so exciting because I get to tell you. Prison reform. Did you know our very own school was built on top of a prison for witches? That sounds horrible, right? Because it was horrible. A bunch of witches' magic is still imprisoned inside. Totally unjust. That's why a bunch of us are gonna free them tomorrow. Fly Fest is sort of a pre-party to get people to sign up. My linked sisters and I are going to lead it with our friend Margeaux. You should sign up! Please say you'll come. It can be our first act together as witches."

"Have you seen LaToya?" I asked. I was trying to catch glimpses of the crowd over Annie's head. Annie's kind of short, but that actually made it hard to look like I was giving her my full attention and look around the room at the same time.

Annie's face changed when I said LaToya's name. "I don't know," she said. "She ditched me. She ditched all of us. Margeaux got hurt and she just cut us all off and left us to deal with it. We went along with it so LaToya let Margeaux off the hook from the time imme-morial future favor she got all of us to give her. Margeaux's only a sixth grader. She didn't know what to do. Thank goodness Kaitlynn stepped in and—wait. I wasn't supposed to say all that. I'm just sup-posed to say, 'LaToya is no longer involved in this project.' But will you come tomorrow? Please?"

"I have to check with my coven," I said.

Annie smiled. "I totally get that now, too. No wonder the four of you have always been so close. Oh! And tell Angelique she should come tomorrow, too. Kaitlynn talked about her especially. She said if she came she could help her with her earrings. And she has some-thing for you and Dee, too. *It might be art schoooool,*" she sang.

So . . . what? Kaitlynn was like the Wizard of Oz now, granting everybody one wish? Wait. Kaitlynn was exactly like the Wizard Oz. Those wishes were fake, too.

I backed away, smiling.

Annie was watching me, so I pushed across the room to give Angelique Kaitlynn's message.

"How does Kaitlynn know about my earrings?" she said, but she was way better at maintaining a party face than me. If I didn't know better, I would have thought she was just saying the DJ was playing a really good song. "Never mind. Let's just find LaToya and get out of here."

Dee was the one who found her, and instead of pointing her out, Dee just vibed in LaToya's general direction. Weirdly, that worked, although how we missed LaToya in the first place I had no idea. She was doing a WeBop dance with a bunch of people. LaToya's dancing was smooth, but I could see underneath it. She wasn't dancing to have fun, she was bringing the fun, desperately hoping that her fake joy would get people to bond with her. It was just a feeling, but I knew I was right the second LaToya looked up and saw Angelique. She smiled. Her real smile. The one she used to use at Social Hour when it was just me, her, and Dee. LaToya was dancing over to where we were until she saw me. She threw me an icy glare, turned, and walked straight out of the tent.

"Dag. She really does hate you," Dee said.

"No kidding."

Angelique followed her out, so we did, too.

"Wait!" Angelique shouted. "Don't go! We want to help you."

For a second, LaToya froze, but then she shouted, "Yeah, right" without turning around or slowing down or anything. "So you figured I'd be just thrilled to see Hasani. That's why you brought her with you, right? I guess I really don't have any friends."

LaToya disappeared into a little clump of trees right before the levee rolled straight down across the railroad tracks. I thought it was magic, until she reappeared a second later on a bike. She had just stashed it there. No magic required as she hopped on and let gravity pull her away.

"Bikes!" Dee smacked her forehead. "Why didn't we think of bikes?"

I don't know, but what was it Grandmé Annette said? If you don't use your head, you will use your legs? Angelique took off running and the next thing I knew, all of us were racing down the levee after a girl practically flying away on a bike we'd never catch. I wasn't even wearing cute shoes, but I was winded by the time we got to the bottom. We couldn't really see her anymore. She'd probably cut into the park. I had visions of slowing her down with egrets and swans, but really I was hoping Sandy had parked her car where she'd dropped us off. It had only been five minutes. Ten minutes, max. Maybe Sandy was waiting for us. I scanned the parking lot, desperately looking. I didn't see Sandy, but I did see Lucy.

"My mom!" I said and took off running in Lucy's direction with a fresh wind.

"I'm not going to ask," my mom said as we climbed in, "but I have tagged Sandy out and I'm not leaving you and we will definitely be talking about this later."

"Thanks, Mom." I gave her a quick hug.

"Don't thank me. Tell me where to go."

"Let me pull it up on your phone?" Dee said to Angelique. Before Angelique could dig in her pocket, my mom had passed her phone to the back seat.

"Here. Use mine," she said.

Dee grabbed it, tapped the screen for a few seconds, and the next thing I knew, we were basically watching LaToya pedal up the street on street-camera view. The camera angle kept changing, sometimes high like it was coming from a light pole, sometimes low like we were watching from someone's porch, but always LaToya streaking past, white dress flying out behind her.

"That's St. Charles," my mom said, pulling out.

"She's headed to school," I said.

"Or the Freret entrance to 3Thirteen," Angelique added.

"Awww," my mom said, glancing at the phone again. "Bless her. She's staying in the bike lane."

"Yeah," I said. "She doesn't want to die." Where else are you supposed to ride a bike?

"Not a given if she's riding straight into a capture."

Moment of silence for the fact that we, too, were driving straight into a capture. Even from the other side of Audubon Park, I could feel it pulling.

"Angelique, honey, use your phone to call Miss Nancy. Her team might still be close by. Right now they're working on creating a new perimeter to stop the capture from spreading farther than it already has. Apparently something is pulling streams of it toward the river, but they're probably going to want to do something to stop her from doing any more damage, poor thing."

"Mom, that's what we're doing." LaToya was way ahead. We were just turning onto St. Charles, but she was already curving onto Carrolton.

"Hasani, this isn't on you. Every single thing is not on you."

"Mom. Trust me. This is my circus. At least it is until I apologize. I wasn't always as good a friend to LaToya as I should have been."

My mom gripped the wheel tighter as we crossed the light at Broadway. I was wondering if she would slow down for yellow, but thankfully we'd had nothing but green the whole way.

"I'm not asking questions," she said, "and I'm coming with you."

"Mom! No!" I said, panic setting in for the first time. "Park outside the perimeter. We'll run the rest of the way. We have Angelique's custodies, remember? Triple-layered protection." I didn't say "We'll be

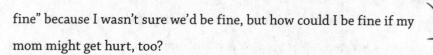

fine" because I wasn't sure we'd be fine, but how could I be fine if my mom might get hurt, too?

"Hasani, I already said I'm not asking questions. That was not a question. I'm coming with you."

"But we don't have anything to protect you," I said.

"I'm a kismet, remember?" she said. "I'll protect myself."

I blinked. "You're gonna count on luck?"

"I'm going to count on the fact that kismets can't waste magic because we can't control it in the first place. If I can't fight the capture, it can't drain me."

I threw my arms around my mom as she rounded onto Carrolton Avenue. Or at least I would have if our car hadn't held me back. Lucy's seat belts don't like sudden moves.

My mom pulled right into an open spot on the corner. I could see LaToya sitting calmly on a concrete bench inside the gate. I know she saw us. At least she did if she was looking our way. But she might have been looking up in the trees like I was.

Half the beads in the trees were white. They looked like ghosts. Decades of Ms. Coulon's work bled dry in an instant. The wind was moving constantly the way it does in video games. I don't think I would have noticed if I weren't watching the beads. They were swirling, like at any second they'd get sucked down the drain.

Angelique and I pulled out our brass glass scopes at the same time. I wanted to see what was happening with the trees before we walked in.

"There's no intentions left in the trees," I said, my mind involuntarily remembering the symphony of light magic.

"Look at the ground," Angelique said passing her scope to Dee.

I did. There were no lights or anything. But then I realized, that was it. There were no lights or anything. Every tiny spark was instantly swallowed by the dark.

"Like a black hole," Dee said.

Angelique pulled the packet of sawdust out of her bag and handed it to Dee. Dee opened it, and it practically leaped into the void. I don't think I would have had the reflexes to close it before it was all gone, but Dee did. The tiny bits of roots in the termite dropping were being drawn to the roots in the tree just like we thought they would be. The three of us nodded, unbuckling our seat belts to get out of the car.

"I never knew your charms sparkled like that," my mom said. By then, she had Angelique's scope. I don't know why none of us had ever thought to do what she was doing. Maybe because we knew our charms were working because we could feel them working. Maybe because our charms were a part of us and you hardly ever look at yourself as much as you look at somebody else.

Right then was no exception. Instead of looking at my charms or Angelique's or Dee's, I turned to look at LaToya's. Her charm made the only sparks of light on the capture. The lights danced, but it felt more like a battle. Like crackles of electricity that got weaker with every heartbeat but kept fighting anyway. The Belles Demoiselles were protecting us, after all. I just didn't know for how long.

Angelique went first. I stuck the scope in my pocket. I didn't want to give LaToya any more of a reason to run again. Although, from the calm on her face, this was exactly where she wanted to be.

"There's nobody watching now," LaToya said as we crossed the gate. "You don't have to pretend to care."

My fleur-de-lis was hot against my skin. The force of the capture pulled harder and harder the farther we went in. It pulled at my stomach and my knees. It must have pulled at LaToya, too, but she sat with her back straight, ankles crossed, just like we'd been trained to do. I don't know how she did it or why I had never really noticed how small she was. For whatever reason, LaToya always seemed so tall. But really she was tiny. And alone.

"Hasani, you better check yourself before you wreck yourself. Step aside before you get schooled. This is nothing for fake witches to play with."

The words were strange. They didn't have any bite. I don't know if it was because of her or if it was because of me. Maybe both.

We kept creeping closer, like LaToya was a baby deer. She didn't run. She made the earth move. Literally. The roots of the trees began to pull and tug, rippling the ground around us as they tried to get away. At least that's what it felt like—like the trees wanted to run and we'd be broken and swallowed in tiny pieces.

"They did it without me," she said. "It was my recipe, and they just did it without me."

A root pulled near us. I put my arm out to steady myself as a wave rippled past.

"I let Kaitlynn have my spellbook. I thought that way, she'd need me. I thought that way she couldn't do it without me. We'd be partners. She switched it up on me, though. That was my fault. I wasn't careful enough. But when I bring her this orb, she won't be able to switch it up again. The wording is perfect and it's on the blockchain. She has to give me my money and my partnership just like she promised when she took my spellbook."

"LaToya," Angelique said. "Stop."

LaToya wasn't listening. Or else she really didn't hear.

"Annie doesn't understand," she said, looking at Angelique for the first time. "I'm the one who has to bring the orb to Kaitlynn. She can't do it. It's my debt. It was my contract. I don't want it to be hers, too."

"That's why you broke the connection with your coven?" I said. I thought I said it gently, but she immediately turned on me.

"No one is talking to you, Hasani." She said my name like it was a curse word. "This is the problem with being in some stupid coven. I only wanted to talk to Angelique, but it's like she automatically comes with stupid Hasani and Dee. Y'all are not one person. It doesn't matter if you're in a coven or not. The only person you can rely on is yourself. I'm one of one."

My fleur-de-lis burned. The ground rippled again. That time it did throw me down, but I got right back up again.

"LaToya, we wanna help you," Dee said.

LaToya didn't seem to hear. "I'm so stupid," she said. "I just trusted Kaitlynn, but I should have verified. Trust but verify. That's why I put it in the rules. But it's good. I needed to learn that. That's what Kaitlynn says. 'Either you win or you learn.' Every time I brought her back a bottle of magic and she'd say 'These are ordinary,' I thought she was lying. Turns out those stupid bottles *make* the magic ordinary. Idiotic, right? Why would anyone want magic to be ordinary? I didn't get it. Now I do. Kaitlynn stealing the orb from me was just business. She got the dragon scale, but the orb was my idea. My recipe. The old people don't always write stuff down, but they can't help but talk. I listen. That's why I learned Kouri-Vini. So I could listen. I didn't do all that work getting everything just right for somebody else to come up while they step over me and leave me and my family behind. Kaitlynn stayed winning and I stayed getting schooled. But not this time. This time I wrote that contract perfectly. When I bring her this orb, she can't say no. This time I'm gonna win."

LaToya closed her eyes. If I thought the ground shook before, I was wrong. The rumble was so strong the trunks of the trees rocked back and forth. I thought they would collapse around us.

"Wait!" I shouted.

The trees froze. I was frozen, too—fixed in LaToya's stare.

I knew that look. It was the look of abandonment. Betrayal. It was the look of not forgiving. I didn't need a mirror to know I looked the same way every time I thought of my father.

"We want to help you!" I said.

LaToya laughed and the ground moved again. "I'm supposed to believe that?" she said. "I'm supposed to believe you want me to be great? You want me to win?"

"Yes, I do!" I said. "There's room for all of us out here. Let us help you!"

This time, the ground didn't stop.

"You think I'm that weak? Huh. I don't blame you for that part. I thought I was, too. Even when y'all showed up at the festival, I still thought I needed somebody. I don't. That's the easy way. I'm stronger than that."

"You're gonna break it," I said. "We came to help. Show her, Dee."

Dee pulled the little wrapper of capture roots out of her pocket. But she couldn't open her hand to show them. The air was swirling all around us, trying to make us resist. Trying to pull us in. So I kept going.

"You don't have to if you don't want to," I said. "You're a witch, and witches always have a choice. But Dee is holding something that will make it easier to get the orb out."

"Dag, Hasani! You've been lying since day one, acting all extra innocent so you'd get picked as the chosen one. It worked. It worked on me, too. But I peeped your game that first night you sneaked out and didn't say a word about it, even though I gave you boukou chances. Why should I believe you now?"

"You're tired!" Angelique said. "You can't last much longer. Let us help!"

But that wasn't what LaToya needed to hear. I knew what she needed to hear and, since I knew it was the truth even if it wasn't everything, that made it easy to say.

"I know you hate me," I said. "I hurt you. I shouldn't have gone off to the Vacherie coven and tried to keep it a secret from you. All of us were new. All of us were struggling. It was wrong that I couldn't see that. It was wrong for me to expect that every single other person was stronger than me and nothing I did could hurt them. I apologize. If I had it all to do over, I wouldn't do the same thing again. You hate me. OK. But when you try to get back at people, it poisons you, not them. I hurt you in the past, but Kaitlynn is hurting you right now.

Maybe you should just walk away. Let us both go. Give yourself a chance to heal."

"Cute meme, Hasani. You can say what you want. Nobody's going to listen to you, anyway. We all know how fake you are. At least Kaitlynn is real. At least with Kaitlynn I know what I'm getting."

"I'm telling the truth! Kaitlynn has been playing you since day one. She wants the signatures in the capture. She doesn't care how she gets them, even if it means destroying you. She's not trying to teach you. She's not trying to help you. She doesn't care about you."

"And you do?"

"Yeah. Actually, I do."

"You're lying! Signatures don't even sell. I tried."

"Then why did Kaitlynn already try to get mine?"

LaToya shook her head over and over again.

"Hasani!" It was my mom yelling. She was standing right on the same ground we were, the brass glass scope pressed to her face, fighting the ground and the wind to get to me. "Your charms." I hadn't been paying attention, but I took that moment to notice. My fleur-de-lis wasn't burning anymore. It was being worn down, but there was still life in it, probably because of the dolphin boosting and feeding it and Angelique's triple-protected earrings. I was scared and I was tired, but I was fine. LaToya wasn't. She didn't have the extra blessings of strangers and family keeping her magic in. No matter how strong she was, LaToya was reaching her limit.

Angelique was holding down her hair, muttering something into the wind. *Kouvèr lamou. Kouvèr lamou. Kouvèr lamou.* She looked scared out of her mind. I had to call it.

"Just give it to her, Dee!"

Dee unclenched her fist and the gift from the termite queen went flying. First up, but then plummeting down, plunging straight into the ground. I meant to let my magic follow the roots down deep as they wrapped around the orb and help LaToya guide it back up again.

But LaToya was right. She didn't need me. She pulled it out on her own.

Less than a second later, the orb came bursting through the ground like a cannon, throwing mud in every direction. The trees rocked, roots pulling out of the ground like a giant with tar under his feet. Dee whipped something straight at the orb as it came down, but that didn't stop it from landing square in LaToya's hand.

The wind died down. The mud settled. Angelique inched closer. Everything about everything said it was over, even the buzz in my fleur-de-lis. Less than a second had passed and it was already refilling.

"It worked," LaToya said, staring down at the orb in her hands like she couldn't believe it.

Kouvèr lamou. Kouvèr lamou. Kouvèr lamou.

Angelique kept muttering.

Whatever awe LaToya felt from pulling the orb out intact melted away.

She only gripped the orb tighter. "Spare me your fake incantations, Angelique. You're not trying to cover me with love. I thought you were different, but being with Hasani made you fake, too."

LaToya turned to walk away. I put up a hand to stop my mom from moving toward her.

"You're a witch," I said. "You don't have to do this. You don't have to give that orb to Kaitlynn."

LaToya looked at me, her eyes totally cold again. "You're a wild-seed. You have no idea what it means to uphold a legacy."

"No," I said. "But I do know what it means to uplift a friend."

She rolled her eyes as she shook her head and ran away, taking the orb completely out of reach.

"Should I call someone? Should we stop her? Why aren't we stopping her?" My mom was frantic.

"Don't worry mom," I said. "She'll be back."

"She'll be back?"

Angelique tapped her empty right ear.

"Yeah," I said. "We put a lock on it."

OPEN, NOT CLOSED

Most of the kids in New Orleans are magic in one way or another, they just don't know it. That's why I started my WeBop, so they could learn a little something and maybe we'd help each other out. But where were they now that I needed them? Nowhere to be found. I couldn't even go to a practice room anymore. Not after Hasani messed with my head. Not with what I was about to do.

No risk, no reward. That's what Daddy says. Taking risks usually worked for him, too. There was only one time it hadn't. The whole family was still paying for it.

I couldn't go home. My parents would ask how I got there. I couldn't go to Auntie Regina's. Not yet. She'd ask too many questions. So I planted my feet in the dirt in the one place I could still work: the library. It doesn't take long to get used to the flashes of electricity arcing from mushroom to mushroom. It's like a lightning storm with no thunder, only the quiet movement of knowledge from one node to another and then to some unknown place on the network. Besides people's phone screens, the sparks were the only light in the room.

I settled down with my back against the bark of a tree, my knees under a large mushroom that was meant to be a stool. I wasn't using the connector node above it, anyway. I'd already checked. Maybe there was something in a private recipe, but there was nothing on the Interweb about breaking into a locked orb.

Open. Open. Not closed, my brain repeated. When Kaitlynn gave the specifications, one of them was that the orb had to be open. If I brought it to her closed, it'd be a failure. I'd be a failure. I'd never be able to look at my father again, and if I did, he would never call me by my name. They hadn't even given me a middle name so I'd have nothing to fall back on. No choice but to win.

Open. Open. Open. Kaitlynn must have said it at least seven times. Every key was unique, but there had to be a way.

I tried all the numbers through 9999. Maybe the key was something after 10,000, but it felt like a dead end.

Open. Not closed.

How could I let them get in my head? Hasani talking about friendship as if I'd ever be dumb enough to trust her again. And Angelique muttering the same words like an incantation, when we both knew it wasn't one. *Kouvèr lamou. Kouvèr lamou. Kouvèr lamou.* It was probably the only Kouri-Vini she knew, and there she was like an idiot just saying it over and over again. *Covered in love.*

It was late. Auntie Regina was probably worried, but I couldn't stop. I had to open it, or that was it. I may as well have let my mom burn out. That would have been better than me digging a hole so deep that my family would never recover. There had to be a way.

The smell of fresh-dug earth filled my lungs, and I almost cried. I couldn't believe that I had ever been silly enough to think any of them were my friends. I was better now. Stronger now. But Angelique's voice still echoed in my head. *Kouvèr lamou. Kouvèr lamou. Kouvèr lamou.*

What if they hadn't been lying?

If they hadn't been, that meant they really were trying to cover me with love.

I sat up, holding the orb out in front of me. The surface wasn't perfectly smooth. There were four tiny dots. I wouldn't have noticed them if I had been able to shake that crazy thought from my head.

I dug into my backpack and pulled out a sheet of graphing paper. I measured the dots on the orb and transferred them over to the paper. If I weren't in Mathletes, I might not have had graph paper with me. But I was, and I did, even if at first I'd only gone to take a chance at Ms. Coulon's glasses. None of that mattered. I found the key, and suddenly, I felt open, too.

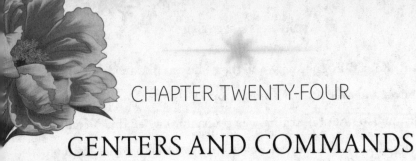

CHAPTER TWENTY-FOUR

CENTERS AND COMMANDS

Miss Lafleur was the very last person I expected to see at the glassworks in Amite. The glassworks was this huge, polished machine, harnessing the power of magic with fire and math and straight lines. Miss Lafleur was the opposite of that. Intense, but focused and wild. Maybe in her Belles Demoiselles suit, she would have looked more like she belonged at one of Ms. Coulon's sci-fi command tables, but she sat there in her overalls staring up at us firmly. Comfortable, even though she didn't match. Maybe that's why they had her sit front and center, where her dark brown eyes could be the most piercing while Dee, Angelique, and I tried not to shuffle back and forth where we stood.

My watch said it was not even sunrise, but at least they let us get some sleep before lining us up for interrogation. The overnight rooms at the glassworks were cool. They had room service and everything. I should have known better, but when I went to sleep, I kind of thought it was over. LaToya had the orb and the world kept spinning. I knew better when I saw all the signatures outside the volcano door. Most of them were unfamiliar, but there were too many signatures there for them to be giving us a rest. Something was up.

"Tell us again what happened yesterday," Miss Lafleur said. "Please include your actions along with your reasoning. Begin with the moment you got in the elevator bound for the Amite subsol station, include how the orb containing countless magical signatures was lost, and finish with this moment."

Dee started. Her mom was there, though Dee tried not to look her way. She tried not to look any way in particular. This was our third time going through the story. It was mostly the same every time, although the first and second times we interrupted each other to add in details here and there. Mrs. Hebert made a face every time the Interweb or mushrooms came up, but other than that, the first time through, all the adults in the room just listened. No one besides Mrs. Hebert seemed bothered, but they all took notes. Miss Lafleur in a hand-pressed notebook with flowers on the cover, my mom in the long spiral notebook she used to make grocery lists, Miss LaRose on a legal pad, and Miss LeBrun on her phone.

The second time we told the story, our version was smoother, but people raised their hands to interrupt us with consequences. Miss Nancy said that the explosive rise of the orb made some of her team's intentions irretrievable. They were left in pieces to decompose into ordinary magic, which was a waste. Miss LeBrun said something about invaluable observations being lost. Sandy said now she'd be nervous every time I left the house. Miss LaRose said that a little of her trust was broken. The consequences were all fears and things that would never be the same. None of them were punishments. I was waiting for the punishments. And no one said anything about us losing the signatures inside the orb.

"Thank you," Miss Lafleur said. She was looking at all of us even though I was the one who had just finished talking. "This has been most elucidating."

People started getting up to leave, but that didn't make any sense.

"Wait," I said. "What about the punishments? We aren't gonna get in trouble?"

Miss Lafleur gave us one of her gentle looks. "This isn't a council of people to judge you. This is a gathering of people who love you. You are witches. Charmed ones, no less. The consequences belong to all of us, but your actions belong to you. Why? Is there something else you wanted to say?"

"Yes," Dee said. "I didn't think about hurting those trees. If anybody is planning on helping them, I'd like to be a part of it. If not, I'm gonna figure out how to heal them myself, and anyone who wants to help me can."

Miss Lafleur nodded.

"I won't apologize for our actions," Angelique said, her long hair covering her bare ear. "We did what we thought was necessary, and even though it was dangerous, we were cautious. Given the opportunity I know I would make the same decisions again. However, I would like to commit to contributing enough funds to repair whatever physical damage there is at Riverbend Middle School. My plan is to lean on the fiat currency in my individual account, but I'll also work to earn credits to cover any magical item balance."

Ms. Coulon and Mrs. Hebert both nodded.

It was my turn. I centered myself. When I did that, it was easy to remember who I was. "I want to thank my mom for letting us try, and for staying close by. I always knew you were smart, but kismet on a capture is some magical genius that needs to be recorded."

"On it." Miss LeBrun smiled.

"And Sandy, I apologize. I guess I have to give Angelique a shout-out here and say I'd probably do it again, but I didn't have to do it the way I did. I should have just told you our plan from the beginning. It's like, I didn't want you to be nervous so I didn't tell you, but because I didn't tell you I guess you're gonna be nervous in perpetuity. I can't control your feelings because, well, they're your feelings. But I didn't have to make you drag the truth out of me. So, from now on I'll try not to do that. I'll try to just say what's going on with me."

My mom smiled and she and Sandy both nodded.

On the subsol back to the city, Miss LeBrun only talked about the trees. Since the capture had been violently ripped out, not coaxed out the way it should have been, the trees themselves were hurting. If their pain wasn't released, they'd wither and die. It went without saying that I wanted to help heal whatever damage there was at Riverbend Middle, but the more Miss LeBrun and I talked, the more I realized that more land than Riverbend Middle needed healing, and I wanted to help with that, too.

"Even though the darkness of the capture was poisoning the trees, they have grown accustomed to that magic," Miss LeBrun said.

"But you said the capture magic was poison," I said.

"Given enough time everything adapts, Hasani, even to unhealthy situations. Change is sometimes painful, even if that change will heal you."

Deep, but OK. Weirdly, it made sense.

"Now that the slow change is no longer possible, we must drain the remnants of the poison as quickly as possible so that the capture is not formed anew. The river grants freedom, especially in moonlight. We can use the full moon today to speed the flow. My team and I are linked sisters, so we can help each other weave channels of intentions to guide the remaining magic to the river. It will be difficult for you to help us, but perhaps you can use your brass glass scope to inspect the work."

"OK. I will, Miss LeBrun."

"Call me 'Mariama' or perhaps 'Miss Mbaye' if using my first name makes you uncomfortable while you're still so young," she said. "If you're ever to come apprentice with me and free more captures, you must learn to call me by my real name."

"That offer still stands?" I asked. I'm not gonna lie, correcting the historical record sounded a lot cooler than it did at "camp."

"That offer still stands. But careful, now. Don't go accepting it until you're ready. Offers of apprenticeship are binding."

I nodded and took my scope down to the edge of the water to look at the temporary intentions that Miss Mbaye was here to fortify. I had to look for the right spot. When I found it, it blew me away. Whoever laid that channel of intentions had done beautiful work. There wasn't a chink in it, at least not that I could see, but I wasn't looking for long before my eyes landed on Jenny.

I wanted to ask her what she was doing there. It was too early in the morning for it to be something normal. But then I remembered that it wasn't my business. If Jenny wanted to poke around the levee at sunrise, Jenny wanted to poke around the levee at sunrise.

She decided to speak. "Hey," she said.

I put my chin up in response but tried to get on with my work.

"They're doing part two of the festival tonight," she said. "I thought they might have set up the tent."

"I haven't seen it yet," I said. "But have fun."

Jenny turned like she was going to leave, but then she turned right back.

"I've been thinking about what you said yesterday. You're right. What I was asking for was pretty messed up. I was out of line. We're not even friends." She should have stopped there, but she kept going. "Well, we were already friends. I guess we just never got that close."

I shook my head. "We've never been enemies, Jenny, but being friends is deeper than that. If you want, we could try hanging out some. See if something clicks?"

Jenny smiled. "Will you consider letting me start a WeBop for Othello? You saw what I did for LaToya's." Then she caught herself.

"That's all right," I said. "I wouldn't want Othello's account to result in world domination. Othello is greedy enough about magic as it is."

I meant it as a joke, but even I didn't find it funny. Jenny was different, though. Or maybe I was different. Either way, that creepy vibe had fallen back a notch or two. Not enough to come back to my house and take videos of my cat, but enough to talk to her out in public without wanting to flee.

"I was thinking more like a group thing," I said. "The trees got pretty damaged yesterday. We're supposed to do a thing tonight to heal them at the peak of the full moon. You could come if you want."

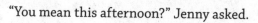

"You mean this afternoon?" Jenny asked.

I looked at her, confused.

"The peak of the full moon is at three thirteen this afternoon. We were gonna do a whole thing around it. For the festival," she said.

I blinked. Not from the time being 3:13 or having way less time I had than I thought, but the idea of a full moon in the daytime. Isn't that supposed to be a night thing?

"Yeah," I said. "Then, I guess, this afternoon."

After Jenny left, I followed the channel of intentions from the trees to the levee and back to the trees. Miss Mbaye said they'd handle it from there. That I should get some more rest before the moon got full. I thanked her and told her the truth: I wasn't going to sleep. I was going to see the two people I had been waiting to see: Luz and Miguel. I just wished I could bring them better news.

CHAPTER TWENTY-FIVE

BARRIERS AND BOUNDARIES

When I got to Luz's house, she had a million questions.

"I would say let's go to your house to talk, but I don't want to leave Miguel, so we have to talk here. What is happening out there? Seriously? I've read the texts, but I need to hear it from your face. What gives? Did you actually let LaToya walk away with that orb thing when you know how dangerous it is? And please, PLEASE tell me it doesn't have your signature inside."

"I don't know," I said.

"Hasani," Luz said, a quiet tear falling. "How are you so calm?"

"I don't know," I said. "I mean, last night I was really scared. Not hide under the bed scared. Action scared. It didn't go exactly like I thought it would, but Angelique captured the capture just like we planned. So it bought us some time at the very least."

"How much time?" Luz was trying really hard to keep her voice down.

"Maybe forever," I said. "Angelique is the one who locked it and she won't even tell me whether she used a pattern or a recipe to do it, so I'd say the chances are really good. Not one hundred percent guaranteed, but good. And we don't have the orb, but the sun came up again and there's a whole team of people including Sandy monitoring the blockchain for the close of that transaction between LaToya and Kaitlynn and it just seems really obvious that we'd know if somebody gets the signatures out of that orb. And in the meantime, there's all this work that I can help with. Things that will make the world a little bit better either way. It stops me from worrying sick about the people I love. Like Miguel. How is he?"

"He felt kind of guilty when he found out what happened to Margeaux."

"Margeaux burning out wasn't his fault," I said.

"I know. I keep telling him that. But I guess he kind of wished it in his head, so now he's worrying about that, which makes me keep worrying about him. It's exhausting," Luz said.

"He's lucky to have you," I said.

"He's lucky to have you, too. Thank you for always looking out for him. It seems like these days you love Miguel even more than you love your dad."

No, but I love Miguel more than my dad ever loved me.

"Sorry," Luz said. "I was trying to be funny, but I'm still scared so my funny wasn't funny. Just tell me. What can we do?"

"Well, we're gonna try to heal the bead trees," I said. "Wanna help?"

Luz felt better when I left, but I didn't. I felt shaky and awful like I had eaten something bad. Like if my body would just let itself throw up, I might feel better—at least until the next wave of nausea came.

I stood on Luz's porch and called my mom even though she was only two doors down.

"Is Lucy charged?" I asked. "Will you give me a ride?"

"To 3Thirteen?" she asked.

I shook my head. "No. Dad's."

Sandy was on magazine duty, but even if she hadn't been, after talking to Luz I really wanted to be with my mom. The fact that she'd almost said no because Lucy was "only on fifty percent" battery didn't help the sick feeling in my stomach.

I knew I wasn't mad at her, but when we got in the car, I snapped anyway. "Mom, I'm a witch. You know I can charge your car, right?"

"I know," she said.

"So then why don't you let me? Do you think I'm gonna break the car or something? Do you just not want me to help?"

"No, I love having your help. But it's not your job to help me."

"So what?" I said. "You're my mom. Of course I want to help you."

"And you do help me. And I hope you always will. But someday you might decide that you don't want to be here. That your life, your destiny is somewhere else. What I don't want is for you to get an opportunity to fly, and you just let it go because your first thought is something like, 'But how will Mom charge her car? She can't live without me.' I want that to always be a choice for you, not some obligation that ties you down. Because the truth is that even though your roots are here with me, I've always had the feeling that you were born to fly."

How my mom knew I was thinking about going to Senegal with Miss Mbaye, I wasn't sure. Maybe Miss Mbaye had told her. I hadn't really seen them interacting much, but they called each other by their first names, so who knew? Or maybe it was kismet. Or maybe it was because my mom really, really knew me. However it was, I was grateful.

We were quiet for a bit. My mom liked to drive the ground route, not the interstate, so there was lots to see. Lots of reasons to look and not talk. After a while I decided to ask her something I hadn't yet.

"What do you think about Dad and Sandy having a baby?" I asked.

"I think 'better them than me,'" she said with a laugh.

"No. I'm serious," I said.

"I'm serious, too. My baby is sitting right next to me, and the only reason their baby affects me is because their baby affects you. How do you feel? Do you think you're ready?"

"No," I admitted. "I don't even know how I'm supposed to be. Like I know I'm supposed to be excited because babies are babies and they're cute and everything, but how do you get yourself hype for your replacement? I mean part of me is like, 'whatever.' If Dad wants to just go off and make a new family, that's on him. I don't care. But . . . I *do* care. I wish I didn't but I do. How do you do it?"

"How do I do what, Hasani?"

"How do you not care?"

My mom frowned. "What makes you say I don't care?"

"You're friends with Sandy!" I said. "You loved Dad, but you're friends with your replacement like nothing bad happened. How?"

"Well, I'm sure part of it is that I know Sandy could never replace me. She can't stand in our memories or be a part of the connection we had. Her relationship with your dad is new and entirely separate from me, just like my relationship with Sandy is entirely separate from your dad. That actually started because of you."

"Me?"

"Yes. When Sandy and your dad were getting serious, she asked your dad to give me her number. She said that, as much as she liked him, she knew that having a healthy relationship with him could only happen if she had a healthy relationship with you. And before she tried to walk that road, she wanted me to have the chance to get to know her if I wanted to. I did. And I liked her. And I thought you might like her, too."

"I do," I said. "She's a way better parent than Dad is. She doesn't even have to be there, but she is. He's supposed to be there, but he isn't."

"Hasani, I love you. I'm glad you're going to talk to your dad."

"Why?" I said. "Because he's my dad and I'm crazy if I don't always just love him no matter what he does? So, like, just because he's my dad I'm not supposed to have boundaries?"

"No," she said. "Your relationship with your dad is between you and your dad. I can't control it any more than I can decide whether or not your dad and Sandy have a baby. But there is a difference between a barrier and a boundary. A barrier is something you put up when you're afraid. It stops you from feeling pain by blocking everything out. They're like painkillers. Barriers don't actually stop what's causing the pain, they just temporarily stop you from feeling it. The pain will always come back because the hurt is still there. Boundaries are different. Boundaries are what you make when you're healthy. When you know for sure that you're worth more than bad treatment, and you're healthy enough to walk away."

"So you think I'm hurt?"

"Baby, I know you're hurt. What happened was hurtful. I just don't want you to double up on the pain by drinking poison."

Uh, poison? I gave my mom a look, which she somehow saw while keeping her eyes on the road.

"Not literal poison. Anger. There's a saying I kept coming across in those text boxes people post on Instagram."

I cocked my head to the side. "A meme, Mom? Are you about to give me advice from a meme?"

"If it's good advice, it doesn't matter where it comes from. The meme said, 'Anger is like you drinking poison and expecting the other person to die.' I hope that you and your dad mend whatever is hurting between you, but whatever happens, I hope that at some point you'll be able to sit in your anger, acknowledge it, and then move past it."

"Oh. So I'm not supposed to just rant, mic drop, and leave? Got it." I smiled, but I was only half joking. "I do all my communications through Sandy, anyway."

"The way your dad does all his communication through me instead of you?" she said. I don't know if she meant that to be pointed or not. Sometimes with my mom it's hard to tell.

"Do you want me to come in with you?" she asked.

"No," I said. "I'll be right back."

I think my mom was telling me not to rant. That I should be having a mature, back-and-forth conversation with my dad that does not get posted on YouTube so it doesn't poison me or something. But when I got inside and the house was beautifully filled with plants and Sandy ran over to hug me even though she was focusing on important stuff in her magazine and my dad was actually the one who answered the door, the last thing I wanted was to go back and forth with my dad, who, instead of saying "hello" or "come in" or something normal said, "I didn't know you were coming."

He stepped aside to let me in, though. And even though part of me wanted to just walk up to my room to show him it was my room and he couldn't turn it into a guest room even if I was hardly ever there, I knew that I couldn't because my mom was right. I had all this stuff to say, but I didn't need to say it to him. I needed to say it to me.

My brain wanted to say so many things that it was racing a mile a minute. So eventually I walked past my dad, sat down on the sofa, and let my brain say what it wanted to.

You can say something if you want to, but you don't have to say any-thing. Actually, I kind of wish you wouldn't because even when you do, you're trying to give the reasons why, when really I just need you to listen. So silence is totally, totally OK. I'm not looking for cool dad quotes from you to post on Instagram. I just want to give us a chance to actually be a family. Love. Not guilt. Not the memory of how things used to be or a feeling you feel but never do anything about. I mean the verb. The action word. The thing you choose to do every day. I show up for the people I love, and the people who love me show up for me, too. Sometimes that means telling each other we're wrong and sometimes we let each other take risks and make mistakes even though we might get hurt in the end because love isn't what you say. It's what you do.

I'm the kid. You're supposed to know more than me. But you don't, so . . . here I am. Then I was thinking, how can your dad love you when he doesn't know you? And before you say you do, no. You don't. Maybe you knew me when I was seven and maybe you even knew me when I was in seventh grade, but you don't know me now. You don't know the person I became when you started to disappear. And you don't know who I am now. Sandy does. Funny how y'all were in the same places, but she got to know me and you didn't. I think it's because she wanted to know me. Even when I was giving her a hard time, she gave me a million chances and just kept being there for me when she didn't have to do anything at all. You're my dad. You're my dad and you didn't, even after I told you things weren't cool.

I don't know if this is a barrier or a boundary and I don't know how many chances this makes for you, but I know I don't owe anybody a million chances, not even you. I wish I didn't care, but I do. I don't know what you're going to do after this, but it kind of doesn't matter because I just need to tell you one thing.

"Dad, I'm a witch," I said.

Sandy looked up from her magazine, her eyes brimming with tears.

"That's all," I said. "I'm gonna go. Mom is waiting outside. We have some stuff to do."

"Hasani."

My dad stood right when I did. He put his hands out to the side. I knew what he wanted. He wanted me to run into his arms like I did when I was little. Like I had only a few months before. I didn't move. It wasn't on purpose. I think my body just knew that I needed him to come to me. At the same time, I think my body was making peace with the idea that maybe he never would.

The next thing I knew, my dad was hugging me. Tight. It felt like it lasted forever. It felt good, but it didn't feel like an ending. A hug isn't enough for an ending, but it also wasn't a bad beginning.

There was a loud tap. Sandy was holding something down on her magazine. I let my dad go and went to see it for myself. I knew what it said, but, for whatever reason, I didn't want Sandy to read it to me.

_LaToyaNull_black_gladiolas palustris_1_1/1

_KaitlynnSkye_orange_bellis perennis_3_1/1

1 globe sunk, rooted, removed, and delivered as specified,
by LaToya and two (2) or more linked sisters
at specified location in peak moonlight to be
completed within forty-eight (48) hours of this
agreement and before the start of the waning
gibbous in consideration of 43.4 credits and the
refund of one future favor TI upon completion or
86.8 credits and the addition of one future favor TI
upon failure. Link requirement waived upon delivery.
Nest Alpha_Beta_Gamma_Delta_Epsilon_Zeta_Eta_Theta_
Iota_Kappa_Lambda_Mu_Nu_Xi_Omicron_Pi_Rho_
Sigma_Tau_Upsilon Final

LaToya had given Kaitlynn the orb.

CHAPTER TWENTY-SIX

SECONDS AND CHANCES

*P*erfect is the enemy of done. It was only two o'clock, and Kaitlynn had the orb. We couldn't wait for the perfect time. Who knew what the world would look like at 3:13 P.M.?

So all of us scrambled to do the one thing we could do before Kaitlynn took over the world. We came together to heal the trees. I messaged everyone that I knew who might want to help. I started with people whose roots in the Riverbend went deep. They didn't even have to be magic. If you weren't you wouldn't see anything, anyway. Even if you were, you might not see anything. So it was better to have everyone who cared. Miss Lafleur and Miss Mbaye thought so, too. So after I ran out of kids whose roots ran deep, I kept going because who was I to say who cared about those trees? And once I let it sink in that it was too late for the orb, I messaged Annie and Jenny. In the end, I even messaged LaToya. LaToya's message wasn't an invitation so much as information. She got what she wanted. We really did want to help. I hoped it worked out for the best. I didn't think it would, but I was doing this one last act.

I pressed Send, stuck my phone in my pocket, and tried not to think of LaToya again. It was surprisingly easy to do.

There were so many other things to focus on. First, I was up where the levee meets the river with Miss Mbaye and her linked sisters, making sure there were enough channels to flush out the roots. Then both the Maries came to get me because they'd finally arrived from Vacherie to bring Miss Lafleur all the samples she needed to encourage the trees' ecosystems to rebalance after the poison flush.

"True health is a community," Miss Lafleur said. "Even we humans are plural beings. Without our bacteria we quite literally would not be able to live."

I imagined her bringing ants and worms and, I don't know, maybe squirrels. Whatever community oak trees needed for their roots to heal and grow. But the only thing the Maries brought was spores.

"Are the trees going to heal by having a better connection to the Interweb?" I said. I was not being serious, but Miss Lafleur was.

"Yes, exactly," she said. "Forcing those trees into a capture severed them from their natural community. Once we've helped flush the remnants of our rather suffocating barriers away, the only thing left is for the trees to reconnect with their community. The mycelium will help them do that."

It was Saturday. Most of the people we invited had stuff to do. Regular stuff like dance class and soccer and visiting grandmas. In the end there were a few dozen of us, mostly witches, although Jenny and Margeaux came through. Luz side-eyed Margeaux really bad and almost said that what happened to her—being burned out—was goody for her, but I stopped her. We did want her to stay away from Miguel, but that was it. Wishing bad on people wasn't cool and, more importantly, it wasn't Luz. Luz said I was right about that. I hope she meant it. By the time we were singing songs and those of us who could were pouring out tiny drops of magic to help whatever was left of the capture loosen up and move through, Luz was smiling again, holding her dad's and brother's hands.

I knew when it was done because through the scope the drops of magic flowing away were more and more clear, until it hardly looked like magic at all. Just water flowing down the channels the Maries made until, eventually, it would go back to the river.

People drifted away in twos and threes. Jenny stopped to thank me for inviting her, but she drifted away, too. Eventually, the only people left were my witch family, which, by then, included Luz. Everyone was there except Sandy.

"Oh no! We missed it?" Sandy said. She was hurrying through the gate. My dad was right behind her.

"We got stuck on that bridge," she said. "It's my fault, though. When the lights started flashing, I wouldn't let Bobby swerve around."

"Good," I said. "That would have been dangerous, and we want to keep you two safe."

It isn't that I didn't want my dad to be safe. Of course I wanted my dad to be safe. It's just that when I said "you two" I meant Sandy and the baby-hopefully-not-called-Bobbi, not Sandy and my dad, Bobby. But my dad is the one who responded.

"I just didn't want you to think I didn't want to be here," he said. "Because I do want to be here."

"I want to be here, too, if I'm allowed," a tiny voice said. It was LaToya. She was wearing regular clothes but pulling a bike with two giant, flowered suitcases attached. The suitcases were connected to each other, so it kind of looked like she was a tractor pulling Mardi Gras floats or the conductor on a train.

"What are you doing here?" Luz said. "Haven't you done enough?" She was holding on to Miguel like at any moment LaToya might jump up and bite him. That's the same way Mr. Jose was holding on to her.

LaToya didn't answer. She just reached down, unlatched both cases, and flipped the tops open for everyone to see. One was full of green crystal bottles. The other was full of pillows and an orb.

Somebody gasped. It might have been my mom. I wasn't sure. I was too busy looking at the orb.

"This can't be the same orb," I said. "You gave it to Kaitlynn. The transaction said 'final.' I saw it. No nesting, no nothing. This can't be the same one."

The orb glistened in the light. No one reached out to touch it.

"I did give that orb to Kaitlynn," LaToya said. "But after what you said yesterday, I knew I couldn't give her the magic inside it. That part I'm giving to you."

"That doesn't make sense," my mom said.

Sandy had already pulled out her magazine.

"We don't believe you," Luz said. "Why would you do that?"

"Kaitlynn knew she couldn't crack the code, so she said it had to be open when I delivered it to her. She never said it had to be full."

LaToya picked up the orb she brought and turned it to the back so everyone could see the creole hoop attached to it.

"You had another custody?" Angelique asked.

LaToya shook her head. "No," she said. "This is just a reflection of the one you used. It'll work just the same, but only for a day or two. Just as long as the potion lasts."

Sandy tapped a page of the magazine, careful to keep her finger pressed down in one corner when she turned it around for everyone to see. There were two entries on the ledger. Both of them LaToya. One of them I had already seen. The other one was an S- Crow inquiry in exchange for a future favor. I didn't even know the magazine could do that.

"Explain this," Sandy said.

"I don't have one of these thousand-hour magazines," LaToya said, "so I had to go to S-Crow to look up a blockchain entry to see if Hasani was lying. You know. Witch Life Lesson #17: Trust but Verify. I had to know for sure. But I had negative credits, so I had to use a future favor."

Sandy did not seem satisfied. "What were you verifying?" she asked.

"You and me," I said.

LaToya nodded. "Hasani said that Kaitlynn had tried to steal her signature before. I didn't believe her, but I didn't believe Kaitlynn, either. So I checked the record. Your story checked out."

"How did you find the key?" Sandy asked.

"Angelique gave it to me," LaToya said.

We all, and I mean everybody, looked at Angelique.

"I gave her a hint. It was in the incantation I used to activate the custody. Kouvèr lamou."

"You said it out loud," LaToya said. "Everybody knows you don't have to say incantations out loud. That one means covered in love."

"Your password is three regular words?" Luz exclaimed. "You may as well have made the password 'password.'"

"It wasn't that simple," LaToya said. "It was an expression of love."

We all switched to looking back at her.

"Being corny is not the same thing as being secure." Dee said it low, but I heard it.

"No," LaToya said. "It's a literal expression of love. Well, an equation, anyway. Look."

LaToya pulled out a notebook and showed it to us.

$$x^2 + \left(y - \sqrt{|x|}\right)^2 = 2$$

"It took me all night to find an equation that drew it just right," she said.

The way Ms. Coulon smiled, I could tell that she had instantly graphed the thing in her head. I was gonna need a paper and pencil.

"Impressive," Ms. Coulon said. She didn't break a smile, though. I think she was waiting to see what LaToya would do. LaToya unhitched the suitcases from her bike and backed her bike away.

"I don't know what to do with them now," LaToya said. "I was hoping you would."

Ms. Coulon nodded and half a second later there were no fewer than eight adult witches examining the suitcases and the bottles and orbs inside. Talk about trust but verify. People were pulling out instruments I've never seen. Sandy used a hairpin. Miss LaRose used a binder clip. And, for what I realized might have been the first time ever, Ms. Coulon put on her reading glasses. I didn't know what they were for, but they were definitely, definitely not plain glass.

After a few minutes, all of them seemed satisfied. Sandy nodded as Ms. Coulon waggled her fingers, so I figured Ms. Coulon had put a lock on the orb's lock. Then, without a word, Ms. Coulon steered the suitcases out of the gate and toward St. Charles Avenue.

"You coming?" I asked. I could have been talking to Dee or Angelique, but I already knew they were coming. So I was kind of talking to them. But I was talking to LaToya, too.

"You really want me to come?" she asked. She didn't say "after everything we've done." We both knew what we'd done.

"Do you?" I said.

"That's not an answer," LaToya said quietly.

"I know," I said. "But it's not on me to give you an answer. Not about this. The river belongs to all of us. You have roots in this place just like I do. So what matters right now is what you want to do."

"I don't have roots here," she said. "My roots are at the Academy. I've only been at this school like a week."

"Feels like an eternity," I said. We both laughed.

"No, but seriously, you don't have to be somewhere a long time to get roots. Sometimes it happens instantly. And oak trees only have one deep root, anyway. All the rest of them are shallow."

"I'm gonna have to look that up." LaToya giggled, and for a second, I forgot we weren't really friends.

"Go ahead," I said. "That's what I did when Ms. Lafleur told me that earlier."

We all walked together to the Fly. Nobody paid any attention to us. A bunch of people pulling two suitcases up the levee was not the weirdest thing that place had seen. In fact, at three o'clock on a Saturday afternoon, we kind of blended in. Angelique put on her new glasses and watched as her mom and Miss Mbaye wove an intention that apparently put all other intentions to shame. At least that's what they kept telling each other with their *Oohs* and *Wows* and *OK? I see you*s after checking through brass glass scopes. The channel Ms. Coulon inspected and declared the best one wasn't one Miss Mbaye and her team wove. Turned out, it was one LaToya made.

"I used a potion to make it," she said. "Kaitlynn kept going on about how important it was to free the capture. I surprised her by digging a channel down to the river that she could use to free the magic. She wasn't happy when she saw it. I should have known then that she didn't really want to free anything."

"You don't have to feel bad about that," Sandy said. "Kaitlynn is very convincing. If it weren't for Beverlyn, she would have gotten me when I first got here, too."

"Mr. Jones wasn't going to ride in on a white horse to rescue you?" Luz joked.

"Oh, I didn't know Bobby then. I came to New Orleans for Beverlyn and the rest of our coven. Well, I guess technically I came here for Jazz Fest, but while I was there, I was open and our magic just connected. I was thirteen of thirteen. It was organic. I didn't have to move here. I mean, Sheila lives in Cleveland. I didn't *have* to move here, but I *had* to move here, you know? Bobby came after. Oh! Looks like we're ready."

Sandy didn't look down at her phone, but when I looked at mine it was exactly 3:11. Two minutes left. I guess she could just feel it. Everybody who wasn't already holding one of the green crystal bottles grabbed one. The idea was that once the replacement orb was open we'd try to fill as many bottles as we could so that the signature magic could cycle back into the ordinary as quickly as possible. It was like expediting freedom after being imprisoned for so long.

Miss LeBrun pick up the orb and cradled it in two hands. A giant marble softly glowing with the faerie lights dancing inside.

"I'm not wearing any special lenses," I said. "Why can I see the magic?"

"That's what happens when you're rooted in a place," Ms. LeBrun said. "Some of those people are your ancestors."

I don't know why, but suddenly I started to cry. I wasn't the only one. Dee, Miss LaRose, and Angelique were streaming tears, too.

"Be careful," Miss Mbaye said. "Funerals are always freeing. But especially in the moonlight, this close to a riverbend, you may find yourself more open than you have ever been. If that is not what you want, this is your chance to step away."

The river frees you, especially in moonlight. It just never occurred to me that moonlight also happens during the day. I looked at Angelique and Dee. They were both looking at me. We were already connected, but we moved to stand shoulder to shoulder next to Luz, anyway. For us, more connection was good. My mom stood next to me. Sandy leaned on my dad. Miss LaRose was across the circle, but Mrs. Hebert stood right behind us. Right behind Angelique. Only LaToya kind of hovered alone. I had a feeling she wouldn't be for long.

Ms. Coulon unlocked the custody, cracked open the orb, and thousands of lives of magic flowed out in front of us. It was too much to catch. Like being at a thousand people's funerals, but where you know every single one of them by name, and even if you don't, you feel it anyway because all of you have the same roots. Too much to contain. Pouring out like a river the second it came out of the orb. A sea of lights that flowed down the channel and into the river.

For a while they hovered like fireworks do in the sky, but gradually they began to fade. I was a little disappointed. I thought that, with all of us being so open, me and LaToya might have found a connection. Once upon a time, we really were friends. And then I realized that, even if LaToya got away from Kaitlynn, that didn't automatically mean she had fixed things with her family, or with me.

But LaToya had connected with someone. She just hadn't connected with us. She had connected with Annie.

CHAPTER TWENTY-SEVEN

HOW DO YOU KNOW WHICH WAY TO GO WHEN THE WIND IS ALWAYS CHANGING?

We spent the rest of that day together. Not LaToya—she went off to find Annie. But everybody else.

Miss LaRose "didn't patronize 3Thirteen," so we decided to hang out at the glassworks instead. Ms. Coulon said the one in New Orleans was too small, so we ended up going to Amite. We also couldn't decide how to get there, but in the end, Miss Nancy drove everybody who wanted to ride aboveground except Miss LaRose, who insisted on driving herself. The rest of us took a subsol from 3Thirteen. Sandy gave my dad one of her guest passes so he could ride with us, too. We stopped in the Rivyèmarché to pick up some food. Sandy sprang for most of it, but Dee was eyeing some cupcakes where the flavors were colors. Red. Blue. Purple. You get it.

"What is greige supposed to taste like?" I asked.

"I have no idea," Dee said. "They look good, though."

"Are you getting some?"

"Nah, bruh. I been listening to Angelique's dad. If you can't buy five, you can't afford one. And right now I can't afford one."

"Why does everybody keep talking about Angelique's dad? What does he do?"

"SmartMoneyDad? On YouTube? Bring your dollars for boukou sense? You didn't know about that?"

I shook my head.

Note to self: Get Angelique to share every detail of her life so you don't embarrass yourself. Again.

We took the subsol to Amite, then flexed in the bubble in front of my dad like we had all ridden bubbles at least a million times each. FYI: Riding in a bubble is still cool. So was eating dinner with everybody inside a volcano. That wasn't the first time Ms. Coulon served a feast in her command room, either. Apparently they do fish fries there every Friday during Lent.

At some point, before everything started to die down, Ms. Coulon made me an offer, Willy Wonka style. "The glassworks could be yours if you want it someday."

"Seriously?" I said. "Little old me? Humble cocaptain of the Mathletes?"

Ms. Coulon laughed and said, "Don't get a big head, Hasani. Angelique would do just as well, but she already turned me down. Apparently Miss T has already won her heart at the library."

"Thank you so much for the offer. I'll think about it," I said. "This place is pretty dope, but I might want to travel the world."

Ms. Coulon nodded, actually looking impressed. With me. "That shows forethought and knowledge and acceptance of self. In other words, it's exactly the response that makes me think I should check in with you again before I'm ready to make the move. Go. Be free."

"Wait," I said. "Wasn't the capture, like, your life's work? What are you going to do now?"

"I have had an offer to do some traveling with Mariama."

Dag. Miss Mbaye was hittin' up everybody . . .

"But I don't think I'll do that just yet."

. . . Aaand getting shot down by everybody.

"I do still want to crack the code on rose-colored glasses, but that is a passion project more than a commercial venture. I don't think the world is ready to have those widely available. Not yet. And don't worry. I'm in no hurry to leave the school."

I smiled. I kind of was worried. "At least we don't have to worry about kids blossoming at Riverbend Middle all the time anymore," I said.

Ms. Coulon raised her eyebrows. "I wouldn't count on that," she said. "The campus is already showing signs of healing. Once it's fully mended, my guess is that it will boost magic even more than the intentions to counteract the capture ever suppressed it. My money is on Riverbend Middle producing more magical middle schoolers than the city has ever seen."

"Well, if you're ever thinking about starting a full-blown magic school, I'd talk to LaToya. Check out her WeBop. She's already got the magical curriculum thing in progress."

Ms. Coulon did not look like she was about to jump on opening a magic school, but maybe LaToya would. She was good at it. As long as she dumped that Hasani wig.

Before we went back to the group, I had to ask Ms. Coulon one more thing.

"So . . . did you, like, influence someone at the school into having kindergarten Mardi Gras parades just so you could hide more magic stuff in the trees?"

Ms. Coulon gave me a slow blink. "I'll try not to take offense at the suggestion that I might stoop to influencing human beings, but the answer to your question is no. It's New Orleans. I threw one bead in the tree to start. The rest did itself."

*E*ventually, after we ate and laughed and ate and pretended to be on *Star Trek*, people started to go home. A few stuck around to see some of the more "artistic" things in the glassworks, like a fire-breathing glass dragon Ms. Coulon had been working on, but when everyone else was saying, "See you soon!" Sandy was still talking about Self-Care Sunday.

"Beverlyn. Come on. We have to. It's a tradition!" Sandy said.

Ms. Coulon gave Sandy a look. "Sandy, this would only be the second one."

"I know!" Sandy said brightly. "Tradition!"

"You're not worried about magic and the b-a-b-y?" I asked.

"Hasani. Honey." Sandy put a hand on my shoulder. "The baby might be able to hear you, but I'm pretty sure they can't spell yet. But also, are you kidding? This baby is the size of a strawberry! If you think I'm missing seven months of mani-pedis over a strawberry baby, you have not met me."

Fair point.

Luz didn't end up coming to Self-Care Sunday. She stayed home with Miguel. I thought she'd be sad about it, but turned out she actually wanted to help him with his *dinosaur toy meets glitter Jell-O world* photo shoot. Luz really was a great sister. I was glad I had her to look up to, especially where being a big sister was concerned.

I was a little annoyed about my dad inviting himself to Self-Care Sunday, but Sandy said, "Oh. I invited him. I mean, now we don't have to worry about him bumping into you and finding out you're a witch before you were ready to tell him. But it's all good now, right?"

"Yeah, but is my dad really a Self-Care Sunday kind of guy?" I asked.

"Honestly?" Sandy lowered her voice. "I thought he was. That's why I invited him. But when he thought it was just me and my circle of friends, he turned me down. When he found out you were coming, though, he totally changed his tune."

Not an end, but a beginning. I don't want to say I was keeping score about how many times my dad made an effort to see me or talk to me, but I was sort of keeping score of how many times my dad made an effort to see me or talk to me. I probably wouldn't do it forever. Hopefully at some point the number would be so big that I would lose count.

Bonus: My dad was pretty chill at Self-Care Sunday. For the most part. Everybody said that he had kind of a freakout when he finally saw the witch who likes to read at the Rivyèmarché while drinking tea and using her white tiger as a body pillow. He swore up and down that it wouldn't have scared him except the tiger "looked hungry," but Angelique, Dee, and I missed that part because Angelique had an appointment at S-Crow and she had already asked us to go with her.

The appointment was about her earring. Angelique was wearing both of them again, but only one of them was still a custody. The one from her biological dad was the one she'd unlocked and used to capture the capture. A pretty dope use if you ask me. She kept asking us if she looked different, by which I'm assuming she was asking specifically if her magic looked different. Like, was her magic looking stronger than it had before. Honestly, her magic looked the same, but *she* looked different. Maybe she was more mature or something? I couldn't put my finger on it. All I knew was she wanted us to go with her, and that was good enough for me.

"I used the credits I got from the library to buy an inquiry at S-Crow the other day," she said. "My mom had the code to my biological dad's earring. She got that doing inquiries for blockchain entries that included 'Vacherie' and just systematically worked her way through. The thing is, until I was officially an adult with a registered signature, she couldn't just search for my name. And since my mom just found out I joined 3Thirteen at that 'Mom's Council' interrogation in the volcano, I beat her to the punch."

"You were hoping your biomom left you something in S-Crow?" Dee asked.

"Kind of?" Angelique winced. "I honestly thought that I was probably wasting my credits. I didn't really think there'd be an entry with my signature at S-Crow, but I got a notification this morning. It says 201817." Angelique turned her phone around so we could see.

"Cryptic," I said. "Should we get Sandy? She speaks corvidae."

"I don't think we need a translator," Angelique said. "There are a bunch of numbered safe deposit boxes in the back. We can start there and grab Sandy if we hit a dead end."

We walked through a bunch of narrow rows, constantly being eyed by crows barking orders we didn't understand until we found row 201. Then a right turn and around a zag to box 817. There was a shabby patch of grass on the front of the box. Angelique wove her signature into it and the door sprang right open. Inside was a folded piece of paper someone had clearly ripped out of a notebook.

"It's a recipe," she said, touching the custody in her ear. "My biological mom locked her custody with a spell. This must be the recipe to unlock it."

She reached in to touch it. She was gentle at first, but her hands shook too much to keep that up.

"What are the ingredients?" I asked, starting to look over Angelique's shoulder, but then Dee put her hand out to cover the page.

"Wait," Dee said. "Angelique, do you want this? Once you see it, you can't unsee it, you know what I mean?"

"I already saw it," Angelique said. "It doesn't matter if I want it or not. One of the ingredients is dragon scale. I'd probably be thirty before I could save enough for one of those. And that's if one even went up for sale."

"You could always go up that mountain to get one yourself," I said. "Isn't that where your mom said Kaitlynn must have gotten hers? From somebody named Sealie on a mountain? Or somebody on a mountain named Sealie?"

I was joking. The idea of Angelique on a mountain was clearly a joke. But Angelique looked like she was seriously considering it.

"Are you talking about Mamie Seal?" Miss Mbaye said.

All of us jumped.

Miss Mbaye was standing right behind us, tightening the tie holding her locs into a bun. Between the boots and the cargo pants, she looked like she was ready to hit up an archaeology site right that second.

"I apologize," she said. "I didn't mean to sneak up on you. I was just looking for my apprentice and possible future apprentice to say that I'm catching the next gondola out. I was going to ask you if you wanted to come out for a few weeks at the end of term to get your feet wet, but it looks like you might be making other travel plans. Finding Mamie Seal would be quite the adventure. I hear she's more than one hundred twenty years old and lives behind an intention so large that it masks an entire mountain. I'm assuming this is about your remaining custody?"

Angelique nodded.

"I understand. You do what you have to do. The two of you would be quite a team, but you should take care of unfinished business first," Miss Mbaye said, shrugging to scoot her leather backpack higher on her shoulder. "Correcting the record of history is hard. Other captures we come across may not be quite as dangerous as this one was, but we will come across others, and I can't say there won't be things that make you sad. We always say, 'You first have to fill your own cup before you can fill someone else's.' If your cup has a hole in it that needs to be healed . . ."

"Not a hole," Angelique said, sounding more like Mrs. Hebert's daughter than she ever had. "Definitely not a hole. More like a curiosity."

"Well," Miss Mbaye said, "I do love a good adventure, too. Just promise me one thing."

"What?"

"Before you start that story, make sure you want to know what happens no matter which way it ends."

I thought about endings and beginnings the whole walk back to the Rivyèmarché.

Luz wasn't there, but I knew she would be there for me. My dad was there, but I didn't know the same thing for sure. It seemed like every time I thought something was ending, it was really something new beginning. I didn't know if LaToya would come back to school or if my dad and I would be close again or if I would ever just have a normal week. Or maybe now this was a normal week. It was like being blown around and around in a hurricane, wind coming from every direction.

But I looked around the table—Dee throwing back another magenta-flavored cupcake; my mom laughing at Sandy's retelling of how she almost got burned out by a solar system necklace; my dad trying to have a clue; Ms. Coulon's explanation of Angelique's code; even Angelique looking off into space, pondering her next move—and I breathed it in. Knowing that things might never land like this again.

Not even the bead trees stayed the same. I knew I wouldn't, either. So I soaked up the feeling and let the wind blow, happy to know that I was rooted so well, that I could go wherever the wind took me.

Mo lib.

To lib.

So lib.

No lib.

All witches are free.

Blockchain entry, refracted view

5781.256.0716

_HasaniMarie_black_ipomoea purpurea_1_2/3

_GTTravelCooperative_null_null_null_null

Passported gondola travel from New Orleans to Dakar for

Hasani Marie Schexnayder-Jones

Passported gondola travel from New Orleans to Dakar for

Nailah Marie Schexnayder

Passported gondola travel from New Orleans to Dakar for

Sandra Elise Freeman-Jones

Passported gondola travel from New Orleans to Dakar for

Robert Alexander Jones

Passported gondola travel from New Orleans to Dakar for

Alex Freeman Jones

Final

ACKNOWLEDGMENTS

Writing is not easy. Even when words flow like water downstream, there is always a log or a boulder or a beaver building something to get in your way. Something that says, "How badly do you want this story? Enough to write it all again, even if most of it is lost?" Because, honestly, sometimes that's how badly you have to want it. That's why, when the logs and the beavers and the boulders try to get in the way, it really helps to have people on your side. No one can write the words for you, but they can tackle obstacles while you do.

Thank you to Jadi, who calmly took a pickaxe to the biggest writing trouble I've faced to date. Thank you to Samantha and Rebecca, who put up with me week after week without fail. Thank you, Jenn, for always coming in clutch with the titles. Thank you to Maggie Lehrman and the whole team at Abrams for making every page a work of art. No need for testing. Every one of you is promising at the very least. Thank you to all the *Cool Aunts,* including Heather. You love and support remind me that all of this is worth doing. Thank you to my nephew, who helps surround me with life. Thank you to my mother-in-law, who was the first person to ever pay money for one of my books and continues to read and lift my writing to this day. And thank you to my father, who saw so much of himself in me that he gave me almost all of his name. I'm glad he did.